# TARNISHED, TEMPTED AND TAMED

Mary Brendan

Published in Great Britain 2015
by Mills & Boon, an imprint of Harlequin (UK) Limited,
Eton House, 18-24 Paradise Road, Richmond, Surrey, TW9 1SR

© 2015 Mary Brendan

ISBN: 978-0-263-24802-9

Harlequin (UK) Limited's policy is to use papers that are natural,
renewable and recyclable products and made from wood grown in
sustainable forests. The logging and manufacturing processes conform
to the legal environmental regulations of the country of origin.

Printed and bound in Spain
by CPI, Barcelona

**Mary Brendan** was born in North London, but now lives in rural Suffolk. She has always had a fascination with bygone days, and enjoys the research involved in writing historical fiction. When not at her word processor she can be found trying to bring order to a large overgrown garden, or browsing local fairs and junk shops for that elusive bargain.

### Books by Mary Brendan

### Mills & Boon® Historical Romance

#### Society Scandals

*A Date with Dishonour*
*The Rake's Ruined Lady*

#### Regency Rogues

*Chivalrous Rake, Scandalous Lady*
*Dangerous Lord, Seductive Miss*

#### The Hunter Brothers

*A Practical Mistress*
*The Wanton Bride*

#### The Meredith Sisters

*Wedding Night Revenge*
*The Unknown Wife*
*A Scandalous Marriage*
*The Rake and the Rebel*

**Visit the author profile page
at millsandboon.co.uk for more titles**

# Chapter One

'So, you are happy to be travelling all alone, then, Miss Chapman?'

'I am, ma'am,' the young lady answered through lightly gritted teeth. She had been asked the same question, in the same scandalised tone, about five minutes previously. Even before then two other women, and a gentleman, had made similar enquiries, couched in a slightly different way. Each interrogator had in turn professed a concern for her welfare rather than an interest in her business. In the close confines of the mail coach Fiona Chapman could not escape the ladies' judgemental eyes or the fact that they were whispering about her behind their gloved fingers. Only the middle-aged farmer had not returned to the subject of her lack of a companion after his initial remark.

A triumphant blast of the driver's horn proclaimed the rattling contraption to be approaching a watering hole. Miss Chapman's fellow passengers stirred excitedly at the prospect of stretching their legs and having some refreshment. A few minutes later, from under the brim of her chip-straw bonnet, she watched them all alighting. The farmer, who had introduced himself and his wife as the Jacksons, had sat opposite Fiona, accidentally banging his tweedy knees against hers every time the coach leapt a rut. Now he kindly held out a hand, helping her to alight onto the cobbles of the Fallow Buck public house. Fiona gave him a rather wistful smile because he reminded her of her late papa with his wispy salt-and-pepper hair and rotund girth straining his waistcoat buttons. But Anthony Chapman had been older, Fiona guessed, than this fellow. Her father had died of a heart attack a few years ago at the age of fifty-two and the sad occasion had been the catalyst to Fiona making this journey.

'Don't be paying heed to my wife, miss.' Mr Jackson patted Fiona's hand before letting it go. 'She's a worrier and not only on her own account. We've two daughters, you see, so know a bit about what girls get up to.' He slid Fiona a startled look. 'Not that I think you're up to anything, my dear Miss Chapman,' he burst out. 'Oh, no…I wasn't suggesting…or prying…'

'I understand.' Fiona gave him a kind smile, taking pity on his blushing confusion. Of course he thought she was up to something…just as the ladies did. And they were right to be suspicious; well-bred young ladies did not as a rule travel unaccompanied on public transport.

'Our two girls have settled down with their husbands. Good fellows, both of them, and Dora and Louise have each got a brood round their ankles.' He gave Fiona an expectant smile, perhaps hoping to hear that such a blissful ending might be on the cards for her before it was too late.

Fiona knew that it was clear to all but a blind man that she was not in the first flush of youth and remaining on the shelf was thus a possibility. She'd no claim to beauty, either, and looked what she was: a spinster in her mid-twenties, with a pleasant rather than a pretty face and hair a disappointing shade of muddy blonde. She spoke in an educated way and that together with her neat attire proclaimed her to be not poor, but not rich, either, holding a status somewhere in between the two.

Mr Jackson poked an elbow in Fiona's direction, offering to escort her into the tavern. While they had been conversing his wife and the Beresford sisters had gone ahead and disappeared inside the open doorway. 'Mrs Jackson is alarmed in case any harm is done you, you see. And I have to admit I share my good lady's worries.'

'I'm sure I shall arrive in Dartmouth in one piece,' Fiona returned with a smile that concealed the fact she wasn't as confident as she sounded. She had left London in good spirits despite her mother begging her not to act so rashly. But the further west she journeyed the stronger grew her doubts over the wisdom of her impetuous decision to take up gainful employment in a strange and remote place.

She'd read about Devon and Cornwall in books and studied pictures of wild seas crashing against rugged coastlines. She'd seen images of country folk dressed in plain coarse clothes and shod in clogs. It was all a far cry from the sophistication of the capital city in which she'd been reared. But then Fiona had never really been part of that life, either, preferring to read or paint than attend society parties with her mother and sister. She'd been sure she was ready for a change, even before change had been forced upon her by her papa's demise and Cecil Ratcliff's arrival.

'You're an innocent, my dear, not used to country ways, I'll warrant,' Peter Jackson broke in on Fiona's deep thoughts. 'There are nasty individuals about these parts who'd rob blind a lady…or worse…' he mumbled. 'So you be on your guard every minute. Before we go our separate ways we'll give you our direction just in case you might be in need of assistance. If your *business* doesn't go the way you want you might need a friend…'

Fiona knew the man was keen to know what her *business* was, but she'd no intention of elaborating. She'd been reared to guard her tongue and her privacy in case the *ton*'s gossips concocted something out of an innocent remark. The fact that her destination was the home of a widower was sure to set tongues wagging; she'd thought carefully about it herself before accepting the post of governess to two motherless children at Herbert Lodge.

'Thank you for you kind advice, sir, I will remember it,' Fiona promised, while holding on to her bonnet as a stiff breeze lifted it away from her crown.

Mr Jackson had introduced himself and his wife to Fiona earlier, when they had set out from the staging post in Dawlish. He'd told the assembled company that he and his dear lady were returning home having attended the nuptials of a niece. Miss Beresford and her sister Ruth had also boarded the coach at Dawlish but were due to alight first. Fiona and the Jacksons were travelling further on into Devon.

On entering the tavern Fiona and Mr Jackson found the trio of ladies already ensconced in comfy chairs around the blazing logs and the landlord dancing attendance upon them.

'Now you must come and sit with us close by the fire, Miss Chapman,' Mrs Jackson called from her cosy position, waggling her fingers to draw Fiona's attention.

'The coffee is very good in here…or I could recommend a hot toddy to warm you up?' Peter Jackson suggested, solicitously drawing closer an armchair for Fiona to sit in. 'We stop here quite often, don't we, Betty, and find the fare very acceptable. I had a beef and oyster pie on the last occasion and very tasty it was, too.'

Mrs Jackson sanctioned her husband's review by nodding vigorously. 'I'd take the rum, Miss Chapman,' she gave her verdict on the beverages. 'I'm having a nip. The way that wind is howling down the chimney the afternoon is sure to turn colder.'

The younger Miss Beresford slid forward on the worn hide of her armchair to whisper to Fiona, 'Pardon me, but are you absconding to elope?'

'No! Indeed, no…' Fiona choked on a half-laugh, glancing urgently about to see if anybody had overheard. Only a serving girl was behind, clearing tables of used glasses, and she seemed more interested in gazing through the window and flirting with the stable hand out in the yard. 'Do I give the impression that I might be a runaway bride?' Fiona whispered.

'I just thought it would be exciting if you were… What an adventure that would be.' Ruth Beresford gave a giggle that sounded odd coming from a woman who seemed at least thirty years old.

'The Duke of Thornley's daughter is getting married.' Mrs Jackson had caught the gist of the young ladies' conversation and thought she'd take up the challenge of prising some information from Miss Chapman. 'His Grace is rumoured to be generous and will doubtless treat his estate workers to a feast during the celebrations.'

'Let's hope he serves pheasant, then,' Mr Jackson said drily. 'The Thornley estate is overrun with the creatures—they're a blasted nuisance, squawking and wandering on to the roads,' he explained when Fiona looked mystified.

'A society wedding!' Ruth Beresford breathed,

and gave Fiona a wink as though they shared a confidence.

'I shall see if our host has a pie kept warm,' Mr Jackson said, changing the subject. He could tell that Miss Chapman was becoming increasingly embarrassed at Ruth's hints she might be eloping. A similar thought about Fiona's lone journey had run through Peter Jackson's mind, but he would never have aired it. 'Would you like to eat something?' Peter asked his wife while traversing the room to the bar.

'Oh, yes, indeed,' Mrs Jackson said.

'I fancy a beef sandwich if the landlord can rustle up such a thing,' Ruth Beresford told her elder sister. 'Might I have my coins?' Valerie Beresford delved into a pocket and drew forth a little pouch she'd been keeping safe.

Fiona was also feeling hungry. She put her reticule on her lap and opened the strings to find some money. The thought of a beef sandwich, with horseradish, was making her mouth water. She decided to add her order to her companions and take up Mrs Jackson's idea of a rum toddy to wash it down and keep the chill at bay. Now out of the coach and relaxing with her travelling companions, she felt her misgivings about her new life fading away. Everything would be fine as long as she kept her mettle…

\* \* \*

'What in damnation are you doing here?' The gentleman's harsh demand suggested an imminent display of anger, but he remained lounging at ease in his chair. A slight hardening in his handsome features was all that attested to his annoyance.

Oh, but he was furious... Becky Peake knew that very well. He hadn't shouted at her, although she knew she deserved it. His voice had been stone cold and so were those eyes that resembled chips of charcoal.

'Don't be cross with me, Luke,' she begged. The landlord of the tavern had shown her to the back room and Becky now skipped over the threshold, closing the door behind her. 'I don't want to be left behind in town when you're so far away.' Approaching his chair, she attempted to perch provocatively on his lap.

But he got up from the table with a muttered oath and walked away.

Becky, always pragmatic, looked at the appetising plate of food he'd abandoned. 'I'm famished...might I tuck in if you've finished?'

He flicked a hand. 'Help yourself.'

Becky untied her bonnet strings, allowing her dark curls to bounce to her shoulders. Loosening the cloak fastened at her throat, she settled down to enjoy the cold meats, springy aromatic bread and cheese piled on to the plate. Suddenly aware that her lover was gazing thoughtfully at her, Becky used the snowy napkin to dab her pout. 'What is it?' She dimpled. 'Do you forgive me? You look as though you do…'

'Well, that depends,' he said with a fractional smile.

'You always overlook my peccadilloes when I'm attentive to you.' Becky sounded confident and got up to sashay towards him, then coil her arms about his strong neck.

'Your impertinence is not a peccadillo and I won't forget it, sweet, but now you're here perhaps there's a way you could make up for it.'

Becky unhooked a few more of her cloak fastenings and shrugged out of the garment. Beneath it she wore a flimsy lemon gown that clung to her curvaceous figure. 'I'll do whatever you say…' she purred suggestively.

'Good…' he growled, removing her arms from about his neck. 'Let me put a proposition to you…'

## Chapter Two

'I'm not set against your plan, Your Grace. I simply think that it is too soon to implement it.'

'Pray, why is that?' Alfred Morland, Duke of Thornley, was not used to being gainsaid, especially by persons of vastly inferior rank. But this was no ordinary man. Major Wolfson was a veteran of the Peninsular Wars and had a catalogue of commendations attesting to his military expertise and bravery. The Duke of Wellington, a mutual acquaintance, had recommended the major's services when Thornley outlined his predicament. Since His Grace was in great need of somebody possessing Wolfson's qualities, he was repressing his temper as best he could while glaring at the tall figure standing opposite. He was a fine figure of a man, Thornley inwardly sniffed, and he could believe Wellington's boast that no sane fellow would cross his former aide-

de-camp without good cause and serious consideration. But having invested much time and
thought in this intrigue the Duke of Thornley
very badly wanted to see action as soon as possible.

Since Napoleon had been defeated, Major
Wolfson had been hiring out his talents; not that
he needed the money—Wellington had let on
that the fellow had banked an inheritance from
his late grandfather that would make Croesus en-
vious. Apparently, Luke Wolfson liked the life
of a soldier and had no interest in settling down
as a country squire in Essex. Such a thrill seeker
had seemed a prime candidate to carry out the
mission, but Thornley could see that the fellow
was not at all impressed with his brainchild to
outwit a local villain.

Luke took a hearty swallow of the brandy the
duke had given him when feeling affable, then
placed the glass on the mantel. 'There is a risk
to a young woman's life which surely makes rig-
orous checks imperative before the point of no
return.'

'I have engaged you, sir, in the hope that you
will deal with any dangers facing the doxy. If
you find the task onerous or beyond your capa-
bilities, you have only to say and I will employ
another mercenary.'

'In which case you will certainly need to delay while you find someone willing to take on the job and infiltrate the Collins gang.' Luke's lips slanted in a subtle smile as the older man brooded on those salient points, like a bulldog chewing a wasp.

'The woman is being paid handsomely for her trouble…as are you,' His Grace sourly reminded.

'Indeed, and I have promised Miss Peake she will be back in town by next week spending her earnings. I would not want to be arranging her funeral instead.'

'Well, tell the chit she might have a bonus if she agrees to expeditiously get this over with.' Thornley gave the major a dour glance. 'No doubt you expect a similar favour even though you have already negotiated a princely sum for yourself.'

Luke gave an easy shrug. 'If you want to offer an inducement to accelerate matters, I will, of course, accept it. But the risks remain the same and I would urge you to think carefully before pelting headlong into this. If Collins smells a rat, you might gain nothing and tempt the gang to persecute you and your daughter. Her welfare is paramount, is it not?'

'It is!' Wolfson's last remark had touched a nerve. The Duke of Thornley adored his daughter. He knew she got bored in Devon confined to the house. But Thornley was loath to let her out much, even with her maid, to enjoy the local markets and emporiums because of the gang of ruffians infesting the area. 'If the blackguard smells a rat it will be because Wellington has overdone your praises. I'm paying you to ensure that Collins suspects nothing.' His Grace thumped down his brandy glass on the desktop, shoving himself to his feet. 'You forget yourself, sirrah, to be lecturing me!'

'I was under the impression you would welcome such advice,' Luke said mildly. 'In fact, I thought you summoned me here for that very reason.' Their combatant gazes tangled, but Luke could see the duke was not going to back down and admit his mistake. 'Jeremiah Collins kidnapped, then returned a young dandy to his family on payment of a hefty ransom some six months ago.' Luke shot the duke a glance and saw him redden. 'You knew about that…got your inspiration from it, I take it.'

'Of course I knew,' His Grace blustered, smarting under the mild accusation of stealing an idea from the very person he wanted to see strung up. 'My friend, Squire Smalley, sits at Devizes. The matter had been hushed up to prevent local folk panicking, but obviously not well enough if *you* managed to find out about it.'

A half-smile tilted Luke's moulded mouth. 'Like you, sir, I have friends in high places,' he said quietly.

'Around these parts…and in London, too, for that matter…*I* am high places.' The arrogant statement had barely quit the Duke of Thornley's lips before he regretted it, but Wolfson had too much to say for himself and needed slapping down. 'You are either with me, Major, or against me. Let me know which.'

'My apologies—it seems we are at odds over this. I couldn't in all conscience proceed knowing I've no faith in the scheme as it stands. I've not gathered enough intelligence to safeguard Miss Peake. And in truth I'd sooner not get any woman involved in such peril.' Luke gave a small bow. 'I will have my lawyer return to you the deposit you've paid and deem the contract void. I'll bid you good evening.'

Luke cursed beneath his breath as he strode for the door without a backward glance. He was willing to forgo his fee; he'd not liked the sound of the job from the start and had only agreed to travel to Devon and discuss it with Thornley as a favour to the Iron Duke.

A mission where a knife might be slipped between one's ribs was par for the course in Luke's line of work, but Becky was unlikely to have encountered anything more perilous than an admirer lying in wait for her on an unlit path at Vauxhall Gardens. Luke preferred working alone. He'd discovered a woman accomplice was needed only after he'd turned up in Devon and Thornley had described explicit details of his plan. Still Luke had bitten back a refusal to get involved out of deference to his old army commander. Over many years the Duke of Wellington had not only been a colleague, but a good friend to Luke, despite the disparity in their ages and status.

Within an hour of concluding his first meeting with Alfred Morland, Luke had contemplated returning to Thornley Heights to express his regrets to the duke and bow out. Then his mistress had unexpectedly shown up, having pursued him to Devon. He'd been both enraged and astonished at Becky's audacity, but had realised that with her love of money and excitement Becky would jump at the chance to get involved in an intrigue. The complication of finding a woman to employ, willing to risk abduction by a gang of smugglers, had been removed; Luke had realised he'd find no better candidate.

Becky was a competent actress; in fact, had

she stayed in London rather than tracking him a hundred miles, she would have been treading the boards in Haymarket as Desdemona. Thankfully, Luke had no further need to be anxious whether his mistress would measure up to the job of impersonating a duke's daughter. He wished he'd never mentioned anything about it to her as she'd boasted from the start that she'd make him a fine accomplice. She'd be disappointed to be sent back to town earlier than expected. But sent back she certainly would be now, because her following him had been the final straw as far as Luke was concerned.

As Luke proceeded rapidly towards the huge oaken doors set at the end of a quiet marble hallway the butler materialised to hand him his coat. Before he could quit the house a young woman called his name, causing him to pivot about.

Lady Joan Morland hastened down the last few stairs, causing the ancient manservant to raise a disapproving eyebrow at his master's eldest child.

'Has Papa persuaded you to get our scheme quickly over with?' Joan whispered once at Luke's side. Joan knew her father would be annoyed to find her apprehending his business associate to grill him for information. But as the business concerned her Joan was of the opinion she was entitled to know about it.

'No…he has not,' Luke replied after a moment's consideration. 'We've failed to agree on some matters so somebody else will take over my role if your father decides to carry on with the plan.' He bowed and proceeded to the door.

Joan looked crestfallen to hear the news and trotted after Luke. 'That's a shame—that odious man is becoming a terrible nuisance. He has beaten up two of our estate workers because they informed against him supplying a dreadful batch of brandy that was so strong it killed people. Now everybody is too scared to even mention his name in the village. But we are not! He'll not browbeat us into putting up with his rampage.'

'Has Collins ever seen you?' Luke asked.

Joan shook her head. 'Not as far as I'm aware. I don't go out much… Papa doesn't like it. But I'm not frightened of such as Collins! I've told Papa he won't keep me indoors, hiding away.' Joan sighed. 'Really I'd like to move back to London where it's gay and there's lots to do.'

Luke allowed a slight smile. She might be young—still a teenager, her father had told him—but she had pluck.

'Collins's luck will run out. I imagine the authorities must be closing in on him and will apprehend him quite soon.'

'People in these parts have been saying that for over a year and still he carries on as he pleases.' Joan dismissed the notion of an early arrest. 'A Lieutenant Brown of the coast blockade was found clubbed in a lane, close to death,' Joan said. 'I think we all know who is responsible for that! And even more kegs of brandy have washed ashore this week…so my maid told me…'

Luke gave an answering grimace that conveyed he wasn't happy to hear the news, but wasn't surprised by it. 'I have to be going now,' he said, bowing politely and giving the young woman a smile.

Lady Joan was trying to prick his conscience and tempt him to again become embroiled in her father's harebrained plot to lure Collins into the open so he might be caught. But in Luke's opinion the duke, being self-opinionated and arrogant, was underestimating the wily intelligence of his foe. Collins was no fool and Luke knew he and the Duke of Thornley would never see eye to eye on how to go about things. Without full control, but with the responsibility of the mission's outcome squarely on his shoulders, Luke couldn't carry on. Besides he had pressing matters elsewhere to deal with.

He wasn't looking forward to his meeting with Drew Rockleigh. But the matter that was threatening their friendship had to be dealt with before he returned to the metropolis.

# Chapter Three

'Are we travelling back to London later today?'

'You are…' Luke said with a smile. Turning to the mirror above the fireplace in the inn's private parlour, he began deftly folding his neckcloth while meeting Becky's gaze in the glass.

'It's too bad of the duke to cancel this escapade.' Becky bit into her toast with an irritated little sigh. 'He should allow me my fee. I want a new hat.' Becky watched Luke's broad back as he shrugged into his tailcoat.

'He didn't cancel it. I did. And I'll give you some spending cash, sweet, don't worry.' He wasn't the only mercenary in the room, Luke realised, suppressing laughter in his throat. But he preferred mistresses who were content with sensual satisfaction plus a generous allowance that allowed them to shop freely, without demanding more of his time and freedom than he was prepared to give. Unfortunately, Becky had been pushing the boundaries of her role. Their last few visits to the opera had seen her becoming tediously jealous, watching his movements around other women. He knew it was time to end their relationship and would do so when he returned to town. He blamed himself, in part, for her stalking him. He'd told her his destination, if nothing else about what business was taking him to the West Country. But he'd never imagined that she'd have the outrageous cheek to come and check up on him.

'Will you return to Eaton Square soon?' Becky knew Luke was still reining in his anger over her unexpected appearance, so sounded quite meek.

She had never set foot inside Luke's Mayfair mansion. As his mistress she'd never be invited to do so and to pay an impromptu visit would be tantamount to professional suicide. No distinguished fellow would pursue a liaison with a courtesan who proved to be an embarrassment to him and his family. Of course, Becky was aware that Luke had few living relatives to upset. He was an only child and his paternal grandfather had outlived both of his parents, but that was the extent of Becky's knowledge of her lover's history. And she knew better than to chivvy for more details of his past.

Becky liked a challenge and had boasted to her friends that she could hook the 'soldier of fortune' as he was nicknamed. And she had. He'd taken her under his protection and set her up in Marylebone almost five months ago. She'd no wish to see their affair come to an end. Luke Wolfson's rakish reputation and his gypsy-dark good looks were irresistible to Becky. But she was a seasoned paramour and recognised the signs of a man preparing to bed hop. She'd noticed him responding to a flirtatious redhead at Vauxhall in that quietly amused way of his. But Becky wasn't too bothered about her, or any *demi-rep* who had a yen for Luke Wolfson. It was another, serious, rival who had her rattled.

'The London Season will soon be underway…' Becky tried another tack to discover Luke's plans as he'd grimaced his indecision in answer to her earlier question.

'What of it?' Luke asked, turning from the mirror.

'Will you stay permanently in town for the Season?' Luke had a vast acreage in Essex. Becky guessed he had a *chère amie* in the countryside to keep him company on his long absences from her bed. But a fat-ankled milkmaid didn't bother her, either.

'Perhaps… Why do you ask?'

'Harriet Ponting has arrived in town with her mother.'

'And?' Luke's expression remained impassive as he straightened his shirt cuffs.

'Oh, you know what's expected of you!' Becky cried, covering her pretty features with her palms. 'Her mama has been spreading rumours for ages that you are ready to pay court again to her eldest daughter.'

'Is that right?' Luke murmured distantly, with an expression that Becky, peeking behind her fingers at him, recognised. He was letting her know that any marriage plans he had were none of her concern and he was displeased that she'd raised the topic.

'I'm going to settle the shot… Pack your things, sweet, we're leaving…'

Becky watched him exit the room, a sulky twist to her lips. In her opinion it *was* her concern. She might not be genteel, like Harriet, but she had plenty to offer a gentleman as his wife. Becky wanted to join the number of other ambitious courtesans who had dragged themselves up by their bootstraps to marry rich and influential men and bear them legitimate heirs. Harriet

Ponting had already turned Luke down once and didn't deserve another chance at being Luke's wife, Becky thought.

'Oh, it's too much to bear!'

'Now, now, calm yourself, my dear,' Peter Jackson soothed his wife. He drew her closer to him beneath the tree so they might get some better shelter from the driving rain.

Fiona had huddled with the Beresford sisters beneath the dripping skeleton of another oak, but as a loud clap of thunder sounded she glanced up warily, through rain-clumped lashes, at groaning overhead branches.

'Perhaps we might be safer out in the open,' Fiona said, pulling the hood of her cloak further forward to protect her face.

'But we will look like drowned rats,' Ruth and Valerie Beresford chorused, shrinking back to the bole of the tree.

'Better that than get struck by lightning,' Fiona pointed out.

She suddenly made a dash towards the coach, which was tilting precariously to one side. The driver and groom were making a valiant attempt to repair the broken front axle, while hampered by the violent elements. The storm had seemed to spring up from nowhere just as they hit a particularly isolated stretch of road. Toby Williams put down his hammer as Fiona stopped by his side. Wearily the coach driver pushed to his feet and patted at the nearest horse, murmuring comfortingly to the sodden beast. The team had bowed their heads beneath an onslaught that was sending rivulets of water dripping down their flanks and manes.

'It's no use, miss, I'll have to return to the Fallow Buck and get help. It's beyond my skill to get this accursed thing again up and running.' The driver indicated his young apprentice. 'Bert here will stay by you all. He can take my blunderbuss for protection. I think you will all be safe enough in the coach—it's stuck firm in the mud so shouldn't tip over. You can't remain out in the open or you'll catch your deaths—'

'Do you think Bert might need the blunderbuss?' Fiona interrupted, suppressing her alarm. The lad had not looked too happy on hearing he was about to be abandoned by his senior and put in charge of protecting the coach's drenched, vexed passengers. Never had Fiona felt quite so out of her depth amongst these country folk and the eerie alien environment they inhabited. She'd only rarely in her life travelled outside London and its bustling, clamorous streets. Then it had been to stay with friends who lived in a quaint cottage in a Hertfordshire village. She wondered if in these parts ferocious animals living in the woods might prey on them, so asked the driver though fearful of his answer.

'Well…you never know, better to be safe than sorry,' Toby Williams prevaricated. He knew very well that any predatory vermin were human, not animal. The Collins gang infested the area from Kent to Cornwall, all along the coast. That group of marauding criminals would think it their lucky day if they stumbled across a party of defenceless people. Jeremiah Collins would relieve them all of their valuables, and the ladies of their virtue, if what Toby had heard about the vile blackguard was accurate.

What really worried Toby though was that his apprentice, Bert, might be relieved of his life. The lad was only eighteen, but already had a wife and child relying on him. Collins was suspected of murdering a Revenue Man in Rye, but he was a wily individual and had been on the run, keeping one step ahead of the law for more than a year.

It was said that Jem Collins felt he had nothing to lose. He knew the noose awaited him and so was on a spree to create havoc and rake in as much profit as he could before judgement day came, as it must in the end.

'I'll tell the others to return to the coach,' Fiona spluttered through the icy rain pounding her face. As she bolted back towards the copse it ran through her mind that the little group would be bitterly disappointed—as was she—to hear the vehicle couldn't be repaired so they could get quickly under way.

'Shall we keep our spirits up by playing a game? We could sing a song?' Fiona suggested in desperation as the weather outside continued to batter and shake the coach. Despite the drumming of the rain on the roof Fiona could hear Valerie Beresford snuffling in one corner of the vehicle. In the other, Mrs Jackson was crying with more abandon while her husband patted alternately at her hands and her shoulders to try to quieten her.

'Well…this is an adventure…' Ruth Beresford said and gave Fiona a nervous grin.

'Indeed…and one I'd sooner not have experienced.' Fiona sighed wryly. She was determined to keep buoyant. She was the youngest woman in the party so should be the strongest, mentally and physically, she'd reasoned. She lifted a corner of the leather blind at the window and peered at poor Bert marching forlornly to and fro, the blunderbuss up in readiness to be aimed.

It was getting dark and Fiona feared that before too long nightfall would overcome them, hampering their rescue team and also throwing her companions further into the doldrums.

'How much longer will that wretched man be?' Mrs Jackson wailed. 'I'm frozen stiff and will catch my death of a cold.'

'Hush, my dear, I'm sure Toby is doing his best. He will be back before you know it.' Mr Jackson again rubbed his wife's sleeve in comfort. When he turned a glance on Fiona his expression showed his deep concern. His wife *was* likely to take a chill from the soaking, as she regularly suffered from such ailments, but it was the vulnerability of their predicament that was frightening the life out of the farmer.

Beneath his breath he was castigating himself for not bringing along a weapon of his own. But he'd taken this route in the past and was aware that Toby Williams always kept a couple of loaded guns on the vehicle as protection for himself and his passengers. An hour or more ago, Toby had unharnessed the youngest horse and taken his pistol with him as his own protection on his gallop back to the Fallow Buck. So now they had just a young apprentice and a single weapon to protect them all.

'A rider is coming!' Bert had whipped open

the coach door to yell that news over the cacophony of wind and rain.

'Close it before we are awash in here, you stupid boy,' Mrs Jackson screeched, beating away a torrent of raindrops with her hands.

Mr Jackson had grown pale at the news of a stranger approaching, but said manfully, 'Let me sit at the front, by the door.' He surged forward, pushing his wife's quivering figure behind him. 'Hold up that gun, young man,' he ordered Bert. 'I take it you're familiar with how to use it and reload it if the need arises?'

Bert wobbled his head in agreement, looking terrified.

'How many riders?' Mr Jackson croaked. He realised it might be Toby Williams returning, but doubted it was; insufficient time had passed for their driver to have reached the Fallow Buck, let alone return with help.

'Just the one, I think, and I only glimpsed him in the distance, through the trees.' Bert swung about at the unmistakable thud of hooves. The lad had sensed that the farmer shared his fears about what might be about to happen: with a whistle, the approaching stranger might bring the rest of his gang swarming out of the undergrowth once he realised how vulnerable they were. Or it could be a lone highwayman, who'd chanced upon them…

Luke slowed to a trot and cursed beneath his breath on seeing the calamity before him. He was only a short distance from his destination and for a split second felt tempted to ride on towards it. He was cold, wet and hungry, but he knew he could not leave the wretches stranded. The least he could do was offer to fetch help, while hoping to hear that it was already being summoned. A horse was missing from the harness and he guessed one of the coachmen had ridden off on it. The young fellow with the blunderbuss looked trigger happy so Luke supposed he ought to quickly declare himself friend rather than foe. But he understood why these folk would be nervous of strangers; since Thornley's daughter had told him of smuggled spirits coming ashore, he'd heard from other sources, too, that the Collins gang were busy.

At the window of the coach he could see a round male face and a woman's pop-eyed stare beaming cross the fellow's shoulder. Dismounting, Luke gave a friendly salute, then tethered his stallion to a low branch and squelched through mud to the far side of the lopsided carriage to assess its damage.

As soon as the rain had started hammering down, he'd rued his decision to travel, but he'd set out in fine weather that afternoon, travelling west, with the intention of visiting Drew Rockleigh who had a hunting lodge in the neighbourhood. He'd visited the place before, then under far more pleasant circumstances than drew him there now. But if a fight between the two men were unavoidable, then Luke would as soon get it over with than it hung over them both like the sword of Damocles.

He squatted, saw the axle was in two pieces and stood up almost immediately. It would be quicker and simpler to get another coach out to rescue these unfortunates than try to repair the sorry contraption. He sensed he was under close scrutiny and through a blur of water dripping off the brim of his hat saw a woman's indistinct features.

'Where were you heading?' A hand swiped the worst of the wet from his face as he walked closer and got a better view of her. She was younger than he was by some years, although not as youthful as Becky, and her severe expression made her look plainer than she probably was.

'Dartmouth...' Fiona knew to be careful with her answers. They didn't yet know anything about this fellow to be able to trust him. Mr

Jackson's instinctive alarm at knowing a stranger was in their midst had made Fiona suspect the area was populated with criminals. 'Where were *you* heading?' she countered, blinking to get a better look at him. When she did focus properly on his lean, rain-sleek visage her breath caught in her throat. He was the most disturbingly handsome man she'd ever seen.

'Lowerton…a village a few miles distant,' Luke explained hoping to put her at ease. One of her hands was holding the open window ledge and he could see the tension in her grip.

'Has somebody gone to fetch help?' Luke angled his head and included the others in the coach in his request for information.

'Our driver has and is expected back at any moment. Would you introduce yourself, please, sir?' Mr Jackson insisted, peering across Fiona's shoulder at him.

'My apologies… Luke Wolfson…at your service…'

'I am Peter Jackson, and this is my wife and these two ladies are the Misses Beresford, and the lady nearest to you is…'

'Miss Fiona Chapman,' Fiona quietly introduced herself as Mrs Jackson's coughing drowned out her husband's voice.

Fiona was feeling more relaxed than she had

moments ago. Mr Wolfson had spoken just a few sentences, yet there was something about his tall, imposing presence that now seemed re-assuring rather than threatening. He spoke in a calm, cultured way and was dressed in expensive clothes, so would indeed be an odd highway-man—although she'd heard that wily miscreants sometimes garbed themselves in stolen finery to mislead their victims as to their true characters.

She sensed that her fellow travellers were becoming equally glad that Mr Wolfson had happened by. Another man—especially one of Luke Wolfson's age and muscular stature—could only be of help, if he stayed around. Fiona wondered if he might soon bid them farewell now he knew help was on its way.

Bert had trotted around the coach to stand by the newcomer's side and gaze at him defer-entially, the blunderbuss pointing at the ground.

'Are you cold?' Luke had seen Fiona huddle into her cloak and pull the hood forward over a bonnet.

'Very cold, sir. We all left the coach earlier so the driver might better attempt to mend it…alas, to no avail.' She gave a small shake of the head. 'Toby Williams has given up on it and returned to the Fallow Buck for a wright with better tools.

The trees gave us little shelter from the storm and we all got drenched through.'

'I'd say this one's beyond quick repair and out of action for a while. Your driver should bring out a fresh vehicle.'

A groan of dismay from Mrs Jackson met Luke's bad news about their transport. Fiona nodded acceptance of his verdict, she'd come to a similar conclusion herself.

'I hope that Toby will return very soon.' She glanced in concern at Mrs Jackson as the woman again started to cough.

'I'll light a fire—you could gather around it and dry your clothes while you wait for your man to show up.' Luke frowned at the nearby copse as though assessing its suitability as a shelter.

'Fire?' Peter Jackson left off thumping his wife's back to bark an incredulous laugh. 'I'd like to think he might manage it, but I doubt it somehow.' He gazed at Luke's retreating figure. 'He'll not find a stick of dry kindling about anywhere.'

'It's good of him to try,' Fiona murmured, also watching Mr Wolfson's impressively broad back.

Twenty minutes later the farmer was eating his words. The driving rain had slowed to a drizzle and meekly Mr Jackson followed the ladies towards the trees where a welcoming blaze could be seen. In a clearing, further into the wood than the little party had previously ventured, a fire was steadily taking hold, protected by a tent of evergreen branches that Luke had propped over the flames. Intermittently there was a hissing sound as raindrops slithered through ivy on to glowing embers.

'I should get out of these wet things—I will be laid up for weeks, I know I will,' Betty Jackson grumbled through chattering teeth.

'Stand close to the fire, my dear, to keep warm.' Mr Jackson took off his greatcoat and used it to shield his wife from view as she shed her sodden outer layers. The Beresford sisters took up position on the opposite side and performed similar tasks for one another, Ruth giggling the while.

Fiona moved away to allow them some privacy while they juggled their coats and shawls and attempted to pat dry their damp bodices. She held out her hands to the flames, but now being a distance from the fire she gained scant benefit from it.

'You're soaked, too—take off your cloak and wear my coat while it dries.'

Startled by the mild command, Fiona stuttered, 'Thank you…umm…for the…kind offer, sir. But it would hardly be fair—it is still drizzling and your shirt will get wet.' She gave Luke a fleeting smile, averting her gaze as his dark eyes bored into her. She turned up her face to the heavens, shivering as a chill mist bathed her complexion. 'I will take this off, though,' she added lightly, removing her bonnet and giving it a thorough shake by the brim to remove rain that had settled in the straw.

Her heart had begun to pound at an alarming rate and confusingly she was uncertain whether she wished he would go away. Yet he'd been unfailingly polite and helpful. Without turning to check if it was so, she was sure their Good Samaritan was still watching her while he removed the long leather riding coat he wore.

'Here…take it…I'm used to braving the elements,' Luke said firmly, settling the garment around Fiona's shoulders before walking off.

With no time to properly protest Fiona pressed together her lips and held on to the garment by its lapels. It trailed on the ground, so long was it, and she tried to hoist it up a bit to prevent the hem collecting mud. The leather held a scent redolent of her dear papa's study. Once the room had been crammed with cracked hide sofas and cigar smoke, but all had been removed and sold since Cecil Ratcliff had married her mother.

Jerking her mind to the present, Fiona quickly slipped out of her soaked cloak and, with Mr Wolfson's replacement garment about her narrow shoulders, she gave her own a good shake to dislodge water from the woollen surface.

The two gentlemen and young Bert were hanging the ladies' outerwear on sticks they'd rammed into the ground about the perimeter of the fire, creating a humid atmosphere as steam rose from the clothes.

Luke returned to Fiona and took her cloak to hang it up.

'I'm famished,' Valerie Beresford moaned, fiddling with the pins in her straggling hair. 'I hope that Mr Williams will bring us back some food.'

'He will,' the absent fellow's nephew assured the company. 'He'll turn up with every possible thing to make you comfortable.'

'A refund on the fare would make *me* easy,' Mr Jackson snorted. 'The contraption could not have been roadworthy to sustain such damage. I took a look at that pothole that overset us. It was not so great an impediment for a vehicle in good order. Highway robbery indeed! These coach companies charge a ransom for inferior transport.'

Mrs Jackson joined her husband in carping

about the cost of their tickets and Valerie Beresford added to the debate, making poor Bert sidle off into the shadows, looking chagrined.

Having found a low tree stump that might serve as a seat, Fiona dusted a pool of moisture from it with a gloved palm, then sat down with a sigh to wait for Toby to return.

# Chapter Four

‘Whereabouts in Dartmouth are you headed, Miss Chapman?’

Having stretched Fiona’s cloak over two staves to aid its drying, Luke had strolled closer to her to ask his question.

After a slight hesitation Fiona told him. She realised there was no reason not to. Mr Wolfson didn’t seem a person given to gossiping. Besides, they would never meet one another again after today so it was unlikely that any confidence she bestowed would be of note to him. Even were it to be repeated, who would care—apart from a few people dear to her—that Fiona Chapman, spinster, had left home, so unpleasant had her life become, to take up employment as a governess.

She had heard her chosen profession could be quite wretched and lonely. A governess was not quite a servant, yet neither was she a member of her charges' family. Her position fell somewhere in between, and she risked being resented by her inferiors and despised by an employer who'd deem her presence an irritating necessity. And the children might be horrors, too...but Fiona was confident she was a capable, resilient sort, content with her own company if no other were to be had.

'Are you travelling on business or pleasure?' Luke asked, turning Mrs Jackson's coat so the lining faced towards the fire.

'Business...' Realising she was staring, Fiona dragged her gaze from where his linen shirt, dampened by drizzle, clung to the muscled contours of his ribs. The buttons at the throat were undone and his swarthy skin gave him a dangerously foreign air. Yet he was a refined Englishman, of that she was sure, although he'd disclosed nothing about himself.

Luke turned to glance at her with an elevated eyebrow, wordlessly requesting more information about her plans.

Again Fiona was tempted to tell him and that was odd for she was normally an extremely private person. In one way she found this gentleman's virility daunting, yet his confident, capable manner was soothing too. The dark, romantic atmosphere of flame-daubed shrubbery and the sound and scent of spitting kindling was having a peculiar effect on her, she realised. She felt enchanted, bound to this good-looking stranger's side, and willing to confess her life's secrets until he chose to draw a halt to their conversation.

'I'm on my way to take up a position as a children's governess,' Fiona said.

'You're brave, then, as well as…foolish…' At the last moment Luke had substituted something truthful yet unflattering for the compliment that had almost rolled off his tongue. He'd astonished himself by being uncharacteristically familiar with a genteel woman he barely knew. Fiona Chapman wasn't beautiful… She wasn't even conventionally pretty despite the sweet halo of fawn curls fluffing about her heart-shaped face as the glow of the fire dried her off. Earlier, when her hair had been sleek with rain Luke had thought her a brunette and her features, though small and regular, were nothing much out of the ordinary. Yet something about her was undeniably attractive to him…and he'd almost told her so.

The spell had been broken; Fiona shot to her feet from her makeshift stool, wondering if he was being sarcastic. She was sure he'd been on the point of calling her beautiful and she knew she was nothing of the sort. Fiona came to the depressing conclusion that Mr Wolfson, despite his worthy practical skills, had a shallow side and it was hardly the time or place for insincere flattery.

'Foolish?' she echoed coolly, hoping to convey she wasn't impressed and wasn't playing his game. 'Pray, why do you think that of me, sir, when we barely know one another?' No doubt he believed she'd be better served seeking a husband to care for than children to tutor.

'You're travelling alone, aren't you?'

'I am,' Fiona crisply owned up.

'Then I'll amend what I said and call you *extremely* foolish. These are dangerous roads stalked by violent criminals, as I'm sure your coachman or Mr Jackson must have told you by now.'

'Even could I afford her, how might a lady's maid protect me from such as highwaymen?' Fiona snapped. 'A female dependant would be a burden, not a comfort, to me for I would fret constantly for her safety as well as my own.' Fiona spun away, ready to march off after her parting shot. She'd taken just two steps when hard fingers clamped on her wrist, arresting her.

'And who will you burden with your safety, Miss Chapman? A middle-aged coachman, or a youth unable to handle a gun correctly? A farmer who has his wife to attend to? Me…?'

Fiona twisted her arm free, glaring at him with tawny eyes that held a feral spark. 'I expect no one to look after me, sir. Least of all you. I can care for myself.'

'Can you indeed?'

The murmured words held a soft mockery that brought high spots of angry colour to Fiona's cheekbones. 'Yes…I can,' she vowed sturdily.

He gave a slow nod, accepting what she'd said, but Fiona knew he was still laughing at her even if he had dipped his head to prevent her seeing the expression beneath his long black lashes.

'Are you going to castigate the Beresford ladies for travelling without a servant?' Fiona demanded. 'Or is it just me you wish to condemn as a nuisance for having the temerity to do so?'

'Just you…'

'And why is that?'

'You are younger and more comely than the other ladies, as I'm sure you're aware. If your coach were held up, you would draw the attention of felons who might want to take more than just material valuables from the women they rob.'

That took the wind out of Fiona's sails and put a deeper blush in her cheeks. She swallowed, said hoarsely, 'You seem to know a worrying amount about it, Mr Wolfson.'

Luke's mouth quirked. 'Over the years I've learned lots of things.'

'I'm sure…and have you now learned not to stop and help stranded travellers, lest they irritate you?'

'I confess I was tempted to keep going.'

Fiona found that admission rather shocking, given that he'd helped enormously, keeping them safe and sound by lighting a fire and drying their clothes. 'It's good to know that your conscience got the better of you in the end, sir,' she said faintly.

Fiona backed off a step, then swung about. A moment later she realised she still had on his coat. Whipping it from her shoulders, she handed it over with a stilted 'Thank you, I've no further need of it.'

This time he let her go and Fiona walked swiftly to where the others were congregated, discussing animatedly how long Toby had been away and when they might expect his return. It was obvious to Fiona that Mr and Mrs Jackson had worked themselves up into quite a tizzy about the calamity, blaming the coachman for all their ills.

As though in answer to Mrs Jackson's prayer—

chanted between coughing fits—the sound of hooves and rattling wheels was heard.

Bert leapt up from where he'd been squatting by the fireside. He picked up the blunderbuss and looked fearfully in Luke's direction for a signal as to how to proceed.

Luke had already removed a pair of duck-foot pistols from his saddlebag and his fists were curled about the weapons in the pockets of the leather coat he'd donned.

A moment later Bert was grinning and rushing towards the road as he recognised his uncle's voice booming out his name.

'I'll bid you farewell now your driver is back,' Luke interjected when there was a break in the frantic conversation batting between Toby Williams and an irate Peter Jackson.

'Our gratitude goes with you, sir,' Peter announced. 'You've done us all a great service.' He held out his hand and vigorously pumped Luke's fingers. 'This fellow has been a godsend in your absence,' he told Toby Williams accusingly.

'I take it you'll overnight at the Fallow Buck?' Luke addressed the remark to the driver.

Toby Williams gave a nod, ignoring the glare he got from Mr Jackson. 'I must thank you, too, for your assistance, Mr Wolfson.' He held out his hand.

Having shaken it Luke bowed to the Beresford sisters, who fluttered about him and offered him their fingers to hold. Mrs Jackson went so far as to give him a motherly pat on the cheek to display her appreciation.

Then he turned to Fiona. 'Miss Chapman...' He gave a slight bow and received a dip of the head in return.

'I hope you reach your destination safely,' he said quietly.

'And I return you that wish, sir,' Fiona replied.

'The name of the family who has employed you is...?'

Fiona no longer felt swayed to tell him anything about herself. She answered him with a concise farewell and a frosty smile before following her fellow travellers towards their replacement vehicle.

But she was acutely aware of every sound behind as a horse snickered on being mounted. When the slow clop of hooves told her he was negotiating a path away from them through the woods she felt a peculiar lump form in her throat. It was nothing more than anxiety over the loss of him guarding them, she told herself crossly.

Once the luggage and the spare horses had been transferred to the new coach, a confab began with the driver.

'In my opinion it's best that we return to the Fallow Buck,' Toby Williams argued with Peter Jackson, who'd said he wanted none of it. 'It's a treacherous night. After all that rain the road will have washed away and it's not a good idea to travel in the dark in any case, what with villains about.' He'd lowered his voice for the last bit so as not to alarm the ladies.

'And I say we carry on,' Peter Jackson declared. 'We have lost enough time already and my wife needs to be home in her own bed. She's caught a devil of a cold and might need a physician.'

'Yes…I…might…' Mrs Jackson stressed.

'I want to get home, too!' Valerie Beresford wailed. 'I wish Mr Wolfson had stayed and ridden alongside us. I felt safe in his company. Will you not fetch him back, sir?' She tugged on Toby's sleeve.

'I think he turned south,' Bert piped up helpfully.

'Never mind him. He's gone,' Toby said shortly, miffed that a passing stranger had thrown his own role as saviour into the shade. 'We should rest the night at the inn and leave the horses we've no need of. Then start off fresh in the morning in good light and better weather.'

'Mr Williams has a valid point,' Fiona ventured an opinion. 'We do not want to end up sliding into a ditch in the dark and again be stranded out in the open.'

'We will not be so lucky next time to be saved by such as Mr Wolfson,' Ruth interjected, wringing her hands. She seemed to have given up on craving an adventure and looked as heartsick as her older sister following their misfortune.

'I say we hurry up in getting home!' Mr Jackson loudly insisted as his wife obligingly started to hack and slap herself on the chest. 'The Pig and Whistle is not so far in front of us and we can leave there the nags we don't need.' He pulled out his watch. 'At a strong pace we might reach the inn by half past midnight and will lose no time at all in ending this infernal journey.'

'Very well…be it on your own heads.' With no more ado Toby climbed angrily on to his perch, signalling for his nephew to join him.

Fiona awoke about a mile into their renewed journey, feeling unrefreshed and rubbing her gritty eyes. Although she'd been wretchedly uncomfortable, squashed in the corner of the seat, she'd managed to doze fitfully. Ruth Beresford was snoring beside her, her head drooping on Fiona's shoulder. Rather than wake her and ask her to shift along a bit to give her more room,

Fiona chose to put up with her cramped position. The mood in the coach as they'd set off had not been happy and Fiona would sooner suffer sore muscles than more moaning.

At first, her companions had agitatedly watched passing scenery to spot lurking dangers until, one by one, they'd settled back into the squabs. Mr Jackson had been last to succumb to the rocking of the coach and to close his eyes. They were making steady progress towards the Pig and Whistle. Fiona was glad, even if none of the others seemed to have been, that Toby Williams was sensibly taking a slow and easy pace along the perilous road, slick with mud.

When they'd started out Peter had loudly commented that Toby Williams was deliberately dawdling to annoy them all. He had hammered on the roof of the coach in protest. Thankfully, the driver had ignored the command to increase speed and they continued to go along at a sedate pace.

Pinned against the window as she was, Fiona had little choice but to gaze into the darkness dappled by the flickering coach lamps. Patches of vegetation loomed into shape, adopting a yellow gloss before returning to an inky outline as the vehicle lumbered past. Fiona shivered, unable to stop imagining that behind the dense bushes unfriendly eyes were watching them.

For all her proud boast to Luke Wolfson that she could look after herself, Fiona knew she couldn't. She was a fish out of water in this rural environment and wished as dearly as did the others that Mr Wolfson had accompanied them on this dark and lonely road. For some reason that she refused to attribute to simple conceit, she sensed that had she asked him to stay with them, he would have agreed to do so. But they'd parted coolly and now he would be miles distant and close to his destination if not already arrived at it.

He'd said he was going to Lowerton, but she doubted he was a local and lived permanently in a Devon village. Fiona imagined he was, like her, from London and wondered if she'd ever passed Luke Wolfson on a city street. Perhaps, without realising it, she might have bumped into him while out shopping, or when socialising with her sister and their friends at the pleasure gardens. She pondered for a moment on the likelihood, but doubted a meeting had occurred; she would have noticed him even if he'd overlooked her.

And he would have done so. Her younger sister Verity had always drawn the gentlemen's attention and their friends, Elise and Beatrice

Dewey, were both blonde beauties, now married to eminent millionaires.

Fiona had been the oldest of their group, but when all the others settled down she had never felt miffed that, being plain-faced, she'd been passed over. Until now. The thought of Luke Wolfson flirting with her sister or her friends irked her and she knew it was ridiculous to feel that way. How could she possibly be jealous of something that hadn't occurred and concerned a gentleman she scarcely knew?

Irritated with the direction of her thoughts, Fiona sighed beneath her breath. She squeezed shut her eyes, hoping to block Mr Wolfson's rugged features and husky baritone from her mind. On opening them again a gasp of shock abraded her throat. She quickly blinked and craned her neck, but the shadowy silhouette she'd glimpsed was lost to her as the coach rumbled on. She tensed, wondering whether to alert Mr Jackson or the driver to what she thought she'd seen, but then if she were mistaken, and there was nothing out there but a deer, she'd just cause more bad feeling. But…it might have been Luke Wolfson who'd felt conscience bound, as he had once before, to help them on their way, her inner voice argued.

Before Fiona could find a solution to her dilemma the coach juddered as the driver reined in and the silence of a moment ago was shattered by shouts from within and without the vehicle.

Peter Jackson fell almost into Ruth Beresford's lap while his wife, who'd been resting on his shoulder, rolled sideways on to the empty seat. Only Fiona, primed to something afoot, had not tipped from her perch at the abrupt halt.

The sound of a gunshot brought in its wake an eerie silence. Then there was another bang and Mr Jackson flung open the coach door and leapt out, flailing his arms for balance.

The sight that met their eyes was shocking enough to make Valerie Beresford swoon against her sister's breast and Mrs Jackson squeak in fright before shouting for her husband.

Only Fiona and Ruth remained quiet, although Fiona imagined that Ruth Beresford was as terrified as she was at the sight of the grinning felon pointing a weapon at them.

She knew he was smiling from the crinkling about his eyes; the lower half of his face was concealed behind a neckerchief.

'Out you come, then, ladies, let's take a look at you,' the ruffian jovially ordered in a voice muffled by cotton.

'You will not lay a finger on these ladies!'

Peter Jackson roared, shaking a fist at the fellow, although visibly perspiring in fear.

Once disembarked, Fiona could see that the highwayman was not alone; his associate was astride a horse a yard or two away. His features were also partially concealed, nevertheless he seemed vaguely familiar to her. And then her eyes fell on a sight that made her groan in dismay. Toby Williams had been unusually quiet following the hold up because he was occupied tending his wounded nephew. Young Bert was lying on the ground and his uncle was crouching beside his still figure, trying to staunch his bleeding.

Ignoring the highwayman's demand that she stay where she was, Fiona spontaneously rushed to help the invalid if she could.

'Is he badly hurt?' she breathed, watching as Toby tried to dry Bert's wound with a handkerchief. But as fast as the fellow turned the wad to find a clean spot, it again became scarlet with blood.

Crouching close to the floor to protect her modesty, Fiona lifted her skirt a few inches and ripped a length of lawn from her petticoat hem. She handed it to Toby who gave her a grateful smile and proceeded to fold it into a thick compress.

'I told Bert to lay down the blunderbuss as soon as I saw 'em flanking us.' Toby shot a baleful glance over a shoulder at the robbers. 'I knew we was done for and no use making it worse than need be,' he added plaintively. 'But the dunderhead loosed off a shot in a panic. Bert never could hit a barn door—now what am I to tell his mother about all this?'

'He will be all right…I'm sure.' Fiona whispered, hoping that Bert, if conscious, would not be depressed by a doubtful inflection in her voice. The boy had his eyes closed and his deathly pale complexion was dreadfully worrying. As his uncle stuffed the linen inside Bert's bloodstained shirt, binding his injury, Fiona tore again at her petticoat to provide a fresh bandage should it be needed.

'You…come here!' the older highwayman barked at Fiona.

Fiona glanced over a shoulder to see that the younger man had dismounted and joined his comrade on foot. They were both levelling pistols, swinging them threateningly between their victims.

The youth suddenly whispered something in his senior's ear and Fiona had an uneasy suspicion that what was said concerned her as two pairs of eyes narrowed on her.

'Come here, you defiant wench!'

The felon strode to Fiona, jerking her upright by the elbow. He propelled her towards the youth who stared at her over the top of his mask.

'That's her, right enough,' the lad said. He turned to whisper in his cohort's ear, 'Running off to be wed.'

'Leave her be, or you'll have me to answer to,' Peter Jackson bellowed. He beckoned frantically to Fiona to come to him, but his efforts to protect her were rewarded with a clubbing from the villainous youth's pistol butt.

Mrs Jackson dropped to her knees beside her prone husband, her wail rending the night air, while the two Beresford ladies began whimpering behind their fingers.

'Let me go!' Fiona wrenched her arm to and fro, attempting to liberate it from a painful grip. 'What is it you want? Money? Here, take it.' With her free hand she pulled from her pocket a pouch containing her coins.

That gesture brought a chortling sound from behind a neckerchief. 'Why, thank you…' the older highwayman said sarcastically, jingling the little bag of money in front of his colleague's face. 'Not enough in there, I'll warrant, to keep us happy.' But despite his contempt for Fiona's worldly goods, he pocketed it before making a lunge for her. 'Whereas you, my dear, are treasure to somebody I know.' Grabbing her behind the knees, he swung her up and over his shoulder.

# Chapter Five

❧

If he'd not been a military man Luke might have mistaken the muffled boom of the blunderbuss for the bark of a deer. As it was he reined in sharp with an oath exploding between his teeth. Another bullet was let loose far in the distance and this time he recognised the retort of a pistol.

The stallion had also heard the sounds and, attuned to his master's need for speed at such signals, required little prodding in turning and flying back the way they'd come over black, muddy fields.

When thirty minutes later Luke reined in his mount its flanks were foamy with sweat. He approached the road cautiously, then, slipping from the saddle, covered the last hundred yards on foot, guided by the stationary coach lamps. Immediately he feared the worst as he heard the sound of groaning and women weeping being carried on the still night air.

His fingers tightened on the duck-foot pistols and his jaw clenched as he glimpsed through the undergrowth the spectacle before him. Having ascertained that the thieves had left the vicinity, he loped onwards, calling out to announce his presence in case a bullet was fired at him.

The Misses Beresford were the first to spot Luke. They scrambled from the coach where they'd been sheltering and rushed to cling to his arms, garbling a version of events.

Peter Jackson was sitting on the ground, a hand pressed to a crust of blood on the back of his head. His wife continued dabbing frantically at his throbbing brow with a rain-dampened hanky and howled curses at the vile cowards who'd caused this mayhem.

But it was the unmoving boy sprawled on the mud with his uncle fussing over him who drew Luke's concerned gaze, but only momentarily. He suddenly realised that the person he most wanted to see was absent. Freeing himself from the spinsters' clutches, he strode to the coach and looked inside.

'Where's Miss Chapman?' Luke demanded, a surge of furious emotion suddenly overtaking him.

'They've taken her.' Peter Jackson shook his head, tears rolling down his face. 'I couldn't stop them, sir—they knocked me down when I tried to...'

'Who was it?' Luke snapped, coming closer, restraining an urge to grab the man's lapels to hurry his answer.

Peter raised his eyes to a flinty black stare. 'There were two of them. They wore masks, but I'm sure that Collins is behind it. The evil black-guard!'

Luke spun towards the driver; Williams was, after all, in charge of his customers' safety, yet he'd offered no explanation or apology for Miss Chapman's kidnap. But the man was distraught and Luke bit back the ferocious accusation he'd been about to let fly.

'I think he's dying,' Toby gurgled, patting Bert's face with increasing strength in an attempt to bring the youth round.

'Get in the coach...all of you...apart from you!' he ordered Toby. 'Help me lift the lad— we'll lay him on a seat and the others will have to squash together on the opposite side. Come, quickly now!' he snapped at Toby in the hope of penetrating the man's shock and galvanising him into action. 'The Pig and Whistle is a few miles away and you can get help for your nephew there. Pray to God we're in time for him...'

The ladies tottered aboard the coach once more, followed by Mr Jackson. Luke and Toby gently lifted the invalid, then settled Bert on the worn upholstery. Although Toby winced on hearing the lad moaning, Luke was gladdened by the sound.

'He has not fallen too far into unconsciousness,' he reassured the driver. Pulling Toby away from fussing over the boy, he slammed shut the door. Once up on the driver's perch Luke took the reins firmly; he didn't want Toby Williams turning them over in a ditch in his agitated state.

'Should you not tie your horse to the back of the coach, Mr Wolfson?' Toby attempted to calm himself and be of assistance.

'No need to worry about him—Star will follow.' Following his concise reply about his finely trained stallion, Luke set the team to a trot. They'd soon cleared the woods and he put the horses to a faster pace, his eyes narrowed and straining to see through the darkness for hazardous obstacles littering the terrain in order to avoid them in good time.

But as much as he was occupied by the job at hand an image of a woman with fawn hair and golden eyes was in his mind, too. Luke knew that if Collins had harmed a hair on Fiona Chapman's head the dragoons on the smuggler's trail wouldn't be needed after today; Luke would find the lawless bastard and kill him himself.

Fiona felt scarcely able to breathe with a silencing gag wedged between her lips. As she'd been carried off she'd kicked, scratched and yelled so much that the two men had reined in after a short gallop to secure her hands and ankles together. They'd called her foul names while roughly curbing her thrashing. Then, when satisfied they'd quietened her, they'd carelessly flung her across the horse's back in a way that knocked the breath from her body and made her feel faint.

Now her head was hanging low, banging against the animal's belly and she could feel a heavy hand pressing down into the centre of her back to keep her from sliding off the beast. A hammering at her temples was making them ache abominably, but instead of feeling frightened she felt enraged, and instead of self-pity she inwardly berated herself for not putting up a greater fight and making good her escape.

She was incensed to be suffering such treatment. No man had ever raised a punishing hand to her, not even her father when she deserved chastisement. When Cecil Ratcliff's attempts to manhandle her had grown beyond bearing she'd hit him across the face with her silver-backed brush, then packed her belongings shortly afterwards.

But she realised others had suffered, too, at the hands of these ruffians. Young Bert might have perished and Mr Jackson was certain to have sustained concussion at the very least. Fiona felt tears prickle her eyes, not just because of her own uncertain fate, but because of that of her fellow travellers.

The junior highwayman had stolen the spare horses, tethering them behind his own mount, and the drumming of a dozen or more hooves was increasing the pounding in Fiona's skull. Just as she thought she could stand no more of the interminable journey, and of struggling for breath while blocking out her aches and pains, the horse was slowed to a trot.

Moments later they were at a standstill and her captor dismounted, pulling her down so she collapsed to her knees at his feet. Her hair, wound neatly at her nape that morning, had escaped all its pins and Fiona could feel its heavy weight on her shoulders and straggling around her face. She remained still, listening, sensing that others were around. She heard muffled male voices, then boots on gravel. A moment later she was hoisted up by an arm and the blindfold and gag were removed.

By a filtering moonlight Fiona saw that a rather thin, nondescript fellow was gazing at her and that they were standing within the grounds of a graveyard. The bulky outline of a church, its spire soaring against a navy-blue sky, was outlined on a mound some yards away. Closer to her were scattered headstones and box-like tombs topped with eerie sculptures. She suppressed a shiver, not wanting these vile rogues to know that they, or her surroundings, intimidated her.

'Jeremiah Collins, at your service, my lady.' He raised a hand, taking a thick fawn tress between calloused thumb and forefinger. 'Would I be right in thinking you are the Duke of Thornley's daughter?' He cocked his head, inspecting her.

'No, you would not, you buffoon,' Fiona snapped, slapping his hand away from her hair.

Jeremiah chuckled. 'She's the spirit of a highborn lass right enough, Fred…but I'm not sure. The major said the jaunt had been cancelled.' He turned to the senior of the two felons who he'd addressed as Fred. 'She's plain as a pikestaff and older than I expected. I think you've brought me a pig in a poke, not a ransom.'

Fred Ruff was embarrassed by his boss's

criticism. He ripped down his neckerchief so he might speak more clearly, uncaring of Fiona seeing his face now. If Collins were right and he'd taken a worthless woman, then she'd need to be disposed of. In that case it would be immaterial whether his victim could recognise him again. 'Mayhap the major's been playing with us so he might keep all the money in his own pocket,' Fred blustered, but shot his youthful accomplice a baleful look. Sam Dickens had convinced him they were on to something big and that Jem Collins would praise them to the skies for using their initiative and abducting the chit.

'That's her!' Sam also removed his disguise while wagging a finger in emphasis. He knew he was in trouble if he'd led Fred up the garden path. 'Megan told me they was talking about the estate and the old duke's pheasants and a society wedding feast. They said about this one eloping…whispering they was like it was a big secret, Megan said.'

'We were! But the Thornley wedding plans are nothing to do with me personally!' Fiona interjected in exasperation. She glowered at the youth. *Now* she knew where she'd seen him before: he was the stable hand who'd been flirting with the serving girl at the Fallow Buck. 'My name is Miss Chapman and I've journeyed from

London.' She realised that the dolts had confused her with a duke's daughter, living locally, and abducted the wrong person. She felt like shouting a laugh. Sooner or later they'd realise their mistake and if her stepfather were approached to pay up for her release the miser would pay them not a penny piece. And her mother had nothing left now of value to offer.

Collins turned towards Fiona, rubbing his chin thoughtfully with thumb and forefinger. 'You might be right, Fred, about the major trying to cut us out of the deal. He might want to pin the deed on us, but keep all the spoils. If that's what he's about, then the fellow will be close by and mad as hell that we've got to this little lady before him.' He circled Fiona, looking her up and down. 'Perhaps you aren't as bad looking as I first thought.' He cocked his head. 'You're Quality, no disguising that, even dressed in these plain things.' He fingered her woollen cloak. 'But then you'd want to look unexceptional, wouldn't you, my dear? Drawing attention to yourself would be a mistake till you'd got your lover's protection.'

'Perhaps her swain would stump up a ransom for her, too,' Sam suggested brightly. 'We could play 'em one off against t'other.'

'He's poor as a church mouse, according to the

major's report, that's why she's eloping—because her father won't hear of the match.'

'But maybe we can't trust *his* word!' Sam exclaimed.

'You're all talking rot!' Fiona shouted in frustration. 'And you might as well let me on my way, for I'm expected elsewhere to take up a position in service. The authorities will be on your tails by now. My travelling companions will have reported this outrage.'

'She's no domestic, I'll stake my life on it! She's lying!' Sam triumphantly declared.

'I'm a governess and I'll be missed by my employer. He'll send a search party if I don't turn up,' Fiona warned.

Jeremiah Collins again raised a hand to touch her, but Fiona stepped out of his reach, glaring at him. He looked quite inoffensive with his wispy fair hair and wiry frame. But she sensed that behind his pale eyes lurked a vicious and devious mind and she wanted to be quickly out of his clutches.

'I think you're a crafty wench, accustomed to lying,' Collins said slowly. 'If you're Thornley's spawn, you'll have been deceiving your papa for some time, gallivanting with a ne'er-do-well to escape being married off to an old roué.' He clucked his tongue. 'His Grace won't be popular if he tries to pass off spoiled goods to his new son-in-law, even though the fellow can match him for years. Thornley will pay handsomely to get you back and keep quiet this escapade.'

A glimmer of revulsion flitted across Fiona's features at the idea of a young woman being forcibly married off to an aged lecher. As for the poor young lady being compromised following her abduction by highwaymen... Fiona realised that fate now applied to *her*. If it ever got out that she'd been in the company of three brutes—and of course it would because many people knew of it—then she would be thoroughly ruined.

Collins had noticed her distressed reaction and smiled with nasty satisfaction. 'Come...come... I have sympathy for your plight, my lady, but I've money to make and pleasure to take before I swing on Gallows Hill.' He strode to his comrades to mutter beneath his breath, 'I think she could be Thornley's brat, but if she's speaking the truth, and is Miss Chapman, we've got ourselves a millstone round our necks. There's only one thing to do with such: cut 'em loose and cast 'em in the sea so they sink.'

'Shall we scout around the local hostelries for the major? If he's still in the neighbourhood, that'll tell us what we need to know,' Fred Ruff hissed.

'If Wolfson's still in the vicinity then we won't need to go looking for him, he'll find us,' Collins answered with a sly grin. From the two meetings he'd had with Major Wolfson, Collins had gauged he was not a man to cross. But then Jem Collins could match any man alive for ruthlessness. Nevertheless, he was regretting agreeing to do business with him.

By straining her ears Fiona could just catch snippets of their conversation. She heard the name Wolfson and a hand squeezed at her heart. 'Are you talking about Luke Wolfson?' she burst out.

Three pairs of eyes were swung in her direction.

'What do you know of the major?' Collins demanded.

'Nothing… I've just heard his name before,' Fiona murmured, feeling as though she'd taken a blow to the stomach.

So, *the major* they were talking about and Luke Wolfson were one and the same. *He* was the fellow these thugs thought had crossed them in a deal they'd struck to kidnap the Duke of Thornley's daughter. But when Wolfson had come across their broken coach he'd had the intelligence to deduce that Fiona Chapman was who she said she was. No doubt he'd gone after the *real* prize…wherever the poor wretch might be.

*Now* she realised why he'd paid her such attention: Luke Wolfson hadn't been flirting with her, he'd been assessing her and, unlike these fools, had come up with the correct answer. She supposed it had been rather good of him to warn her about the hazards for a young woman travelling alone! He was preparing her for villains such as himself who preyed on female victims.

Suddenly Fiona felt very alone and frightened. From the moment these thugs had hauled her away from her travelling party she'd harboured a tiny hope that Mr Wolfson would somehow discover what had happened to her and ride to save her from these savages. But he was no better than them and he'd provide no service she'd welcome! Of that, Fiona was certain.

From the age of sixteen, when she'd left her home in the countryside to make her fortune, Becky Peake had regularly used payment in kind for things she wanted but couldn't afford. But rolling in hay with a yokel for a ride on his cart was a new low for her. She felt ashamed of herself and wished she'd not spent all the cash Luke had given her on a fancy hat and a night of gambling at the Red Lion at Exeter. Then she might have had the wherewithal to hire a tired nag, or a two-wheeled gig, to follow her lover without resorting to soliciting.

Luke had paid for Becky's coach fare back to London but, on impulse, she'd disembarked before the vehicle had travelled east far enough to cross the county line. Her need to stay close to her lover, lest he replace her with somebody else, was lately always on her mind.

Becky doubted that she would ever love Luke Wolfson in that selfless way her mother had adored her father, but she did know that she craved his company. Major Wolfson was the most attractive and exciting man Becky had ever known; she wanted to be permanently in his life, sharing his adventures and his riches. She fantasised that they would have a brood of beautiful children and then, if the fire in her blood was quenched by the passing of the years, she'd settle into a comfortable life in Essex as lady of the manor with five handsome sons about her silk skirts, and her husband providing her with every little luxury that her heart desired.

'Take you on a foo more miles if yer like.' A gap-toothed fellow shattered Becky's delightful daydream with his coarse country brogue.

'Here will do very well, thank you,' Becky replied in her crispest tone. She continued tying her garters and ignored the farmer grinning at her while he buttoned his trousers. She brushed down her dress and stood up, picking bits of straw from her bonnet.

A moment later Becky was at the barn door and peeking through a crack. Nobody seemed to be around so she slipped out and sashayed off towards the village square, tying her new hat in place as she went. She was hoping that Luke would still be lodging at the same inn; she knew he'd planned to see a chum before heading home. He'd not told her any more about it, no doubt chary of her turning up unannounced at the fellow's home. Becky knew she might have been tempted to do so, too, in her obsession with Luke. But she was sure he'd again put up at the King and Tinker on his way back so she headed in that direction to wait for his return.

'How is he, sir?'

Luke had been saddling up in the stable yard of the Pig and Whistle when he spied the doctor exiting the hostelry. He had quickly intercepted the physician, keen to know how young Bert fared now he'd been ensconced in one of the inn's bedrooms.

'I've dosed the patient with a sleeping draught to aid his recovery.' The doctor gave a grim shake of the head. 'His wound is clean now and luckily the bullet passed through. Bert Williams is young and strong, but he's bled a lot.' He sighed pessimistically in conclusion, then climbed aboard his trap and flicked the reins over the pony's back.

Luke was about to swing into the saddle when he saw Mr Jackson and Toby Williams coming towards him at quite a pace. He hesitated and patted the flanks of the replacement beast he'd hired. Star was limping a little after his punishing ride and Luke didn't want to risk a lame horse hampering him in his search for Fiona Chapman.

'What are we to do about…you know…?' Mr Jackson blurted in a whispering hiss. 'My lady wife and I cannot in all conscience proceed on our way and just ignore the fact that Miss Chapman has been kidnapped by those beasts.'

'I know, sir, but I've asked you to give me a day or so to find her,' Luke replied in an equally muted tone. 'You and I both know that an unmarried young woman's future would be blighted for ever by such a tale becoming common knowledge. And it will, if the authorities are alerted to her abduction. Better I try to get her back and help her to reach her destination. Then she might pick up her life where it left off before this disaster befell her.'

'But the poor lass is bound to be in hysterics and will give the game away herself,' Peter Jackson argued.

'She put up quite a fight, as I recall,' Toby Williams pointed out, sounding in awe of the young woman's pluck.

Luke gave a wry smile; he recalled very well his chat with Fiona Chapman and he sided with Toby's opinion: she was no pushover and he doubted that any lasting harm would be done... as long as he reached her in time. He knew how Collins's mind worked: he was a businessman above all else and if he thought he could turn a profit from Fiona Chapman he'd try to sell her back to her family. To do that successfully, he'd need to return her intact. What was puzzling Luke was the reason he'd taken her in the first place. The other travellers hadn't had any valuables stolen and he found it hard to believe that Collins would think Fiona's ransom might turn a tidy sum. From her appearance, and her need to seek employment, her family connections were modest, Luke reckoned. And if Collins sought simply to use her for his own amusement... Luke's jaw clenched and he suddenly mounted the horse.

'Blight the poor lass's life, good 'n' proper, it would,' Toby stated bluntly. He was feeling better now his nephew was abed and sleeping soundly. 'My young niece was led astray by an older fellow…married her, though, he did…albeit with a gun at his back.'

'I don't think it's seduction or a wife Collins is after,' Luke said drily. 'Give me a day or two and I will return with Miss Chapman, God willing.'

# Chapter Six

Fiona knew she had only one chance at escaping her dank stone-cold cell that reeked of mildew. If she failed to make her getaway the Collins gang would thereafter guard her like hawks. Also, they might kill her for making the attempt, thinking her too much trouble to contend with. Eventually her captors would realise she was who she said she was and they'd want to quickly rid themselves of her.

She was thankful they had not yet discovered that she had little monetary value. Nevertheless Fiona didn't relish the idea of being stuck with this motley crew for weeks while they tried to negotiate a price for her return with her stepfather. They'd certainly dispose of her rather than drag her along while trying to outrun their pursuers. Cecil Ratcliff would enlist the help of the authorities rather than part with any cash to have her discreetly returned. Her mother might weep and protest about the cost to her daughter's reputation should the disaster be broadcast, but Ratcliff wouldn't care about that.

Fiona shifted position on the straw pallet on which she was perched. It had served as a very uncomfortable mattress last night, not least because she feared beetles were also using it as a bed. She had sprung up at one point when the night was at its blackest, having sensed a creature on her arm. Fidgeting to and fro, she studied the bed for movement, wondering if she'd been bitten by bugs.

Her hands had again been tied, but her feet were free and the gag left off, no doubt because her screams would go unheard in this isolated spot. After her capture yesterday she had been dragged, kicking, into the derelict church and down into the crypt to be locked in. But she could hear the gang members coming and going. Fiona's greatest fear was that her gaolers might all be shot and killed by the dragoons without giving her location, leaving her to starve to death in her grisly prison. Fiona knew she'd sooner perish quickly than endure that fate and it renewed her determination to flee for her life at the first opportunity.

She started on hearing footsteps on the stairs,

then the key struck the lock and she knew Sam was bringing her supper. He would untie her hands so she might eat, as he had earlier, when bringing her a lump of greasy pork she'd been unable to stomach. But he'd not been so squeamish; when he'd returned to again fasten her wrists, he'd gobbled up the meat before leaving her alone.

The youth sauntered into the room and put down a plate of bread and cheese on the rickety stool below the window. The single-square pane was set high up and looked far too small for Fiona to slip through, even had she managed to reach it to break the glass. Earlier, she'd used the three-legged seat to stand on to test whether it would be possible to wriggle out into the graveyard. It had proved a fruitless exercise; the tempting glimmer of light had remained beyond her stretching fingertips.

Awkwardly Fiona pushed to her feet by using her clubbed fists. The muscles in her legs were horribly stiff and unobtrusively she tried to ease them by flexing them beneath her skirts. In a moment, if luck were with her, she must run as fast as she could.

Alarmed, Fiona saw the youth turn towards the door without approaching her. 'What about my hands?' she burst out. 'I cannot eat like this.'

Sam turned back, looking churlish. His master was above stairs and had told him to take no chances with the sly minx. 'You can if you're careful…see…' Sam mimed having his wrists tethered in front of him and picked up a crust, taking it to his lips.

'Please…I cannot…I have pins and needles because the twine is too tight.' Fiona raised her arms. 'See how white my hands have become.'

Sam tutted impatiently, then, after a moment of pursed-lipped consideration, his conscience got the better of him and he drew a knife from a pocket.

'Thank you, Sam,' Fiona said in a shaky voice. 'You're kind…not like the other two…'

'Don't try to sweet-talk me.' Sam spat. 'I can be as tough as me pals. Don't go thinking different.'

Fiona nodded to humour him. 'I can see you're a strapping lad. Megan is your sweetheart, then?' She held out her wrists for the binding to be cut, hoping that if she kept him talking she might eventually win him over and make him see how stupidly he was acting. Then he might not only free her hands, but assist her in escaping. He looked to be no more than seventeen, yet he was risking a premature and degrading end on the gallows by associating with Collins.

'Ain't telling you nothing, so keep quiet.' Sam slashed the rope.

'Megan will be distraught if you're sentenced to hang,' Fiona persisted.

'I said keep quiet!' Sam snarled and raised the knife to touch her throat.

Fiona sadly realised he might be young, but he seemed as steeped in evil as his older colleagues. She stole a glance at the oil lamp on the floor. If she could just get him to turn his back for a moment she'd swing the stool at his head and dart outside. She didn't want to hurt him, but then she feared that Sam Dickens would have no qualms about hurting her...perhaps fatally...

'Would you light the lamp for me? It's getting dark.' Fiona indicated the brass implement on the cold stone floor opposite the stool.

Sam muttered in irritation, but drew forth a tinderbox from a pocket and crouched down. Silently Fiona lunged for the stool, sending the plate of bread and cheese flying as she swung the wood with all her might at his bowed head.

Sam grunted and toppled forward, but beyond that Fiona didn't tarry to see what damage she might have done to him. She flew out of the door and up the narrow winding stairs, holding her skirts high to prevent them tripping her up. She could hear Sam groaning a vile curse after her, but Fiona plunged on, the thud of blood in her ears making her deaf to any more of his abuse.

She cried out in despair as she felt a hand manacle her arm, dragging her up the final steps. Throwing back her head, she gazed in shock at the swarthy features of Luke Wolfson. But a glimmer of hope that he'd come to rescue her was soon quashed.

'If this is the best you can do, Jem, I'm astonished you're still at liberty. Can your men not even keep a woman under lock and key?'

Luke pushed Fiona in front of him, but she sensed that his callous fingers held a secret tenderness.

'She's a spirited lass…these high-born women are bred to it.' Collins was seated on the end of a pew and swigging from a bottle. Outwardly he appeared little bothered by his captive's attempt at escape. Inwardly he was seething at Sam Dickens's incompetence and the fact that this man had witnessed it. Jem was proud of his reputation as a ruthless villain and resented being shown up in such a way. 'She's been too spoiled by her doting papa, I'll warrant. Though I imagine the duke might take a lash to her back when next he sees her.' Jeremiah wiped his mouth with a hand. 'This brandy is not as good as the last lot we took off the Frenchies.'

'She's not Thornley's daughter, I've told you that,' Luke said mildly. 'Lady Joan is not yet turned twenty and this one is probably half a decade older.'

'I'm almost persuaded to believe you...' Collins's tone hinted that he believed the opposite were true. 'She says she knows of you.'

'She does, but not as well as I'd like to know her,' Luke said with deliberate lust roughening his voice. 'We met on the road when the carriage she was travelling in came a cropper.' Luke tilted up Fiona's chin with a dark finger. 'She's Fiona Chapman and on her way to be a governess.'

Fiona jerked her face away, but not before she'd given him a ferocious glare from amber eyes bright with despising. Accusations were circling her mind, but much as she was tempted to spout her opinion of Luke Wolfson's vile character she sensed it best to appear subdued and focus on her escape. She'd not yet given up on renewing her attempt to flee these criminals.

'You'd tame her, would you?' Jeremiah Collins snorted a laugh, having seen Fiona's defiance. He stroked his chin in that thoughtful way he had. The major had given the same name as the woman had herself, so Jem knew that Ruff and Dickens had brought him a hapless impostor. But it seemed she interested Wolfson or why would he bother coming after her? Miss Chapman might yet turn him a profit, Collins realised.

'If you're right, Major, and she's a governess,' he purred, 'of what use is she to you?' Collins got up and sauntered closer to the couple. 'She's no beauty and thin with it. I heard you've brought a pretty little ladybird with you to warm your bed at the King and Tinker.' He gave Fiona an insultingly thorough look. 'She has a certain buttoned-up charm, but I can't see a rake like you falling for it.'

'I like *unbuttoning* prim spinsters,' Luke murmured, tightening his grip on Fiona who'd spontaneously stiffened on hearing Collins's description and Luke's lewd response. 'The sport's in the chase and the conquest, not in bedding jades.'

'Where's that vicious bitch!' Sam had crawled on his hands and knees up the stairs and now staggered to his feet, blood dripping from his skull on to his shirt.

Instinctively Fiona shrank back against Luke as the youth's lips were flattened against his teeth and he lunged at her. Luke immediately floored Sam with one easy punch.

'Come, have we a deal?' Luke sounded impatient. 'You might as well let me take her. The people she travelled with have reported the incident and you'll have abduction and rape added to your crimes.'

'And so will you, by the sound of things, Major,' Collins returned smoothly.

'No woman's accused me of force and neither will this one when I've finished with her.'

Collins burst out laughing. 'Take her, then, before I do. You've given me a hankering for Miss Chapman with such rousing talk.' He leered at Fiona and wound a long loose tress about his hand, then gave it a possessive tug.

'Leave her be, she's mine,' Luke said, deceptively mildly.

Fiona sensed the atmosphere between the men change and held her breath, wondering if they were about to fight over her. But Jem slowly withdrew his fist and her hair spiralled to her shoulder in a soft ringlet he'd formed.

'When you've done with her, Wolfson, let me know and perhaps I'll buy her back…at a reduced price, of course…' He gave Sam a punishing kick as he passed his sprawled body. 'What of the Thornley business?'

Luke shrugged. 'I think her father's got her under lock and key until he walks her down the aisle. I'll take a bottle of that brandy off you, too. Put it on my bill.'

'Fred will get it for you,' Collins said. 'Are you staying in these parts?'

'Who knows?' Luke replied. 'I go where the money takes me.'

'A man after my own heart.' Collins chortled.

'And where are you headed?' Luke asked.

Collins shrugged. 'To the beach to collect some kegs, then, like you, Wolfson, I'll be following my next fortune.'

Luke smiled but he knew, as did his adversary, that neither of them trusted the other and thus would not disclose a single word about their plans. Suspicion was as thick as smoke in the air. Luke drew from his pocket some cash and tossed the notes on to the pew, keen to get going before Collins's mood changed.

'That should cover everything.' He pushed Fiona in front of him towards the exit.

'Boss says you want one of these.' Fred Ruff had been busy packing barrels of contraband spirits into a freshly dug grave atop a grassy knoll. Some of the liquor had been diluted and decanted into bottles, ready to be supped by the gang. The brandy in the kegs was so strong that it could kill a man if drunk neat. Instances had been recorded of poor wretches, ignorant of the danger, made mad or suffering a painful death from imbibing smuggled brandy straight from the barrel.

The bottle that Fred handed over hadn't been diluted, on orders from Collins, and he turned away, grinning, as Luke stuffed the poison into his saddlebag.

Unceremoniously, Luke girdled Fiona's slender waist with ten firm fingers and swung her up to sit sideways on his horse. Immediately he mounted behind her before she'd time to spring down.

Luke set the chestnut to a trot, weaving between graves till he neared the lychgate, a controlling arm about Fiona's middle. He dipped his head to hers in a way that might have seemed amorous to his audience. But though his lips hovered inches from her small ear his instruction was not sweetly voiced.

'Be still! I've come to get you, not hurt you, you silly chit!' he growled.

Fiona bristled at that. Silly, indeed, she thought, to have ever imagined it had been a boon to have this fellow cross her path! She tensed in his arms as a thumb on her ribs shifted leisurely to and fro, perhaps involuntarily, perhaps in a crafty caress. She knew it would be easy to succumb to his warm strong body and nestle into him. And, as he'd boasted just a short while ago, Luke Wolfson considered himself a master of seduction. Fiona craved somebody to trust and help her out of this dreadful mess, and he'd seemed sincere earlier when protecting the coach passengers. But then she'd not been alone with him and as vulnerable as she was now! Other people had been present and so had loaded weapons ready to be used to see off marauding strangers.

Luke Wolfson and Jeremiah Collins were colleagues, she reminded herself. With her own ears she'd heard them discussing their business deals. They'd plotted to kidnap a duke's daughter and she knew if *the major*, as Collins had named Wolfson, were ready to risk the consequences of mistreating a powerful aristocrat's child, he'd have no qualms about ill using her before discarding her.

Once out of the graveyard Luke urged the horse to speed up along the lane, but still Fiona sat rigidly on the animal, arching her spine to put space between their torsos.

'You'll fall off like that.'

His mild amusement put her teeth on edge, but she refused to comment or tussle with him when he suddenly jerked her back against his chest. She knew he was quite aware of her intention to escape him at the first opportunity. So she would need to seem compliant, even resigned to her fate if she were to outwit him. Luke kicked the animal to a faster pace and it leapt forward, causing a rush of chilly air to spike Fiona's cheeks. She turned her face into his coat to protect it from the chafing cold. *Jump and run* was the phrase pounding in her head in time with the beat of four hooves. She'd sooner take her chances alone than in the company of this rogue. The main roads were dotted with cottages and taverns and Fiona was confident she'd stumble across a place where she might seek help from decent people.

Luke could feel the tremor in her. He knew he should pull up and do his best to reassure her that his intentions were honourable. But it wouldn't be easy quickly convincing her he wasn't in league with Collins after what she'd heard. And he didn't have the time for a lengthy explanation about his work for the Duke of Thornley. Luke knew that presently his priority must be to get as far away from the smugglers' base as possible.

The gang consisted of more men than those currently congregated at the church that served as a temporary camp and contraband store. Jeremiah could call on a dozen or more fellows to boost his gang's numbers, if need be. Luke wouldn't put it past the treacherous devil to re-

nege on the deal they'd just made. Collins might
send men after them to snatch back Fiona, then
God help her…

The horse responded to his renewed prodding,
but it wasn't an Arabian like Star and lacked
a thoroughbred's agility and pace. He knew he
couldn't rely on a tired farm animal to outrun
any pursuit.

After a mile Luke turned abruptly off the
highway and headed into undergrowth. If Collins did intend to double-cross him he'd send
men along the main routes. Luke knew he didn't
have enough ammunition in the duck-foots to
hold off a sustained attack so would need to rely
on evasion rather than aggression to get them
to safety.

Fiona chewed her lower lip, her heart pounding. There was no reason why he should divert
from the beaten track if his intentions were to
help her rather than himself. She knew the further into the woods he took her the more nefarious must be his intentions and the more difficult
it would be for her to find her way back. She
could twist about and demand he tell her what
he was about…or she could act unsuspecting,
then catch him by surprise with a distraction
that would allow her to spring down and flee.

His arm had loosened about her, but she had previously felt the muscle beneath his sleeve and knew it would tighten like a vice the moment he sensed her pull away.

With an inner prayer, and feeling guilty for doing it, Fiona kicked backwards into the horse's flank. The beast reared and, as she suspected, Luke's instinct was to control the animal rather than her.

Beating at his face and chest with her fists, she managed to wriggle and squirm to the ground. She ended, with a thud, on her knees and, though winded, was soon on her feet again. Ignoring his harsh command to halt, she bolted, her skirts held high as she leapt over scratching brambles and undergrowth. She stumbled between dense dark bushes, carrying on swerving to and fro till her burning lungs felt they might burst and she could go no further. Clutching at the gigantic bole of a tree, she looked up and glimpsed through whispering leaves a silver disc strung with cloud. She listened, straining her ears for sounds of pursuit, but could hear nothing but the raucous rasp of breath in her throat.

After waiting what seemed like an hour, but was probably less than fifteen minutes, she slowly slid her back down the tree trunk till she was squatting close to the ground. She pulled her cloak tighter about her and settled her chin down low into its woollen folds.

She wondered if he'd gone off and left her, thinking her not worth pursuing. Luke Wolfson had a woman ensconced at the inn, so Collins had said. Despite his boast about liking a chase, Fiona reckoned the major would take his pleasure with the waiting jade rather than exert himself further. Fiona let out a quiet sigh, settling her back against the rough bark of the tree. She'd no chance of finding her way back to the road in the dark so she'd need to wait till morning before making a move.

## Chapter Seven

'Right… I've let you sleep for ten minutes, now it's time to go…'

A rough hand shaking her shoulder brought Fiona awake with a start. Her head jerked away from her clasped hands, pillowing her cheek on the forest floor. A second later she realised her nightmare had become reality, but her scream had barely quit her throat when cut off by five hard fingers.

Luke had sat beside Fiona, curled up on her uncomfortable mould bed, for more than half an hour. He'd watched her small features twitch and her brow crumple as she dreamed of something unpleasant…him, he'd guessed. Still, he'd not the heart to wake her till the nightmare worsened and she'd moaned in a way that reminded him of Becky in the throes of passion. So he'd sprung up, knowing it was time to leave.

He could easily have outrun Fiona and captured her within a few minutes but he'd not wanted to lose their transport. The untrained nag would probably have bolted had he let go of it. Without a horse—even one such as the aged chestnut mare—they'd be yet more vulnerable to Collins's malice. Stupid as the thought was, Luke was beginning to wish he'd brought Star along, lame or not. But that stallion had been with him for two years and served him faithfully. He'd no wish to see a fine beast that suited him perfectly, irrevocably damaged...whereas this shrew was testing his patience to the limit and he was sorely tempted to go and leave Fiona Chapman to her own devices.

Dragging Fiona to her feet and ducking her small fist, he snaked an arm about her waist, tugging her spine back against him to avoid being kicked on the shins again.

'For pity's sake!' Luke snarled in exasperation, knowing that to quieten her he'd need to get rough. He thrust her fighting form away with such force that she collapsed to the musky earth. He followed her down, barring her escape by pinning her torso on the dirt with one arm braced across her bosom. His hand went to her face, steadying its wild movement so her eyes, still heavy with sleep, were level with his.

'Shall I take you back to Collins?'

That dreadful threat brought an instant response. Fiona gave a quick shake of the head, terrified that he might be mean enough to do such a thing. She'd fallen into such a deep, troubled slumber that she'd not heard him approach and couldn't yet force her wits to function properly. But she was alert enough to know she still didn't trust him. She was conscious, too, of the familiar scent of his riding coat and the long muscled body imprisoning hers. Her lips parted as though she'd say something, but the words jumbled into chaos in her mind.

'Do you want my help to carry on to Dartmouth so you might take up your employment?'

Fiona blinked, wondering why he would offer to do that. It was certainly the better of the two options so she nodded slowly, humouring him. By the filtering moonlight she saw his eyes drop to her parted mouth and quickly pressed together her lips, looking away.

'Well, Miss Chapman,' Luke said huskily, 'let us go then before Collins's men turn up. I've an inkling they might and they've nothing good in store for either of us.'

Fiona allowed him to take her elbow and haul her to her feet. He released her and went to the horse tethered to a branch. She darted a scout-

ing glance about, teetering on her toes and un-
wittingly betraying her intention.

'Please don't,' Luke said, barely sending her
a glance. 'I'll catch you and tie you up because
you're becoming tiresome...'

*'I'm becoming tiresome!'* Fiona echoed in an
outraged whisper, abruptly finding her voice.
The muzz in her head had cleared and she
marched towards him, but he continued seeing
to the horse rather than paying attention to her.
'I've been abducted, gagged and bound, fed dis-
gusting scraps and threatened with...with vile
abuse...'

'You can't blame me for any of that,' Luke
drawled.

'If my memory serves, I think I can, sir!'
Fiona fumed, incensed by his nonchalance.

He turned and looked at her through the
patchy, silvery light. 'You're questioning my
seductive skills?'

Fiona moistened her lips. She sensed...hoped...
he was being humorous, but was in no mood for
levity. 'I'm questioning everything about you, Mr
Wolfson,' she retorted hoarsely.

'And with good cause, but I've no time to explain any of it right now. I didn't have to come
and get you, you know. I've business to see to

and could have let the authorities take on the job of searching for you.'

'Why didn't you, then?' Fiona demanded, hoping to corner him into admitting his guilt and association with the gang.

'I had an idea where they'd taken you and that things might turn extremely unpleasant for you, my dear. The dragoons have been after Collins for more than a year—still he's at large because they've failed to catch up with him. By the time they found you, you'd have been dead…or wishing you were…' Luke gazed at her. 'Collins wanted a profit from snatching you, even after he'd accepted it was a case of mistaken identity. He'd not have harmed you until he'd approached your family for a ransom and been unsuccessful. I'm guessing that as you're seeking employment, your parents are not financially well off.'

'How astute of you,' Fiona breathed, then felt foolish for resorting to sarcasm. He'd only pointed out a glaring truth. 'And why would you feel responsible for rescuing me, Mr Wolfson?'

'I'm damned if I know,' Luke muttered.

'And how is it that you knew where to find me?'

'That's one of the questions I've no time to answer right now.'

'But I'd like an answer, please. As you've correctly guessed, there's no reward on my head. If you think because you seem a well-bred ruffian you stand a better chance than Collins of prising cash from my stepfather, I can assure you, you won't. I'm no use to you, you know,' Fiona taunted.

'I wouldn't say that…' Luke returned softly, a dangerous glint in his eyes letting her know she insulted him again at her peril.

For a moment Fiona felt unable to avoid his black diamond gaze. She knew what *use* he'd hinted at and was glad that the dusk hid the blush warming her cheeks. Suddenly she sensed how very alone and lost she was. Canopies of branches overhead swayed, giving tantalising glimpses of the open sky, but all around thickets hemmed her in. She was completely at this stranger's mercy.

'You're a boost to my eternal salvation, my dear,' Luke muttered on a short laugh that shattered the tension between them.

Fiona was not fooled by his self-mockery or the intention behind it; he'd let her know that he'd sooner keep her docile, but if she challenged him he also held the power and the means of retaliation, should he choose to exercise those.

Abruptly he lifted her on to the mare, not with swift mastery as he had before but with a touch more gallantry. 'Now…as I hold all the cards, don't argue, just do as I say and all will be well,' he growled. 'If you want something to occupy that busy tongue of yours you might pray to the Almighty that the gang are too busy collecting kegs on Dawlish Beach to come after us.'

'I'm back at Dawlish?' Fiona forgot in her despair to leap off the other side of the horse. She'd lost two whole days' travelling if she were now again at that staging post.

'You were taken some distance…' Luke mounted in a lithe movement, then turned the horse's head and they picked a path through the shadowy forest towards the road. Just a clop of hooves and chirruping night-time noises broke the eerie silence until a fox shrieked close by, making Fiona almost jump from her skin. Again she felt that small movement against her ribs as his thumb brushed slowly to and fro in reassurance. She felt in such a state of confusion that she had difficulty making sense of her predicament or deciding how to act. Trying to escape again, so soon after the last failed attempt, seemed idiotic. Memories of the home she had left behind collided with thoughts of the uncertain life she was going to. The fate of those she'd travelled with, and her own safety, were also vying for her concentration. Yet…her greatest concern was about her captor. She wanted to believe him honest and sincere, with her best interests at heart, despite everything indicating that the opposite were true. Nothing made sense, and the more Fiona picked at the different strands of information in her mind, the more her hopes that Luke Wolfson was a decent fellow unravelled.

She had quit her home in London because her life had become unbearable. Now she felt she had jumped straight from the frying pan into the fire. Yet, regret was absent; she didn't trust Luke Wolfson and he frightened her, but, oddly, the idea that she might never have met him seemed worse.

Maude Ratcliff bitterly regretted marrying for the second time. She had dearly loved her first husband and missed him more every day now that she had a spouse she feared and despised.

Had Anthony not succumbed to a heart attack she'd still have a comfortable life and her eldest daughter living with her. Now Maude felt quite alone in the world. Losing Fiona's company was a torment. And it was all her own fault for being a stupid woman flattered by a younger man's lies.

Verity, Maude's second child, had been married for several years and had two delightful ba-

bies and another on the way. Writing to Langdon
Place in Shropshire and worrying her daughter
and son-in-law was not an option for consideration as far as Maude was concerned. She would
have to try and solve the crisis alone. And, of
course, she could only do that if she had some
cash of her own to back her plans to abscond
from the man making her life a misery.

With a glance over a shoulder Maude took out
her jewellery box from where she'd hidden it in a
blanket ottoman. She knew that Cecil had gone
out, yet sometimes he returned quietly and she
was constantly alert to him creeping up behind
her to spy on her. Lifting the lid of the casket, she
sifted through the pieces for something to sell.
Her husband had already taken to the pawnbroker all the fine gemstones. But he'd overlooked
these insignificant items and thereafter Maude
had kept them out of sight. She was hoping he'd
forgotten about them, but doubted he had. Despite their great sentimental value, she'd sooner
part with the trinkets and have the cash herself
than let him appropriate the proceeds of the gold
and silver her beloved Anthony had lavished on
her. She fingered a small locket, the best piece,
wondering if its value would provide enough
gambling chips to give her a chance of winning

a hundred pounds or so with which she might disappear.

When Anthony had been alive they'd often played piquet and he had praised her skill in the game. The locket was gold, studded with turquoise chips, and had been an anniversary gift when she was a woman of about Fiona's age. But by her mid-twenties, Maude had two daughters, although she'd never borne more children. It was a great sadness to her that Anthony had never had the son he'd wanted.

If she had had a boy all would be well, she told herself. She would be able to confide in her son and he would protect her from the avaricious monster who'd sneaked into her life by deception.

Attuned to every sound, Maude hastily dropped the locket and closed the lid of the box, shoving it out of sight. She must assume the role of devoted wife even if in reality she'd sooner stick a knife in Cecil's back. Maude knew the only way she'd ever get free of him was to play him at his own fraudulent game.

'Ah, there you are, my dear…'

Cecil Ratcliff was a fellow of thirty-five, so in his prime, and a decade younger than Maude. He had an average height and build and regular features although his brown hair was already thinning. He was nothing out of the ordinary. But he thought he was, and by some peculiar quirk he'd managed to persuade several women he was, too. Then, when he'd got them hooked and within his power, they discovered he was nothing but a selfish parasite.

At the moment he was posed against the door frame, gazing at his wife with mild blue eyes. 'Should you not be downstairs arranging dinner, Maude?'

'Rose knows what to cook. I spoke to her earlier.' Maude got up from the dressing table, and to conceal the quiver in her hands she clasped them behind her back. She hated herself for feeling too intimidated to order him away from her. Her daughter was gone now and couldn't be harmed, but Maude knew the man she'd married still had her to punish. 'We have some mutton left…and a caper sauce to go with it…'

Cecil tutted, coming further into the room. 'You know I have no liking for such scraps. A joint of beef and perhaps a duck is always more to my taste.' He took one of Maude's cheeks in thumb and forefinger and pinched in a way that seemed playful. 'You'd prefer that, too, wouldn't you, dear?'

'The butcher's bill must be paid before he'll deliver…' Maude began, her hands gripping tighter behind her back as she eased her face from between his bony fingers.

'Bumptious fellow.' Cecil flicked the small pearl ear-clips she wore, then, raising both hands, tugged them together from her lobes. 'Very well, if the upstart wants something, we'll give him these and have a fine feast on the proceeds.' Pocketing the jewellery, he sauntered from the room.

Maude watched him, her eyes brimming with tears and loathing. She knew very well that her earrings would buy her husband a night of carousing, not a dinner for them both. But the loss of her possessions she could tolerate. The loss of Fiona was harder to endure. And how her daughter must hate her for bringing such as Cecil Ratcliff into their lives.


'I like Mr Wolfson and I really think we should persuade him to come back and help us, Papa.'

'I shall determine what to do!' The Duke of Thornley shot his daughter a stern look over the top of his newspaper, but he never remained cross with her for long.

After his wife had died he had gained great comfort from his eldest child's companionship. Joan had only just made her debut at sixteen and a half when her mother expired after a long illness. The duke had wanted Joan to make her come out when older but his beloved wife had desired seeing Joan launched into society, so he had relented. They both knew the time left to them, as a family, was short. Then on the twelfth of August that year—the Glorious Twelfth—with dreadful irony, the duchess had been buried quietly, as had been her wish, in the small graveyard surrounding the chapel on the Thornley estate.

So Joan had been propelled into adulthood before Alfred Thornley would have liked. But the girl had always been mature for her age, although she had an adventurous side better suited to her having been born a boy.

The duke yearned it might have been so. His wife had left him with a son and heir, but at seven years old the boy was too young to be of interest to him and was mostly away at school. Thornley sighed; Joan was right: if he were to do what he saw as his paternalistic duty as largest and wealthiest landowner in Devon, and rid the county of the Collins gang, he'd need assistance from the likes of Wolfson. But the mercenary was no longer at the King and Tinker. His Grace had sent a servant to the inn and the message from the landlord, relayed back to him, had been that Luke Wolfson had travelled west towards Lowerton. But the major had left his doxy still ensconced there, reassuring Thornley that the fellow would return to collect her before heading to London. When Wolfson did show up the duke knew he'd have to eat humble pie if he were to gain the man's attention. The major had always been impeccably polite, but Alfred sensed he didn't suffer fools gladly. He knew he'd been idiotic, allowing pride to make him deaf to the mercenary's advice.

'We cannot keep up the pretence of planning a wedding with a fictitious groom for ever, Papa.' Joan had been buttering her breakfast toast while pointing out a salient point. 'We must strike soon or the opportunity to tempt the reprobate into the open will be lost. The longer it drags on the more likely it will be that Collins might spot the ruse.' She sipped her tea, gazing fixedly at her father to hurry his response. When none came she continued, 'Mr Wolfson might still be lodging at the inn. We should send one of the boys to give him an invitation to dine this evening.'

'He's gone off to his friend's hunting lodge at Lowerton and from there is heading back to the city. The landlord has sent word of it. I doubt Wolfson will be back.' His Grace thought it best not to mention to his dear child that the fellow *would* pass through again…just to collect his concubine.

'Well, we could send word to the hunting lodge; Lowerton is not so far—'

'We will not!' the duke interrupted tetchily before adding in a conciliatory tone, 'I've told you that I have arranged to dine with Squire Smalley this evening.'

'Oh…I forgot…' Joan said meekly; her father had indeed informed her earlier in the week that he was visiting the widower. She always received an invitation too, but found an excuse to stay at home. She had no wish to listen to two fellows reminiscing about their late wives, while drinking themselves silly. Joan brightened. 'Lowerton is a sleepy village; there cannot be more than one hunting lodge in the vicinity…'

'Mmmm…' His Grace mumbled, looking up as the butler entered with the post on a silver tray.

Alfred glanced at the parchments, tutting as he recognised the heavy black script of a fellow magistrate on one of them. There was no need to open the missive to know its content. It would again be complaints about the smugglers stirring unrest among commonly law-abiding folk. Thornley knew he was likely to hear similar concerns from his friend Smalley when they dined later on. Folding his newspaper, he pushed away his untasted plate of kedgeree, feeling irritated.

Again he admitted to himself—if not to her—that his daughter had spoken sense when mentioning the matter ought be attended to before it was too late. Having intentionally leaked the news that he'd set up a match between Joan and a non-existent rich friend, due to return from overseas, it seemed daft not to proceed quickly. The duke had been criticised behind his back for forcing Joan to wed a middle-aged man against her will. But generating juicy gossip that might reach the ears of the gang had been the intention from the outset. To outsiders, father and daughter were at loggerheads because the girl had settled on marrying a secret lover. In order to preserve the scheme's authenticity most of the servants also believed it to be true; just the housekeeper and butler and a few close friends—sworn to secrecy—knew the truth. So deceit had crept into Thornley Heights and His Grace didn't like that one bit. But his daughter—proving her daredevil nature—had been all for the scheme from the start. She still was, hence her constant badgering to get Wolfson to put it into action.

Thornley picked up his post from the table-cloth, pushing back his chair. 'I must attend to business, my dear.'

Joan watched her father depart without mentioning Wolfson's name again. From experience she knew that her father was best left to stew on matters if he were not to become extremely stubborn. But time was not on their side.

Having finished her breakfast, Joan returned to her chamber and gazed out across verdant parkland while her mind bubbled with activity. Her father wouldn't hear of her getting personally involved in the plot. If any harm were to befall her it would be the end of his sanity, he'd declared. So, after a sulk, Joan had agreed to a stand-in. She wondered who Wolfson had chosen to play her part in the drama. Was the young woman the same age and dark-haired, like her? Her impostor must be a brave soul to undertake the grave risk. When local gentry visited her father Joan had overheard them all discussing the increasing savagery of the gang. The evil reprobates took their work very seriously and would kill or maim to get, and keep, their riches. Recently there had been a report that the smugglers had turned on some of their own: two known criminals had been found with slit throats, no doubt executed for a betrayal.

Joan wrapped her arms about herself. But the thrill shivering through her was not simply caused by unpleasant thoughts; she wondered what it would be like if she truly *did* have a secret lover to elope with. But there was nobody she'd yet met that she fancied in that way. Even Wolfson, handsome as he was, didn't make her heart *really* flutter…but she did trust him to do the deed and get her father a victory against the gang.

Joan turned from the window with a thoughtful smile. Lowerton was not *so* far away. And her father was out this evening. She could reach the village, deliver her plea to the major, and be back before morning. Her father always returned from his friend Smalley's, sunk in his cups, and staggered straight to bed. So he would not even know she'd been out…

# Chapter Eight

Fiona's head had fallen against Luke's shoulder as the chestnut cantered through tall meadow grass with dawn breaking at their backs. Surfacing from her doze, she heard the mare whinnying a protest and realised their mount was being forced to speed up and veer to the left.

Blinking open her eyes, she saw they were exchanging mild brightness for cool shade. Once behind a tall screen of hawthorn Luke pulled the horse about to face the way they'd come. He murmured to the exhausted beast, then leant forward, fondling the animal's nose to quieten its snorting.

'What's happened?' Fiona started to ask, conscious of his cheek shaving her complexion. She'd only previously seen him through dusk and drizzle and flickering lamplight. Angling back her head, she looked at him now in pale daylight and with a solemn intensity that she didn't understand. But it seemed he did and her avid interest amused him.

Oh, he knew he was good looking, Fiona thought sourly, and no doubt believed she'd be putty in his hands should he choose to lay them on her. Well, the conceited devil would find that she'd have no difficulty in resisting him! 'Why have we stopped?' she demanded, squinting into the bottle-green depths of the copse.

'Because they'll catch up with us soon.'

'We're being followed?' Fiona forgot about seeming aloof and stared at him in alarm.

'They've been behind for some miles, but are now closing on us fast. This poor nag can't outrun them so best let them pass. If we keep giving them the slip, they'll tire of the game and head back to lucrative business in Dawlish.'

'We must quickly find an inn and seek shelter in case they don't give up!' Fiona blurted, eyes widening in apprehension.

'In these parts you never know what help to expect,' Luke returned ruefully. 'Some people don't take kindly to interfering strangers. They like buying cheap goods from smugglers. Not everybody is against the gang.'

That information came as a great shock to Fiona. She knew nothing of rural codes. Her attempt to escape had been thwarted, but it hadn't once occurred to her she might have been foiled, not by Luke Wolfson or the Collins gang, but by country folk who'd betray her for the price of a barrel of brandy.

'We'll carry on to the King and Tinker and make plans there for your onward journey.' One of his fingers was placed against her mouth, silencing her immediate protest at the delay, before it was pointed at the road.

Fiona heard the drumming of hooves before watching, from behind their leafy camouflage, two horses thunder past.

'It's Sam Dickens and Fred Ruff!' She was fully alert now and had identified her two kidnappers with no trouble, her eyes remaining fixed on their figures until they were just dark specks in the distance. 'They intend to steal me back from you and try to ransom me.' Fiona couldn't control the wobble in her voice, but she refused to display any other sign of fright.

'They won't succeed, trust me.' Cupping her sharp chin in his hand, he turned her head towards him. 'Trust me…' he ordered huskily. 'I swear I won't harm you, or ransom you.'

As their gazes merged, Fiona noticed that his eyes were sepia brown and fringed with long child-like lashes. It would be easy to feel overwhelmed by his masculine charm, she realised. But unanswered questions about him were still cramming her mind and she was determined to have at least one puzzle solved before they set on their way.

'How did you discover I'd been abducted? You were long gone when our coach was held up by those two.' She nodded at the horizon over which the smugglers had disappeared.

'I heard the gunshots and turned back. I regret that I wasn't in time to help.' Luke swung out of the saddle and held out his arms. 'Come, it is an opportunity to stretch your legs. The immediate danger is past.'

Fiona allowed him to help her down, her mind now buzzing with thoughts of the people with whom she'd travelled. 'You saw the others? How were they all?' she demanded. 'Poor Bert had been shot and Mr Jackson hit over the head. But of course you must know that,' she rattled on. 'Oh, please don't say that either fellow has…' Her words tailed away and she blinked back a sparkle of tears. She had only known her travelling companions for a few days, yet so much had happened to unite them that they seemed like her old friends.

'Nobody perished from the attack,' Luke said gently. 'When I left them all at the Pig and Whistle they seemed as well as could be expected. The sisters—especially the younger—seemed to have controlled their hysterics. As for the two invalids, a doctor attended to Bert and Mrs Jackson adequately patched up her husband. The man seemed almost good as new. The couple were very concerned about you, though.'

'And I have been fretting over how they all do. Thank goodness they are safe. Had I known you'd seen them I would have made you tell me about them sooner.'

'*Made* me?' Luke challenged.

'Asked you, then…' Fiona amended, turning from him. 'I wouldn't like you to think *I'm* a bully, Mr Wolfson.' Her tone dripped irony.

'I wouldn't like you to think I am, either, my dear, but I fear you do, despite my selfless and costly efforts to rescue you,' he mocked.

'And why would it worry you what I think?' Fiona snapped, pivoting back, determined not to be bested in this verbal duel. 'You hold all the cards, as you made sure to impress on me, and are playing them close to your chest. I still know nothing about you or your association with Collins. But associated with him, indeed you are! And you're probably no better than he is!'

'Shall I take you back to him, Fiona, so you can know the difference between us?' Luke advanced a pace. 'No?' he taunted on seeing her blanch and retreat. 'I'm stuck with you, then… I doubt Jeremiah would refund my money, in any case.'

'But I will, sir, at the very earliest opportunity,' Fiona retorted, her pale complexion flushing with colour. She put her hands behind her to clutch at a thick tree trunk. His undue familiarity had unsettled her despite her liking the way his husky voice formed her name. 'Don't think for a second that you have bought me!' she whispered.

'But…I have…' Luke pointed out in an infuriatingly confident drawl. 'And it's unlike me to lose on a deal.'

'You will not lose! You will have my price and interest, too,' Fiona spat, tossing her face proudly aside. It was a moment before she realised she had no idea just how much it was that she owed him. And she was chary of asking. She had no money, not even the cash she'd saved for her travelling expenses. That thieving wretch Fred Ruff had pocketed her coins, despite sneering at the paltry amount. All she had left in the world was a gold locket, worn hidden beneath her bodice since her avaricious stepfather entered her life. The small oval had been her twenty-first birthday gift from her parents and was the only piece of jewellery she now owned.

She'd be heartbroken to lose it. But she would hand it over to Luke Wolfson before they parted. From its worth she hoped he might recoup the many banknotes she'd seen him give to Collins and that there would be sufficient left to settle the cost of her coach fare from the King and Tinker to Dartmouth.

For weeks past her mind had been constantly occupied with her new job, but since this man had burst into her life she'd barely given a thought to being a governess. And she must, for what else was there for her? She just hoped that she still had a position to go to and her new master would be sympathetic to her tardy arrival, once he knew some of the facts behind it.

'There's no need for you to feel under any obligation to reimburse me.' Luke had spoken while kicking together some twigs. He squatted down with a tinderbox and put a light to the pile of kindling.

Fiona watched tendrils of smoke transform to baby flames as he teased the fire to take hold. She sensed he'd become bored with their cat-and-mouse game and was now being serious. 'I insist on settling my debts, sir,' she said distantly.

'From a governess's pay?' He slanted a look up at her.

Fiona bristled beneath his quizzical stare.

Days ago he'd chided her for travelling alone as a vulnerable female, now she felt he was ridiculing her ability to earn enough to pay her dues. And, of course, on both counts he was right. He'd said her safety could turn out to be a burden on him…and so it had proved. As for her salary, she'd be lucky to save pennies from it after the cost of her board and lodging, and other necessities, had been deducted.

About to pull the locket into view with a flourish Fiona instead pressed her small hands to her stomach to smother its embarrassing gurgling.

'Are you hungry?'

She nodded, avoiding his eyes. She'd not eaten properly since having a beef sandwich at the Fallow Buck. When was that…yesterday, the day before? She realised she was losing track of time.

Having acknowledged she was famished, she suddenly felt quite giddy with fatigue, too, and sank on to her knees in case she swooned. 'Might I have a small drink from your brandy, Mr Wolfson?'

Luke took the bottle from the saddlebag and, pulling the cork with his teeth, upended it so the spirit poured in an amber stream to the ground. 'It's lethal,' he explained to Fiona, who was watching him with an indignant frown. 'A swig of that could kill you.'

'Why ask Collins for it, then?'

'I wanted him to think I trusted him enough to sell me a drinkable bottle. I tasted a drop earlier and knew it for poison.'

'So…if he thinks you've drunk some, and perhaps me, too, he might believe us to be dead in a ditch somewhere,' Fiona suggested.

'He might…' Luke gave a twitch of a smile, realising she had a quick intelligence. 'But I doubt it…' He stood up now the fire was blazing. 'Jeremiah Collins is not easily outwitted, and neither am I. I think we have each other's measure.' He hunkered down in front of her. 'If I go and find us something for breakfast, are you going to behave nicely and stay right where you are?'

Fiona's feline gaze flicked sideways at him; his lean stubbly jaw was mere inches from her and the warm male scent of leather and wood smoke about his person was pleasant and reassuring. 'If you're going to find a place to buy bread, I'll come, too.' She suddenly realised she didn't relish the idea of being left alone with the smugglers prowling in the vicinity.

'There's no bread to hand, but perhaps a rabbit or hare might let me snare them,' he explained, half-smiling. 'And I'll find us something to drink.' He glanced up. 'I spotted a heron earlier so there's water about.' He'd added that comment while getting into the saddle.

'Keep the fire alight, but don't use damp wood or it'll create smoke and attract unwanted attention,' was his parting advice.

## Chapter Nine

A short time ago Fiona had been desperate to escape Luke Wolfson; now she wished she'd insisted on staying with him, she realised, as the sun climbed higher in the heavens and still he'd not returned.

Every unfamiliar rustle and creak made her start and peer apprehensively into undergrowth. She'd tolerate sharing her little woodland glade with wild creatures, but not with Jeremiah Collins's savages. She constantly fidgeted to and fro, on the lookout for approaching horsemen while her mind concocted dastardly betrayals as the reason why Wolfson had not reappeared. Pacing from oak to ash and back again, she'd soon convinced herself that he had tricked her into believing he'd gone hunting. In reality, he'd had enough of her and was bartering with the gang to get his money refunded. He'd told her to stay right where she was so Fred and Sam would quickly locate her and carry her, again bound and gagged, back to Jeremiah Collins's lair...

The sudden, unmistakable sound of a horse snorting made Fiona whip behind a tree trunk, heart pounding, in readiness to flee for her life. The sight of the chestnut being steered about a bush was so welcome that Fiona forgot herself and broke cover to run to him.

'You were a very long time.' She'd sounded like a carping wife, she realised, and lowered her eyes.

A quizzical sideways look from Luke let her know he also thought her a nag. But his smile was not *too* mocking as he dismounted. 'Sorry... I didn't think you'd miss me so much. I'm out of practice trapping.'

He dropped a brace of hare to the ground and immediately set about stoking up the fire that she'd forgotten to feed while in a stew over his absence.

'Do you know how to skin an animal?'

Fiona's retort, that she'd not missed him at all and was simply keen to get going, withered on her tongue. She gazed at him as though he were mad. The only hare she'd ever seen had been either running in a field or jugged in a pie. She found the idea abominable that she might strip a creature of its fur.

Having seen her pallor, Luke took out a pen-knife. 'Right… Gather up some more firewood while I prepare the carcase,' he ordered. 'Collect dry leaves, too, if there's not much seasoned timber to hand.'

Watching the first cut into the lifeless beast was enough to make Fiona spin away and start foraging on the ground. She didn't stray too far and soon was drawn back by the appetising aroma of roasting meat, carrying an armful of the driest twigs she could find.

As she dropped the kindling Luke immediately built up the blaze, then handed her his water bottle for a drink. She brushed together her gritty palms, then gratefully accepted, waiting for him to furnish a cup of some sort.

'Straight from the bottle,' he told her, turning the game slowly on the spit fashioned from a sapling branch braced between a pair of forked sticks.

Fiona watched him as he worked and juices dropped to sizzle and steam on the embers, curious as to how a refined gentleman came to acquire such marvellous skills.

And despite everything she sensed Luke Wolfson was from good stock and had the benefit of an excellent education. Her father had held a similar station in life, yet she was certain Anthony Chapman wouldn't have had the slightest inkling how to trap or camp or consort with villains.

When her father had been alive they'd been comfortably off and kept domestics to deal with menial tasks. Since her mother had remarried the cook had gone and a single maid had been burdened with everything, including cooking and serving at table. Fiona and her mother had feared poor Rose would hand in her notice before too long. Fiona realised the woman might by now have gone and Maude alone waited hand and foot on odious Cecil Ratcliff.

'Are you an officer serving in the army?'

'Not any more.' Luke hadn't raised his eyes from the browning meat while speaking.

Fiona pondered on how to make him divulge more about himself. She concluded that there was no subtle way of being inquisitive. Before she could stop herself she rattled off, 'Have you fallen on hard times? Have you joined those criminals to earn some money? Did you not really want to take part in kidnapping the duke's daughter?'

He slanted at her an impenetrable look and for a moment Fiona thought he might tell her to mind her own business. 'No, I've not fallen on hard times and, no, I wouldn't have been paid by Collins. As for the kidnap…you're right on that score; I didn't want to get involved because I thought it a stupid scheme from the start.'

'So why *did* you get involved?' Fiona was elated at getting him to spill a few beans.

'As a favour to a man I admire and to collect a fee.'

'So you *do* need the money.' Fiona pounced. Since her own downturn in fortune, she could understand how the prospect of destitution might ruin a previously upright character.

'No…I don't.'

'Why do it, then, with so much at stake?' Fiona was beginning to think he was deliberately talking in riddles to deter her from pursuing the subject.

'I'm starting to ask myself the same question.' Luke stood up, walking towards her.

He held out a joint of hare and Fiona took it, tossing it from hand to hand as it singed her fingertips. 'Hot…' she murmured with a bashful smile that incorporated her thanks. Her stomach was rolling in hunger and she took a cautious nibble, unable to wait for the food to cool. It was surprisingly tender and delicious and she told him so, then greedily tore again at the meat with her small teeth.

'Have you fallen on hard times, Fiona?' Luke

had returned to the spit to break off a leg for himself while speaking.

Fiona wiped her mouth with the back of a hand, staring at him. She hadn't expected him to turn the tables on her. 'Why do you ask?' She took another bite of succulent meat and chewed slowly.

'Because…like me…you seem to be undertaking something at odds with your class.'

Fiona curled her legs under her on the ground and paid full attention to her food. 'My father died and my mother remarried,' she explained, sure he'd not remove his eyes from her profile until she did. 'Our circumstances changed. I felt it wasn't fair to burden my mother with the cost of keeping me any longer.'

'You don't like your stepfather,' Luke stated bluntly.

'No…' Fiona said, discarding the bone she'd stripped bare on the ground beside her. 'I should like to get going, Mr Wolfson. I was expected in Dartmouth this morning.'

'Why haven't you married?'

Fiona shot him a glance, shocked by his crude enquiry. 'I think that is none of your business, sir, and rude of you to ask.'

'I didn't complain when you pried into my life.' He sliced another joint from the cooked carcase and lobbed it towards her. It landed, perfectly positioned, on the grass next to her.

'I did not pry!' Fiona spluttered. 'I simply enquired…' She tailed off, knowing full well that she'd done her utmost to prise information from him.

He sent her a smile. 'If you want to know more about me, you'll have to furnish me with some answers in return. Quid pro quo, Fiona.'

'I'm a spinster because I've never received a proposal. And you? Are you married, and if not, why not?' she retorted in retaliation.

'I'm a bachelor…because I've never issued a proposal.'

'And had you done so, sir, you might still be a bachelor having been turned down,' Fiona pointed out sweetly. She ignored the silent laugh her barb elicited. He was obviously unrepentantly arrogant. 'Well…now we have that out of the way, I'd like to journey on, Mr Wolfson.' The savoury smell of the roast game, laying inches away, was tempting; she'd not eaten her fill, but she stubbornly resisted picking it up.

'I'm not ready to go. Eat your food and stop sulking.' Luke's white teeth ripped off what meat remained on the bone hovering by his mouth. The waste was thrown over a shoulder and he upended the water bottle against his mouth.

'Don't you dare order me about,' Fiona burst out, jumping to her feet. She felt irked at having been made to admit—to him of all people—that no man had ever wanted her as his wife.

'You say your stepfather won't pay out a ransom on you? I'm not surprised he won't have you back.' Luke pushed to his feet and kicked dirt on the dying fire. 'I doubt he's missing your acid tongue and lack of gratitude any more than I will when we go our separate ways.'

That comment made Fiona wince. 'Again you are being impertinent, Mr Wolfson,' she uttered coldly. 'You know nothing about my stepfather. If you did, you'd understand he'd lure me again under his roof as long as it cost him nothing.'

'I think you should explain what you mean by that.'

'And I think your explanations are due first, sir, so don't dare to interrogate me!'

Luke cursed beneath his breath for pushing her too far; he had been enjoying their lively talk despite the fact she could be the most insolent chit alive…and the most alluring. He wasn't sure why he found her fascinating, but the longer he was in her company the more he appreciated her mild loveliness. Here, amongst nature, she seemed to blend in. Her slender graceful body and fawn colouring reminded him of a woodland creature, as did her disposition. She'd attempt to bolt or snap at him the moment he made a move to touch her. And God only knew he was feeling tempted to do so.

Fiona sank her teeth into her lower lip to still its angry tremble. She'd thought they had established a tiny bit of harmony while preparing their meal, but it had soon evaporated. It was her own fault for having brought up the subject of her stepfather; she found it hard to suppress her despising when speaking of Cecil Ratcliff. Even the Collins gang were no worse, in her eyes, than the man her mother had vowed to love and obey. At least those wretches took their plunder openly rather than by stealth.

'I believe I've been more than fair with you, Fiona, but I realise that you have reason to think me a deceitful villain.' Luke broke the silence, hoping to soothe her.

'And are you a deceitful villain?'

'Not in the way you think, and only for the greater good,' Luke replied wryly.

'An answer that says little,' Fiona returned with a sparking glance. Her intuition told her that his casual manner concealed an unrelenting character. She was in the company of a soldier-turned-hireling who was used to giving nothing away. He was sparing with his information and his generosity, she guessed. Wolfson, if honestly acting as her saviour, would expect to be paid for his services.

'You need not fear that I cannot settle your fee.' Fiona fished the locket from inside her bodice and held it extended on its fine chain for him to see. 'I will hand this over when we reach the King and Tinker. It is solid gold and quite heavy,' she added, as she saw his eyes drop to it only fleetingly before returning to her face.

'I've told you I want nothing from you.'

'But I insist you take it.'

'Why?'

'Because I would not have you believe you have bought me, sir.'

'Forget I said that—it was a joke.'

'Not to me…'

'Then you must see yourself as a chattel more than I do.'

'I assure you I do not! I am my own mistress and nobody else's.'

'It never occurred to me you might be otherwise, my dear,' Luke drawled with lazy amusement, brushing a leaf off a sleeve.

She was a genteel spinster, not a prospective paramour, he reminded himself as he watched her blush beneath his insinuation. It was time to get going and find her a suitable chaperon to keep him at bay. Then, once she was on a coach heading west, he could have his belated meeting with Rockleigh before returning to London. The coming tête-à-tête deserved some preparatory thought, he impressed upon himself, as it was certain to turn unpleasant.

Luke knew he was attempting to force his mind to something…anything…that dampened the tormenting heat building in his loins. The longer he was with this provocative woman the more he felt sexual frustration gnawing at him. He avoided looking at her, concentrating on the imminent confrontation with his friend, wondering if it would be as well to ignore the appointment and head straight back to London. The idea of offering to marry Drew's niece because the silly chit wouldn't stop flirting and getting herself into scrapes was absurd and he was itching to tell Rockleigh so. But the matter would wait and perhaps in the interim his friend might accept he'd acted hot-headedly.

In his present irritable mood, Luke knew *he* might act hot-headedly and what had started as a minor problem could escalate to pistols at dawn. Better he got himself away from Fiona Chapman as soon as he could and follow Becky home. He'd pay his mistress one last visit before approaching the pretty redhead he'd seen at Vauxhall to replace her.

Then there was the question of Harriet Ponting. Once Luke had thought himself in love with the blonde. When she'd rejected his overtures on her parents' advice, he'd realised he wasn't, because he'd not felt heartbroken, just humiliated. After that he'd never again been tempted to find a wife, even though he'd since inherited land and wealth from his grandfather that made him a prime target for debutantes. Now he could afford to provide even a rich aristocrat's child with the sort of life she'd been reared to.

Harriet Ponting was still porcelain pretty and on the few occasions that their paths had crossed her big blue eyes had signalled that she still liked him. Luke knew she'd make a good wife; from a couple of brief amorous encounters they'd snatched when unobserved he'd guessed she'd also make a reasonable lover. Her social graces were more highly polished than his own, so he'd no qualms about her being a skilful hostess. It was time he started thinking about settling down for the benefit of future generations of Wolfsons.

He'd considered heading to Eaton Square to accept one or two of the invitations that always piled up on his desk during the height of the Season. Yet suddenly he felt no inclination to return

to town to socialise and pick a wife. With startling clarity he knew that a mild physical attrac-
tion and good manners weren't enough to tempt
him to remain faithful and give up carousing
with courtesans like Becky. The idea of adul-
tery was sordid to Luke. He knew a great many
wealthy husbands did flit between two or more
women, but for him the subterfuge made a mockery of taking vows.

Fiona was aware of his sudden preoccupation
and of her inexplicable hurt at his implication
that she was too plain for a gentleman to want
her as a paramour.

But whatever careless remarks he lobbed her
way Fiona had glimpsed the desire burning at
the backs of Luke Wolfson's eyes. Simply because he could, he might take the opportunity
to prove to her his powers of seduction while
boosting his ego. And with a pang of raw emotion that stole away her breath, she realised that
she wanted him to.

With clumsy fingers she undid the locket and
stood up with it enclosed in her fist. She marched
unsteadily over rough ground and very deliberately dropped the gold to the earth at his feet. 'I
have worked out for myself that you are a mercenary of some sort. Your payment, sir, for res-

cuing me and escorting me to safety. You might as well take it now, as later.'

Luke gripped her wrist before she could withdraw and slowly, with her struggling to free herself, brought her down to kneel in front of him so their faces were level.

'How do you know I'll keep my end of the bargain?'

'I don't,' Fiona breathed. 'But soldiers of fortune gain work through recommendation, I imagine, and if you cross me I will make it known you're corrupt.'

'You'd ruin my reputation, would you?' he murmured, amused.

Fiona gave a brief nod, wishing she'd not used the threat for it seemed to have had the opposite effect to its purpose. She was acutely aware of her imprisoned wrist and although his fingers had relaxed on her she knew they'd tighten in a second if she attempted to rise.

'Perhaps I might ruin yours first.'

Fiona's golden eyes clashed with his dark sultry stare. 'I think it rather late for that, sir. My reputation was in tatters the moment that highwayman tossed me over his shoulder.'

'Nothing to lose, then…' Luke's tone was silky, his eyes watching her tongue tip darting to moisten her top lip.

'Pick up your payment and take me to the King and Tinker!' Fiona ordered shrilly, aware that he was backing her into a corner with his clever words.

'I'm sorely tempted to do without any more of your snapping and snarling and leave you here.' Luke's voice was mellifluous, at odds with the threat in his words. 'Shall we call a truce for what remains of the ride to the inn?'

Fiona pursed her lips, but nodded while twisting her wrist in a renewed effort to liberate it. Unable to do so, she turned her head from him. 'I think it best we don't converse, sir,' she said icily. 'All we do is rub one another up the wrong way.'

'That's an interesting thought…' *And one I could have done without,* he inwardly mocked himself. He released her straining form so abruptly that she fell sideways on to the turf, her skirts askew, displaying her lissom shapely calves.

It was too much temptation for Luke to resist. As Fiona wriggled to straighten her petticoat he braced an arm over her, all thoughts of Harriet and Becky gone from his mind. Immediately Fiona became still, her eyes engulfed by a heavy-lidded blistering gaze.

Luke touched a long forefinger to her softly panting mouth. 'Let's not fight and argue, sweet,' he said huskily. 'We've some hours of travelling in front of us… Better we ride together as friends?'

Mesmerised by the soft finger outlining her lips, she could do no more than wait to see what he might do to her next. She had been kissed before by the more persistent of her suitors, but never, when with those gentlemen, had her heart battered at her ribs, as it did now, in a mix of excitement and trepidation.

Fiona watched his dark head dipping closer, his mouth nearing hers and although a sensible inner voice urged her to beat him off, she could not. He wasn't pinning her down as he had before when she'd fled from him; nevertheless, she felt trapped by her own need to have a small taste of being seduced by Luke Wolfson. Still he teased her as his face scuffed her cheek and his breath bathed an ear, then upwards skimmed his fingers to touch back from her forehead stray tendrils of silky hair.

He stroked his lips to a corner of hers and with a moan Fiona swung her head so their mouths collided.

Luke was lost in her sweet enthusiasm. A courtesan might put up a better fight before going down.

But he knew that Fiona Chapman had no sophisticated tactics to use to increase his desire; neither did she need them. She tasted smoky and sweet from the spit-roasted meat they'd eaten and he could sense a faint scent of lavender on her skin.

As his tongue skimmed her lower lip Fiona wound her arms about his neck, instinctively pressing up against him, to increase the chafing pressure of his chest on her bosom.

Luke drew her up further as he sensed her need, deepening the kiss, teasing her with the plunge of his tongue until she met him with shy touches of her own.

Somewhere deep in his consciousness he knew he should stop this madness before it went too far. But he was in an agony of arousal and his hands were already straying to open her cloak and slide within to caress her.

Fiona gasped as a large warm hand cupped her breast, teasing her nipple through her bodice. When his hand slipped free some buttons and thrust to touch her nude skin she moaned in delight at the sensation of hard fingers tantalising every inch of warm satiny flesh. His head lowered, his mouth circling the sensitive little nub before suckling hard and fast and making her cry out in wonder as fire streaked through her veins. Luke positioned her legs astride him, drawing

back her skirts, but allowing her some modesty
by not lifting them completely. He curved a hand
about her nape, drawing her head down to his,
tempting her back into their shared web of sen-
suality while loosening his trousers. The sweet
feminine core of her felt slick as he teased her
with a fingertip…then two…that began easing
fractionally further into her. He knew that, vir-
gin or no, she was ready for him and he'd only
to free himself and ease her hips down to impale
her, because he was more than ready for her.

Fiona's breath was rasping in her throat and
the sound was so foreign that it startled her into
parting her lashes. Her eyes merged with his,
pleading for she knew not what. Despite drugging desire she understood she was risking everything for this man…a stranger who did deals
with criminals. But it was the memory of something Collins had said that finally brought her
to her senses. Luke Wolfson had a woman waiting for him at the inn they were about to head
towards…

Luke sensed the change in her as she blinked,
put up an inner struggle to defeat his boast of
conquering a woman by seduction rather than
force. Before she could push him away, he tum-
bled her so she lay sprawled beneath him, then
very deliberately he touched together their lips

before getting up with an oath exploding between his teeth.

He scooped up the gold locket from the peat
and was gathering the mare's reins by the time
Fiona had scrambled to her feet.

Slowly he approached her with such an impenetrable expression that Fiona stumbled back a
pace, wondering how he could seem unmoved by
what they'd just done. Without a word he lifted
her on to the saddle, mounted, and within seconds the refreshed mare was hurtling out of the
woods and towards the road.

His arm encircled her waist with such confidence that Fiona knew he was challenging her to
break her silence and object. But she'd no intention of speaking to him because she might betray feeling a dreadful jealousy for the mistress
he had waiting for him at the King and Tinker.

# Chapter Ten

'Yours, I believe, sir.' The fellow propelled the girl forward by her shoulder. 'You should take better care of her, or teach her how to behave.'

The Duke of Thornley gawped at the stranger who'd just addressed him as though he were an incompetent nanny who'd failed his charge. But what angered His Grace the most was having the upstart do so in front of his daughter while manhandling Joan to boot! And all at such an ungodly hour of the morning! He'd not been abed more than a few hours when a servant had woken him and told him he'd a visitor demanding an urgent audience.

Alfred Thornley had had a good dinner with his friend the squire and they'd swallowed much port and brandy to wash down the game that His Grace had magnanimously supplied from his own larder. He'd not reached home till three hours after midnight and had been helped up the stairs to his chamber by two trusty footmen. His head was thumping from over-imbibing and he was struggling to make sense of the scene in front of him.

'I beg your pardon!' he finally thundered. Alfred tightened the belt on his dressing gown with hands that shook with suppressed rage.

'And so you should.' Drew Rockleigh was in no mood for humouring the fellow, duke or no.

Yesterday evening he'd opened his door at gone ten o'clock at night not to the man with whom he had a grievance, but to a young woman searching for the same fellow. She'd told him she was a duke's daughter and he'd snorted disbelief at that. At first. Then he'd realised she was not some opportunistic doxy, but exactly who she said she was. Joan Morland would not tell him what she wanted with Wolfson or why she'd travelled late at night on perilous roads with just a frightened-looking youth driving her two-wheeled gig. Drew's increasingly wrathful demands for information had all been met with the same answer: it was a secret. Finally, in exasperation, he'd ordered the chit back aboard her transport and escorted her home.

'What the devil do you mean by that remark? Beg your pardon? Why should I, you young pup?' The duke planted his fists on his hips, his small black eyes sparking dangerously. 'What the deuce do you think you are doing here? What is it you want? Make it quick before I have you removed,' Thornley rattled off, his face glowing puce. 'Are you a madman?' he spat out in conclusion.

'Papa—' Joan started in a strangled voice, hoping to make her father cease insulting the fellow who'd brought her safely home. She was in terrible trouble, she knew, but her fears were for her father. She wanted His Grace to calm down in case he burst one of the blood vessels she could see throbbing at his temple.

She darted a quick look at the stranger. She guessed him to be about the same age as Luke Wolfson, but he was very fair rather than dark like the mercenary. He'd remained dour-faced and silent for the duration of a very strained homeward journey. She'd begged him to allow her to return in the way she'd arrived, with just Pip driving her. In that way she could have slipped in to Thornley Heights discreetly, in the same way she'd slipped out. But Rockleigh would not hear of it and had ridden at the side of the trap, right the way up to the vast front steps before hammering on the front door and bringing the footman running.

'Go to your room,' the duke snapped at Joan, wanting to deal with this matter in private. 'Why are you up so early, anyway? It can't be much past nine of the clock.'

Drew Rockleigh glanced at the girl, wondering if she was going to answer that one. She lowered her nervous eyes beneath the sardonic enquiry in his stare. 'Your daughter is not up early, Your Grace, she's not yet sought her bed. Last night she paid me a visit in the hope of finding Luke Wolfson, because she has an urgent message to give to my friend. More than that I cannot say…it is a secret, you see.'

Joan winced beneath the sarcasm she heard in Rockleigh's voice, but she kept quiet and tightened her fingers together behind her back until the knuckles showed ivory.

The duke remained facing his unwelcome visitor with a ferocious expression, as though he still believed him a raving lunatic. Then, after a full minute of unblinking deliberation, he very stiffly turned to his daughter, his eyebrows slowly elevating.

Joan hung her head, then with a shuddering sigh gave an imperceptible nod.

'Go to your room.'

Joan recognised that whispered tone of voice only too well; her father was enraged and she

defied him again at her peril. 'Papa...please listen—' she began.

The duke had his open hand knocked aside
in mid-air before it could make contact with his
daughter's cheek.

'You may chastise her, if you will, later,'
Rockleigh said, lowering his arm. 'First, I have
more to say and would ask you to listen so I
might get about my business without further
delay.'

Joan, ashen-faced from her father's attempt
to slap her, turned tail and, gripping her skirts,
rushed to the stairs and disappeared up them.

The Duke of Thornley stalked to a nearby
doorway, leaving his visitor standing alone on
the marble flags. Before entering the room he
turned, announced regally, 'I owe you my apologies and my thanks, it seems, sir. Do come in
so we can become acquainted...there is much
to discuss.' He flung open the door to the small
library and stomped inside.

Maude knew she'd need to choose the time of
her departure carefully. Her husband had been
watching her again, and she hoped it was not because he'd guessed her intentions. Maude was
under no illusion that Cecil Ratcliff would try
to stop her leaving him because he loved or de-

sired her. She aroused no sweet emotion in her husband, and never had, despite his ardent protestations when wooing her. She knew it all for lies now.

But, crafty as Ratcliff was, he couldn't disguise some aspects of his character. He was an arrogant fellow who put much store in his status and keeping up appearances. He would not want the neighbours, or the gentlemen he classed as his peers, to gossip behind his back that his wife had run out on him. Cecil would always want the upper hand and Maude suspected that he was ruminating on when to leave *her*. Of course, he would not do so while there were still things of value in the house that he might sell off to fund his roistering.

A small canvas was on the drawing-room wall that Maude had hoped had escaped his eye being muted in colour. But she'd noticed him in front of it the other day, fingering his chin, and her heart had sunk.

Having heard the crash of the front door, Maude trotted to the window that overlooked the street. Concealed by the curtain, she peeped from behind it as Cecil swaggered off along the pavement, hat at a jaunty angle, swinging her late husband's silver-topped cane as though for all the world it was his. And of course it was.

Everything Anthony had owned was now Cecil Ratcliff's to do with as he would.

Seeing him flourishing her dear Anthony's favourite walking stick hurt Maude more than anything and she twitched the velvet back in place and made a snap decision.

At this time of the day Cecil would be going to his club and often didn't return till dinnertime. Maude knew she might have up to six hours' grace before he again was home to harry her with his snide remarks. Hurrying to the bed, she pulled out the packing case beneath it. She'd already told Rose they were taking a trip and to be prepared to leave at a moment's notice. She'd also told the maid, unnecessarily, to keep her lips sealed on the plan. Maude hadn't elaborated because she hadn't needed to. Rose had eyes and ears and had given her mistress a knowing smile and a nod. The maid hated Cecil, too, no doubt because he'd treated her as a slave rather than a paid employee ever since he'd arrived.

Maude took some scissors from the dressing table then, perching on the mattress, drew a pillow towards her. Carefully she snipped the threads she'd put in a few days ago and withdrew her folded bank notes from where she'd secreted them inside the linen cover. She beamed, raising her winnings to her lips to kiss them in gratitude.

After selling her few remaining items of jewellery she'd done a fine job of turning five pounds into fifty at Almack's faro table. It wasn't the small fortune she'd hoped for, but it would have to suffice because she could stand not another single day beneath the same roof as her husband.

She and Rose would travel to Devon to find her daughter. Once she'd begged for forgiveness from Fiona for subjecting her to Cecil's Ratcliff's odious presence, they would turn their thoughts to their uncertain futures. But Maude knew she must remain optimistic. Fate might yet smile on them. Something *would* turn up…and in case it did not, she was going to fetch the small oil painting from the drawing room and wedge it into her portmanteau. Even if it were not as valuable as she hoped, it might cover the cost of a week's board and lodging for them all.

Fiona realised that the brunette must have been watching for her lover's return. Barely had Luke dismounted in the stable yard of the King and Tinker when a voluptuous young woman hurtled out of the low sloping doorway and straight at him.

Without uttering a word Luke removed Becky's clinging hands and turned to Fiona to help her down from the chestnut mare. But his features were so tensely set that his mistress—and Fiona, too—could not but be aware of his latent anger, if unsure of its cause.

'Where have you been, Luke? Thank goodness you're back at last...' Becky rattled off with a winning smile, twirling a dark ringlet about a finger. When Luke continued to ignore her she flounced about to narrow her eyes on the woman with him.

Fiona had winced on hearing Wolfson's mistress quiz him over his absence using similar words to those she'd fired at him hours before when he'd returned from his hunting trip.

Planting her hands on her hips in a combatant manner, Becky demanded, 'And who is *she*?', while grabbing Luke's forearm in a way that seemed to Fiona both punishing and possessive.

The fact that his mistress had disobeyed him and returned to Devon to hound him rather than travel home with her dignity intact had stoked more than rage in Luke. He'd made it clear to Becky he didn't want or need her company, yet still she clung on determinedly. He realised that the fire had gone out of his anger and his lust for her, and disgust and pity had taken the place of those emotions.

Behind Becky was someone else Luke would rather not have encountered at this precise mo-

ment, leaning on the whitewashed wall of the
inn. Rockleigh's face displayed mild amusement as he watched the scene, but Luke knew
his friend well enough: Drew was here to exact
a promise, not to be humoured. Disentangling
himself from Becky's renewed clutch, he ignored
both his friend and his mistress and turned to
Fiona.

'I'll get you a room in the inn,' he stated quietly.

'There's no need, sir,' Fiona responded coolly.
'If there is a coach setting off west, at any time
at all of the day or night, I wish to be on it.'

Luke watched her tigerish eyes flit past him to
settle on Becky before skittering away. He knew
there was no point in making introductions, or
excuses; Collins had already done the damage
on that score. At the time, Luke hadn't cared
what was said. Now he did. He cared greatly
that Fiona Chapman thought him a lecherous
reprobate who dragged a woman with him on
his travels to warm his bed.

'Surely you'll want some privacy to freshen
up?' he suggested in a voice only she could hear,
while fighting the urge to lift her again onto the
horse and ride off with her into the unknown.
And damn the lot of them. From Rockleigh's
stance, he could see that the man had grown im-

patient waiting to resolve matters and was itching for a fight. And his mistress appeared to be similarly boiling with resentment.

The time spent with Miss Fiona Chapman might have been short and fraught with danger for them both, but it had been rather wonderful, Luke realised. And he didn't want it to end yet. Inwardly he mocked himself for confusing lust with something finer. The reason he wanted to keep Fiona's company was because the desire he felt for her remained unquenched. It was even now a weighty throb in his pelvis.

And it would stay that way, until Becky, or one of her ilk, soothed it for him. Fiona would avoid him like the plague now she'd met his mistress and he would do the decent thing and allow her to.

The idea of a wash and a rest on a proper bed was so tempting that Fiona was on the point of agreeing to take a room; then she remembered she had no money and she'd be damned before asking him to settle any bill other than that of her coach fare. 'I'm very well as I am, thank you,' she said, forcing a lightness into her tone that she was far from feeling. But she wouldn't have him think for a moment that the sight of his paramour bothered her.

Again Fiona's eyes were involuntarily drawn

to the brunette. Despite a sullen droop to her full lips she was very attractive…and young. Fiona guessed that Luke Wolfson's mistress was at least five years her junior and for some reason that hurt more than feeling dishevelled and ugly in comparison. With small movements she brushed down her crumpled skirts, then attempted to twist her tangled fawn locks into a neat bun at her nape. She knew she must look a fright after her ordeal, but refused to feel apologetic or ashamed about it.

'I believe your friends are awaiting your attention, sir,' she remarked briskly. 'You need not think that I expect a long farewell between us. Thank you for the service you provided…I am glad it is over. If you will purchase my seat on a coach from your payment, I would be most grateful. Goodbye, Mr Wolfson.' She extended a hand and shook his fingers firmly before immediately turning away. She had seen the sardonic set to his mouth as she dismissed him from duty, and despite the hammering in her chest, and the weakness in her legs, she was pleased to be able to steadily walk away from him.

Thankfully she could approach the saloon bar of the King and Tinker without passing the young woman watching her with eyes brimming with suspicion and dislike. No doubt Luke would soon soothe the pretty brunette's sulks over a possible rival by saying Miss Chapman had been a client who'd unexpectedly landed in his path and that his fee for the mission had been a gold locket. He might give the necklace to her!

That awful thought shocked Fiona like a dousing with icy water, provoking a physical pain to twist in her gut. But aware of being still under observation she tilted up her chin and drew her cloak about her in instinctive protection. Her twenty-first birthday present from her parents had saved her from the Collins gang so it had been worth parting with such a precious gift, she impressed upon herself. Head high, she entered the low, thatched building determined to find the innkeeper and quiz him over the time of the next coach heading to Dartmouth.

While negotiating a warren of narrow corridors Fiona forced herself to forget the people outside and concentrate on mundane matters. She remembered that she must discover the whereabouts of her packing case. On the last occasion she'd seen the battered leather trunk it was being transferred with the other luggage from the damaged coach to the replacement Toby Williams had driven from the Fallow Buck.

In one of their less challenging conversations Wolfson had told her that the vehicle and remaining passengers had journeyed on, with his help, to the Pig and Whistle following the hold up and her abduction. Toby Williams had been distracted by his nephew's bullet wound that dreadful night, but Fiona hoped that the driver had had the good sense to leave her belongings at the Pig and Whistle for collection. She had nothing but the clothes she stood up in and on arriving at her destination must suffer the ignominy of requesting an advance on her wages. She could only hope that her employer would be sympathetic and hand over a few shilling for incidentals she might require.

A fellow of ample girth and bald of pate with a food-spotted apron hanging below his big belly suddenly rounded a corner, almost colliding with Fiona.

'Well, now, madam, what can I do for you?' He backed off a pace, looking surprised to see her wandering alone. 'Stanley Robley, patron of this establishment at your service, you see.' He followed up his introduction with a jaunty bow and a tobacco-stained beam.

'I am Miss Chapman, sir, and wonder if you can tell me when the next coach is leaving for Dartmouth? I shall need to stop at the Pig and Whistle en route.'

'One doo in tomorrow morning, but might

be full, you see.' He sucked his teeth pessimistically. 'Most of 'em are—coachmen don't like empty seats, you see.'

'Yes…I see…Mr Robley,' Fiona concurred, feeling her spirits sink. In her agitated state it had escaped her mind that it could be a long wait for a vehicle to turn up with spare room on it. 'I am overdue in taking up my employment, so would be very grateful if you could secure me the very first available place, sir. Outside will do.'

Stanley Robley tapped the side of his nose while his other hand snaked out, palm up.

Fiona realised he was expecting her to either give him an inducement for the favour she'd asked, or the cost of her fare, or perhaps both. Whichever it was she had nothing to hand over.

'Mr Wolfson is…umm…an acquaintance and he will settle with you.' Her voice had been level, but she couldn't prevent embarrassment colouring her cheeks. Her blush increased when she saw the landlord's goggling eyes slyly gleaming.

'Well… Of course I know *that* fine fellow and, being the soul of discretion, miss, never would repeat what you said.' He dipped his shiny head to whisper close to Fiona's ear. 'Specially not to his *other* girl. Hellcat she is!' he hissed. 'Nearly had my daughter's eye out with her claws and all my Sally was doing was serving Mr Wolfson his dinner, you see.'

'Mr Wolfson and I are just…' Fiona's indignant response faded away. The landlord's insinuation that she was another of Wolfson's paramours was not *so* far off the mark. How much of a hypocrite was she prepared to be? she taunted herself. She might try to block the memory of her shameful wantonness from her mind, but she couldn't lie to herself. Had Luke Wolfson not let her go when he did, she would have willingly let him take her virginity…just as he'd known she would. He'd made Jeremiah Collins cackle when bragging he could make any woman want him…and Collins had offered to buy her back when Wolfson had done with her. And to her utter humiliation it seemed he had done with her, without even bothering to complete the deed. He obviously preferred his jade to the buttoned-up spinster after all.

Mr Robley broke into Fiona's reflection. 'You and Mr Wolfson are…?' he probed, giving her a salacious wink to reassure her any answer would be safe with him.

'Mr Wolfson and I are simply business associates,' Fiona burst out, then cleared her throat.

Again Mr Robley's fat forefinger patted his nose and he endorsed his trustworthiness with a slow nod. ''Course...' he whispered. 'Doing business...I understand, you see...'

Exasperated by his attitude, Fiona turned away. 'Is there a room where I might wait till the coach arrives?'

Again a pudgy palm wove towards her.

'Is there somewhere free to sit down?' Fiona sighed.

'Till morning?' Mr Robley queried with a squint of astonishment.

'Yes...' Fiona said faintly. She'd not contemplated the discomfort of having nowhere to rest her head overnight.

Mr Robley gave Fiona's arm a paternalistic pat. 'He's been a generous sort so I 'spect he'll stump up for a room and dinner for you as well t'other one. Don't you fret, I'll speak to him, about it, miss, you see—'

'You will not!' The idea that the landlord would demand Luke pay for her to be fed and watered as well as his mistress was mortifying. Fiona was coming to know Mr Robley and reckoned the landlord might want a tidy profit from her board and lodging before eventually 'finding' her a seat on a coach, days hence.

As she could think of nothing further to say Fiona gave the landlord a nod, then retraced her footsteps outside and was relieved to see that

Luke and his companions had disappeared. Aimlessly she wandered about the side of the building that led to a large kitchen garden. Several paths criss-crossed beds filled with vegetables and herbs, and bathed in morning sun was a wooden bench set against a mellow brick wall. She walked towards it and sat down. The golden glow on her face was pleasantly warm and Fiona was glad that at least the weather was in her favour. To keep out of the landlord's speculative sight she'd spend as much time as possible waiting outside for the coach to take her on to the Pig and Whistle. She gazed over the sunlit fields, thinking that she had missed much peace and natural beauty by living in the metropolis for twenty-five years. The signs of spring buds breaking open on the trees and the fresh verdant landscape lifted her spirits, despite the problems besetting her. Her fingertips skimmed the low bushes beside her and she breathed in the scent of rosemary and sage, then picked some purple-tinted leaves to chew on.

She didn't hear Mr Robley approach until he was almost upon her. Fiona jumped up, wondering whether he'd come to tell her that sitting on his bench and eating his herbs would cost her.

He was carrying a steaming plate of food and

she thought that odd as nobody else was outside to have ordered it.

'Would you like to eat here? I can bring a table…'

Fiona glanced at beef stew and dumplings and felt her mouth water. Stupidly stubborn earlier, she'd not eaten her fill of hare and was still hungry. She glanced away from the tempting meal, angry with the landlord for going against her. 'Have you asked Mr Wolfson to pay for my keep even though I said not to?'

'No…honest…' the landlord avowed, slowly shaking his perspiring head to impress on Fiona his truthfulness. 'Never did say a word to him. Mr Wolfson settled his shot and yours, before he went, you see, and wouldn't hear no more said about it.'

Fiona had started off towards the inn as though to find Luke and speak to him. Now she pivoted back. 'Went?' she echoed weakly. Despite what she'd said to him about brief farewells, she'd imagined…hoped…he might come and see her one last time before leaving.

'Gone off with his friends, you see.' Balancing the plate in one hand, the landlord gave her arm a pat. 'The other one's got her claws deep in him, that's what it is, my dear. You're much nicer, I reckon.' Mr Robley mimed the action of savage talons with his free fingers and drew a tiny giggle from Fiona.

'That's better,' the landlord chirped. 'Plenty more fish in the sea, eh, and where you're going, down Dartmouth way, there's sea aplenty.' He beamed at his little quip and nudged Fiona with an elbow. 'Now sit you down and eat this up.'

For some reason Fiona did as she was told and allowed him to place the plate and shiny cutlery on her lap.

'You let me know what else you might like. There's ale or tea or anything you fancy. All paid for...' He gave her a sideways smile that transformed into a chuckle. 'Mr Wolfson might change his mind and come back looking for you, I reckon, when he's got rid of t'other one.'

Fiona picked up her knife and fork, wondering how she would feel about that if he did.

The landlord watched contentedly as Fiona tucked in enthusiastically to her dinner. He liked to know his cooking was appreciated. He could be avaricious if the opportunity presented itself, but also a kindly, tolerant soul. He made a good living from gentlemen and young ladies, not always their wives, taking trips and stopping off at his hostelry, so had nothing against illicit shenanigans going on beneath his roof.

'When you've had your fill I'll have the gig

brought round. Can't say it's a comfy ride, but as you're keen to get on—'

'What?' Fiona interrupted, using her handkerchief on her lips while frowning intently at him.

'Mr Wolfson's paid for the hire of my vehicle to take you on to the Pig and Whistle. He said you'd got to collect your case from there. You'll be able to get to Dartmouth from that tavern.'

Fiona surged to her feet, handing Mr Robley her half-empty plate. Seeing the disappointment on his face as he studied the half-eaten food, she blurted, 'Oh, thank you, it was delicious, Mr Robley, but I must get going, sir. If I don't turn up soon I won't have a job to go to.'

'Oh, well…if you must…' The landlord dug a hand in the pocket of his apron. 'Left you this, too, he did.' He handed over a small package, then nodded eagerly at it to hurry Fiona opening it. With a sigh Fiona did so, knowing he wouldn't go till his curiosity had been satisfied. She'd an inkling of what might be within, but it felt heavier than expected. On unfolding the parchment wrapper she glimpsed a glitter of gold. But it wasn't just her precious locket within: three sovereigns were stacked on top of the delicately etched oval. With the weight of her riches in one hand Fiona turned the paper, hoping to see a note from him, but the sheet was blank.

Mr Robley's jaw had slackened at the sight of the treasure but he suddenly clacked together his brown teeth and chortled. 'He *do* like you the best, you see…'

## *Chapter Eleven*

She was finally drawing closer to her destination and the knowledge should have brought more contentment with it than it did, Fiona realised, as the gig set off west at quite a pace. She waved to Mr Robley who was flapping his dirty apron at her in farewell. As she settled back on the hard seat she put her pensiveness down to the likely reception she'd get from Mr Herbert when she eventually turned up days late.

The stable hand driving the one-horse contraption was called Bob and he was the landlord's son, he'd told her. Bob gave her a grin, but Fiona's eyes were drawn to a couple of older fellows who'd clattered off the cobbled courtyard to trot alongside the gig. When the road narrowed they dropped behind to follow it.

'Who are they?' Fiona asked.

'Them's me brothers.'

'Oh…' Fiona said. 'Do they also need to go to the Pig and Whistle?' She held on to her bonnet as a stray branch in the hedgerow scuffed it.

'They do today, miss, 'cos Major Wolfson's paid 'em to.'

'For what reason?'

'Escort duty, 'case we meet undesirables on the road. Michael and William have got guns on 'em, see.' He gave Fiona an admiring glance. 'Becky Peake don't get this special treatment. She just got put on the London mail last time he sent *her* home.'

So, it seemed that Mr Robley, despite his winks and nose-taps, wasn't the soul of discretion he'd said he was. The landlord had told his sons that she was one of Luke Wolfson's women. Only she wasn't…and neither did she wish to be! And it certainly wasn't the thought of never again seeing a mercenary that was making her feel oddly wistful, Fiona impressed upon herself, pursing her lips.

Becky Peake was welcome to him and the first opportunity she got to reimburse him, she would. She was glad to have her locket again securely beneath her bodice and, she had to admit, she was grateful for the sovereigns, too, although she wished he'd not been so ridiculously generous. One of the coins would suffice so she'd put the others away in their parchment wrapper, ready to be sent back.

Without money for her fare she would have been stranded at the Pig and Whistle. Although she'd already paid for a place on Toby Williams's coach she doubted he would be willing or able to take her on to finish her journey. If he were still at the hostelry he'd be watching over his nephew, and it would be a mean person indeed who'd expect him to abandon a gravely ill relative to drive her to Dartmouth.

Her thoughts veered back to the debt she now owed. She'd little chance of saving her locket's value and a sovereign. Even should she miraculously manage to gather the sum she'd no idea where to post his payment. Luke had told her nothing about himself, other than he was a bachelor who'd served in the army and was out of practice at trapping. Suddenly her mind pounced on the fact that he knew someone living locally. He'd been on his way to Lowerton to pay a visit on the first occasion they'd met. Nostalgically she recalled the stormy night he had built a fire to dry their clothes and they'd stood talking together in firelight while dripping trees made music in the background.

It all seemed now such a long time ago, yet only days had passed. Fiona wondered if the moody-looking fellow with Becky Peake was Luke's friend from Lowerton and whether they were all finished with Devon and returning to London. She'd never discovered the tale behind the aborted kidnapping of the duke's daughter and it irked her that she probably never would. She had suffered at the hands of the Collins gang because of it and felt she was at least entitled to know why.

Fiona sighed, wanting to stop dratted Luke Wolfson from dominating her every thought. Determinedly she turned her concentration to the people she'd travelled with on Toby Williams's coach. She wondered if the Jacksons and the Beresford sisters were now safely home. Fiona very much hoped they were. Yet she was worried that she'd not had an opportunity to beg them to guard their tongues over her abduction. No lasting harm had been done to her and she'd have liked to tell them so, if she could.

'I suppose you think you've been very clever, don't you?'

'What?' Luke was in no mood for jokes or for humouring his friend. He needed this argument with Rockleigh quickly sorted out so he could make sure Fiona had arrived safely at the Pig and Whistle.

Having taken Becky to the coach station, he'd left her there once he'd extracted her sulky promise to go straight home. Then Luke and Drew had travelled on to Lowerton. Luke no longer cared if Becky again defiantly loitered in Devon. He wouldn't be returning to the King and Tinker so if she went back there she'd be wasting her time.

A clinking together of crystal brought Luke's brooding thoughts back to the present. He was seated opposite Rockleigh at a table in the hunting lodge, a decanter and a glass midway between them on its surface. Another tumbler, half-filled with brandy, was shoved towards him over glossy mahogany.

'Turning the tables on me like that was a low trick. I'd not have thought you'd stoop to it.' Drew sat back in his chair, shrugging as though he blamed himself for being naive. He took a gulp of his drink.

'I've not the vaguest idea what the hell you are talking about.' Luke took a large swallow, too, returning the brandy to the table with a thump. He was still only half-listening to his friend's barbed remarks because images of Fiona's enraptured features were monopolising his mind. The silky feel of her skin and hair were ghostly phantoms beneath his fingertips, but it was her sweet instinctive response to his passion he couldn't forget. His hand clenched more tightly about the cooling glass as he became aware of the heat in his body. 'Can we get this business about Cecilia out of the way?' Luke began drumming some fingers on the tabletop. He'd turned sideways on his chair, a dark-sleeved arm resting on the back rail ready to push him to his feet. 'I'm sorry, Drew, but I've something vital to do.'

'Have you now? Well, sorry to hold you up.' Drew's drawling tone was scathing. 'But, by chance, I've also got something vital to do… and say. And you have more to apologise for than dismissing my niece as though she's one of your fly-by-night doxies.'

Luke discerned from his friend's tone of voice that he was about to hear something significant, and unpleasant, that was additional to the matter that had brought him here. His fingers ceased their tattoo. 'Enlighten me, then,' he invited with an impatient gesture.

'I've a meeting with the Duke of Thornley in the morning to impress on him that I will not be proposing to his daughter, despite his threats of dire consequences if I refuse to do so.'

Luke had taken an ill-timed mouthful of brandy; what he'd just heard made him choke, then splutter, 'If the Duke of Thornley, owner of five titles and six estates, would have you as a son-in-law, I'd sign up for it, Drew.' He dried his mouth with the back of a hand. 'No offence—I know you've got pots of money, but I fear you've not got the credentials where the fair Lady Joan is concerned.'

'Having compromised herself she's not quite so fair now…perhaps that's got a bearing on the matter of my eligibility,' Drew said silkily. 'But of course you know all of this. I made a few enquiries and was told she was planning to elope with a lover to get out of marrying some old roué her father found for her.' Drew cocked his head, resting his chin on forked fingers in a deceptively casual manner. 'I can't make up my mind if you're the old roué or the rake she's rumoured to want to run off with. Did you get cold feet and need a patsy? Or is it you're simply out to foist her on to me from spite because I've demanded you marry Cecilia?'

Luke's glass had hovered by his mouth and he'd stared at his friend over its rim while listening to Drew. The drink was placed back on the table and Luke stood up. 'I think you'd better explain that riddle.'

'I'd rather you did,' Drew returned, also getting to his feet.

The two men faced each other across polished

timber, knowing that before too long a punch would be thrown. The silent atmosphere crackled as much from antagonism as burning logs.

'I've had recent business with His Grace, but what that is to do with you, I've no idea,' Luke said shortly.

'It's damn all to do with me!' Drew roared. 'And I don't appreciate being dragged into it so you can wriggle out of facing up to the consequences of kissing my niece at the Hancocks' ball.'

'I wasn't kissing the hoyden!' Luke bawled back. 'She was kissing me…after a fashion. She is only sixteen, after all.'

'Exactly!' Drew barked. 'And that's why you're damn well marrying her.'

'I'm not.' Luke spat through gritted teeth. 'And at the risk of repeating myself—if her mother had taught Cecilia the rudiments of good behaviour we wouldn't be having this conversation.'

Drew's lips tightened although the slur wasn't unjust. His sister had always been too wrapped up in herself to teach her only child her manners, especially around men. Cecilia had been his ward since his sister's widowhood and, like it or no, he'd been the closest thing to a father the girl had had for three years past. He'd already accepted that Luke was innocent in all of this and had been prepared to apologise, days ago. Drew knew it was his responsibility to do the best he could for his spoilt niece, yet wished her sire had taken a stick to her back years ago to discipline the wilfulness out of her.

Drew had said something very similar to the Duke of Thornley about his shortcomings as a father and about his daughter's wild character. Yet he'd instinctively prevented the old boy from chastising Joan with a slap. And God only knew she was an infuriating individual; Drew had felt sorely tempted to shake the life out of her when she refused to answer his questions about why she'd risk everything to seek out Wolfson at dead of night. Instead of an explanation the minx had given him a challenging look.

Drew was determined to get the full story from Luke because he couldn't believe the girl had called on him by accident. If he discovered that Luke had used Thornley's daughter as a pawn to get even with him, he'd call him out. They had been at school and at university together, but Drew had already accepted that this evening their friendship might be irrevocably broken.

'Did you go to Thornley Heights looking for me when I didn't show up? Is that where you met

Joan?' Luke demanded. He always kept details of his work confidential so his friend knew no more than he had business in the area.

'No, I didn't go looking for you,' Drew snapped.

'Well, how in damnation did you manage to put yourself in Joan's path? Her father rarely lets her out because of the Collins gang.' Luke had failed to make any sense out of his friend's tale.

'She rarely goes out…the shy little thing, yet here we are about to get engaged if the old boy has his way.' Drew gave a mirthless chuckle. 'Which he won't…'

Luke forked five fingers through his hair in exasperation. Memories of Fiona were again nagging at his mind, despite the gravity of his friend's predicament. He closed his eyes against the strength of the need to see her again. 'Look… whatever's gone on, Rockleigh, I can't help solve it. Whatever you've done—'

'It's not what *I've* done, is it?' Drew snarled. 'All *I* did was escort the chit home when she came here to find you.'

'Joan Morland came *here*?' Luke barked an astonished laugh.

'Indeed she did, alone…with just a lad driving her,' Drew stated.

Luke swore beneath his breath. His mind had pounced immediately on the only reason there was for Thornley's daughter to do that. He'd told Joan he wouldn't take on her father's contract, yet it seemed she'd not accepted his decision and had acted recklessly in her attempt to change his mind.

'Nothing to say?' Drew taunted, feeling his temper bubbling dangerously.

'How in God's name did she find out I was coming here?' Luke blasted.

'Well, someone told her and I imagine it was you. The way I see it, a woman would only take such a risk for a lover.' Drew's control exploded and he launched himself at Luke, swinging a right hook. Luke staggered, but hit his opponent back, harder. Drew fell, sprawling, across the table, sending the decanter skidding perilously close to the edge.

'We'll have to sort this out another time. I need to go,' Luke shouted. He knew he owed his friend an explanation if not an apology. But he'd not the time to spend talking now. He needed to catch up with Fiona to make sure she was safe.

Drew leapt between Luke and the doorway, barring his exit as he strode towards it.

'You're not going anywhere till I know the

details. If you've seduced Thornley's daughter, then you can marry her.'

'What…and Cecilia, too?' Luke snarled sardonically. 'Bigamy's not my style.'

Infuriated, Drew bounded at Luke again.

'Don't be damned ridiculous, Drew!' Luke sidestepped and put out his hands in placation. 'I haven't seduced Lady Joan or even flirted with her—I barely know her.' He wiped a smear of blood from his mouth with a curled finger. 'I've only spoken to her a couple of times and your name and this lodge never cropped up between us. My business was with her father.'

'Did the duke know you were coming to see me?'

Luke searched his mind for such a conversation…and found one. A whistling sigh was expelled through his teeth. 'I told Thornley I was heading to a hunting lodge at Lowerton to see a friend before returning to London.' Luke leaned his back against the wall and tilted up his head, staring bleakly at the ceiling. If Joan had been eavesdropping on that occasion, or the duke had told her where his mercenary had gone, then she would have known where to head in an attempt to intercept him.

'So do you want to tell me all about it or are we going to fight some more?' Drew went to the table and poured himself a drink. He emptied the glass before adding, 'You blasted well owe me the truth, Luke.'

Luke couldn't deny it, so as briefly as possible he outlined his business in Devon with the Duke of Thornley. He also told Drew why he'd missed their first appointment, and how he'd helped stranded travellers whose coach had come a cropper. But he stopped short of mentioning Fiona and her ordeal at the hands of the Collins gang. That was too private, and, Luke realised, too precious, for even an old friend to know about.

Drew poured two drinks this time and moved one in Luke's direction.

'It sounds like some melodramatic romance novel my sister would read.' Drew shook his head in a mixture of mockery and despair.

'I know.' Luke crossed his arms over his chest. 'But unfortunately, it's no fiction.' He speared a glance at Drew. 'I'll speak to Thornley and explain.'

Drew snorted a mirthless laugh. 'His daughter's already tried that several times.'

'How do you know?'

'She sent me a note telling me so.'

'You've not blamed her in any of this, I notice.'

Drew shrugged. 'Young women can be impulsive and excitable—'

'Like Cecilia, you mean?' Luke interrupted drily.

'So, if you told the duke you were coming to see me, and he let on to his daughter about it, he's at fault.' Drew ignored the reference to his errant niece. 'I didn't have to escort Joan home, or put His Grace in the picture over what had happened. I could have packed her off in her trap and let her fall straight into Jeremiah Collins's clutches.'

'A point worth bringing to Thornley's attention tomorrow at your meeting,' Luke said. 'And while we're talking of gracious gallantry…no more did I have to bring Cecilia home from the Hancocks' ball that night before she disgraced herself any further.' He approached Drew, held out his hand in a peace offering. 'Send her off to her aunt's out in the sticks. Better still, send her off to finishing school somewhere.'

Drew took Luke's fingers, testing their strength with his own in a single shake. 'Do you think Thornley will send his daughter away? Not that he needs to—nobody knows but us and them.'

'What does she say about it all?' Luke asked. 'Apart from sorry.'

'I wouldn't marry him if he were the last man

alive.' Drew had squeaked his answer in a childish treble.

Luke gave a gruff chuckle. 'Well, there you are, then. His Grace might huff and puff, but he'll give in to her in the end. Unless Joan Morland decides she wants you, you're quite safe.'

'Well...go on, then.'

Luke frowned.

'I know you're itching to get away so you can meet a woman. And it's not Becky, is it?'

'Becky's on her way back to London, as far as I know.'

'I'm heading back that way in the morning,' Drew said. 'Perhaps I'll catch up with the minx...'

'Be my guest,' Luke said.

'So...tell me about the woman who's got you dangling on a bit of string.'

Luke turned for the door, giving his friend no more response than a smile.

'The lady you were with at the King and Tinker?' Drew guessed. 'I reckon you've rescued that fair maiden...and put yourself in peril instead.'

Instead of telling his friend to mind his own business Luke made a rather rude gesture, but, worryingly, he immediately understood what Drew had hinted at.

It wasn't love…it was lust, he told himself, banging the door shut after him as he heard Rockleigh erupt in laughter.

## Chapter Twelve

'Oh, how lovely to see you!'

Fiona had spotted the Jacksons as soon as the Pig and Whistle's creaking sign hove into view. She waved furiously in greeting, allowing Bob Robley to assist her down in the tavern's court-yard, then sped towards the couple. They appeared to have been awaiting her arrival, so she blurted, 'Did you know I'd be coming by today?'

Mrs Jackson took Fiona's hands in her own and gave them a fond squeeze. 'Indeed we did expect you, my dear! Mr Wolfson sent a note ahead of you to ask us to welcome you. Not that we needed him to tell us to do that! You cannot know how happy and relieved we felt to discover he had you under his care. It is wonderful to see you, you poor child.' Overcome with emotion Betty Jackson sniffed and enclosed Fiona in a motherly hug. 'Are you *well*, my dear?' She gave the younger woman a significant look, then glanced about to make sure that nobody was within earshot. 'You understand what I mean by *well*?' she hissed, raising her eyebrows, but her weathered features were shaped by concern rather than prurience.

'I'm very well,' Fiona answered quietly.

Mrs Jackson persisted. 'Mr Wolfson caught up with you in time, before those fiends…?'

'I was…am…perfectly fine,' Fiona interrupted with a faint blush. 'My dignity came off the worst,' she quipped. 'I was tossed about like a sack of potatoes.'

'Savages!' Mr Jackson interjected. 'I'd like to get my hands on those two.'

'Did they take you to that monster, Jeremiah Collins?' Betty Jackson whispered, aghast.

'I did meet him and he's a very insipid individual in the flesh.' Fiona gave her opinion of the notorious criminal.

'It's the quiet ones you have to watch,' Peter Jackson growled. 'The sooner the devil's at the end of a noose the better.'

Fiona nodded, feeling a little shiver race over her as she recalled Jeremiah's boast: *I've money to make and pleasure to take before I swing on Gallows Hill.* She sincerely hoped that the law caught up with him soon.

'Mr Wolfson is so brave!' Mrs Jackson's clasped hands were pressed to her bosom. 'How could he attain victory against such ruffians?' she asked rhetorically, eyes glowing with admiration.

'He is a military man, so used to employing tactics when skirmishing,' Mr Jackson opined. 'Nevertheless, praise where it is due for the feat of rescuing you so quickly, Miss Chapman.'

Fiona smiled faintly, wondering what the couple would think if they knew their hero was, or had been, a colleague of the wretch they'd see hung. And how would these fine people take knowing she'd come closer to being ravished by her saviour than by any gang member?

But Fiona knew she'd never discredit Luke Wolfson to anybody and not simply because of the service he'd done her. She sensed, deep within her heart, that he was a good man despite indications to the contrary and so little time spent with him to judge. But more than that, she felt oddly loyal to him, in the way she did to her mother. Maude had chosen to go ahead and marry Cecil Ratcliff despite her daughter's warnings about the man. Even before the banns had been read Cecil had tried to insinuate his fingers beneath Fiona's bodice on two occasions. Yet her mother had been angry to have her com-

plain, insisting Cecil had simply been overzeal-
ous with his hugs. Now Maude knew the truth
about the man she'd chosen to believe over her
daughter, but it was too late. Maude had failed
her child and no amount of bitter regrets would
ever put things back as they'd been between
mother and daughter.

'Mr Wolfson made us promise to keep quiet
about your kidnapping,' Mrs Jackson whispered.

'Not that he needed to tell us to do that, either,' Mr Jackson emphasised. 'We would never
have risked a slur on your reputation. We had
faith in him when he promised to put things
right.'

'Thank you for being so considerate…' Fiona
said huskily with tears in her eyes. 'I *have* been
worried about gossip.'

'We have spoken to nobody about what happened to you,' Mr Jackson quickly reassured.
'Obviously the Beresford sisters and Toby and
Bert know, but I'm sure they'll heed Mr Wolfson's words on it and button their lips.'

'How is Bert? All of you have been constantly
in my thoughts,' Fiona said earnestly.

'Bert is on the mend. Toby has travelled back
to the Fallow Buck so he might be reunited with
his own vehicle, if not his stolen nags. I doubt

he'll see those again.' Mr Jackson sorrowfully shook his head.

Fiona realised that the loss of the coachman's animals would be a great blow to him.

'Toby planned to get Bert quickly home to his own bed from the Fallow Buck. On his last visit the doctor said the lad had made a remarkable improvement and should fully recover.'

'That's wonderful news,' Fiona breathed. 'And the Beresford sisters?'

'Oh, I imagine they're back at their own fireside now. They left with us their very good wishes for you.'

Fiona smiled on hearing that. All had turned out better than she had dared hope. If her employer were to be understanding about her delayed arrival, then her life would be no better, or worse, than before calamity struck.

'Well, let's find a quiet spot to sit down inside the inn. There's lots to talk about and I expect something to eat wouldn't go amiss.' Mr Jackson held out an elbow to both ladies and the trio proceeded into the Pig and Whistle.

'The duke would like an audience, sir.'

'I have an urgent appointment, but you may tell His Grace I will be back this way and will call in tomorrow to see him at Thornley Heights.'

'But it is of the utmost importance, Major Wolfson, he bade me impress that upon you.'

Luke walked out of the farrier's into warm sunlight so he might converse privately with Thornley's steward. He'd been forced to break his journey towards the Pig and Whistle because the mare needed shoeing. As well as heading there for Fiona's sake he had to return the horse to its owner and collect Star, full of beans no doubt after his enforced rest in a strange stable.

But Luke was being dogged on all sides by holdups. He cursed beneath his breath in frustration. He realised his obsession with Fiona Chapman was illogical, and out of character, yet still his mind persisted in returning to the spinster he barely knew, but desired so ardently that every fibre of his being seemed to have grown uncomfortably tense. He accepted, with wry self-mockery, that his desire for her company was probably not reciprocated. Indeed, he'd got the impression when they'd parted at the King and Tinker that she couldn't remove herself from his presence quickly enough. But he'd also noticed that she'd glanced at Becky with an amount of female pique and he'd enough experience with the fairer sex to recognise a jealous woman.

The smith walked out of his workshop, leading the mare. Having paid the fellow for his work, Luke turned again to the hovering steward. About to send him on his way by repeating the message he'd already delivered, he thought of Drew. His friendship with Drew had stood the test of time, but it might not outlast this crisis. He owed it to Rockleigh to speak up on his behalf and make the duke see sense about Joan's folly. Luke couldn't believe that Alfred Thornley would shackle his cherished daughter to a fellow she didn't want. His Grace, despite his undoubted fine intelligence, tended to act first and think second when in a passion over something. Luke had first-hand experience of the man's arrogance. He guessed that Joan's father had already calmed down enough to see the flaws in an enforced marriage. But he was too obstinate to admit he'd been wrong and was seeking a way out that would leave his pride intact.

If he rode hard for Thornley Heights then back again, he'd be delayed by no more than a few hours, Luke realised. He trusted the Jacksons to care for Fiona in his absence. And he did at least have the comfort of knowing that she'd arrived safely: he'd quizzed Robley's sons and been assured they'd seen her go inside the Pig and Whistle with a middle-aged couple.

Luke gave Thornley's man a brief nod. 'Very

well—you may tell His Grace I will arrive by two of the clock this afternoon.'

Maude had never travelled on a mail coach before although she was no stranger to the hired cab. With a public hackney one had the chance to be private, rather than assailed by the touch and odour of strangers' bodies. She hoped the infernal bone-shaker would stop soon so she might get off to have some refreshment and cool down.

It was late April but the atmosphere seemed as hot as the month of June and the interior of the coach was smelly and steamy. Maude cast a jaundiced eye on her maid; Rose seemed unperturbed as she snored with her chin resting on her chest. Irritated, Maude realised that her servant had a better seat than she did being next to the window with air stirring her wispy brown hair. Maude wondered whether to wake Rose and tell her to change places, but of course that would entail bumping into the other occupants of the congested coach and Maude would sooner suffer cramps than risk physical contact with any of them. Stiffly, she straightened her legs beneath her skirts to ease their position.

She stopped fidgeting on hearing the blare of a horn. She avoided the eye of a labourer seated opposite who'd given her several lewd winks

and beneath her breath muttered a little prayer
which was answered: the vehicle slowed down
and pulled into a wide tavern courtyard.

'Might we have a pot of tea, my girl, and some
biscuits or cakes?' Maude asked the servant as
she and her maid settled down in chairs by the
hearth.

'I'll fetch scones and bread and butter with
your tea, madam, if you like.'

Having received an agreement to her sugges-
tion, Megan headed off with the order, her rosy
lips forming a kiss for Sam as she spotted him
through the window. She sashayed towards the
kitchens, knowing her beau was watching her
while using the currycomb on a horse.

If anybody suspected that her sweetheart was
a member of the Collins gang, they knew better than to say so outright. Most local people
took the view that the less said openly about the
smuggling trade, the better. Turning a blind eye
to nocturnal visits by fellows carrying kegs was
accepted behaviour in this neck of the woods.
Megan knew that her employer filled his cellar
with contraband, but instead of personally taking deliveries, he'd leave the barn door ajar on
an appointed night. So that he could honestly
claim not to know the criminals he'd hide pay-

ment behind a brick in the wall for furtive collection. Since the landlord of the Cockerell had been found stabbed, no innkeeper had reneged on paying up for supplies brought on trust.

Megan had no family living close by; she'd left home in Exeter at sixteen to make her way in the world. The landlord and his wife provided her board and lodging and she had nothing but tips from the customers to put into her purse. So Megan appreciated that her Sam was often flush from running with a powerful man like Jeremiah Collins. In the past Sam had treated her to lengths of smuggled French lace and perfume.

Of course, Sam's parents suspected what he did to boost his meagre regular wages, and made no bones about it. With five younger brothers and sisters to feed they were grateful for whatever merchandise their eldest boy brought home. They asked no awkward questions as to how Sam came by sudden riches.

Maude gave the servant a gracious smile; the girl seemed keen to please, she thought, as Megan put down the tray filled with food and tea things and offered to pour.

Megan's pleasant expression turned sour when the maid started pouring tea and waved her away without offering her a tip.

'I do hope we find my daughter quickly.'

Maude sighed as she watched Rose replace the teapot on the tray. 'How am I to know where to look for Fiona? It was bad of her to go off without leaving me her proper direction. Devon is a vast place.'

Rose gave her mistress a sympathetic look, but refrained from pointing out that Miss Fiona had probably been reticent so her stepfather didn't discover her whereabouts. Not that Mrs Chapman—Rose refused to think of her mistress as anything other than the late master's spouse—would have willingly betrayed her daughter. Rose knew Cecil Ratcliff for a bully. If he'd wanted to have Fiona brought home, he'd have eventually got out of his wife where to look for her. But Rose reckoned that Cecil had bigger fish to fry: she had opened the door to duns a few days ago. Now Cecil had almost emptied the house of furnishings, the property would be sold off next. In Rose's opinion, even if Mrs Chapman decided to return to the thieving wretch with her tail between her legs, she'd have nowhere to call home.

'I wonder if my daughter stopped here for refreshment?' Maude looked about the interior of the heavily beamed tavern. 'I'm sure she would have broken her journey as we have. Mayhap the serving girl might remember her,' Maude ventured brightly. 'It would not hurt to ask—she seems an obliging young woman.'

'More tea, madam?' Megan had quickly responded to the customer's beckoning finger. A few coppers as a tip could yet come her way.

'Do you know if Miss Fiona Chapman stopped at this hostelry? It would have been quite recently—she is my daughter, you see...' Maude tutted as the girl began loading crockery onto the tray as though deaf to her question. 'Did you not hear what I said, miss?'

'I...I don't recall that name,' Megan lied, flustered. 'Sorry...I've to wash up.' Picking up the tray, she hurried off.

'Well...really! It was a simple enough enquiry,' Maude huffed loudly. 'I'll ask the landlord instead.'

Megan heard that threat and immediately reduced her pace to begin mulling things over. She stopped and put down the tray on an empty table, then glanced over a shoulder at the two women. Pursed-lipped, she thought harder about things. She didn't like the fact that her Sam was involved in holding up coaches, or that he threatened people with guns to rob them. But he'd sworn to her that it was Fred Ruff who'd fired the shot at Bert Williams, winging him. Megan had been mightily relieved when Toby Williams and Bert had turned up yesterday to collect their repaired coach. Bert had looked poorly, but at least he was again on his feet; he'd even managed to give her a wink and she'd teased him, what with him being a married man. But neither of the Williamses had said a word about an abduction and naturally Megan couldn't say she knew one had taken place when the coach had been held up. So she'd realised that the two men were being respectful of the victim's reputation.

Kidnapping was something new and *very* bad for Sam to be involved in and Megan had told her sweetheart her thoughts on it. Not that he ever took any notice of her; Sam was too eager to please his boss because he liked his pockets jingling and he didn't intend mucking out stables all his life, so he'd told her.

But an idea was taking root in Megan's mind, making her slowly retrace her steps towards the seated women. The Chapmans were not first-rate Quality; if they had been, Mrs Chapman wouldn't be travelling in a mail coach. But she was genteel and such people hated scandals. The mother couldn't yet know what had happened to her daughter, but when she found out she'd want to protect Fiona's marriage prospects and whip her back to London. In Megan's opinion, that couldn't happen soon enough. The longer

Mrs Chapman hung around asking questions, the more likely it would be that the whole story might emerge. The locals tolerated the Collins gang for the sake of cheap tea and brandy, but they'd be outraged to hear of an innocent woman's kidnap and furious if dragoons started turning houses upside down in their hunt for the perpetrators. Megan knew that if her sweetheart were arrested he stood little chance of acquittal.

Sam had told Megan of Fiona's eventual fate: Major Wolfson—who the gang suspected was a turncoat—had bought her from Collins to be his paramour. Jem had regretted bartering his prisoner and had sent Sam and Fred to snatch Fiona back, but they'd been given the slip. Miss Chapman was not the aristocrat's daughter they'd first thought her, but Wolfson's interest in her had piqued Collins. Jem had told his men he reckoned Wolfson saw Fiona Chapman as good for a profit as well as a roll in the hay.

'What is it you want?' Maude had turned and seen the serving girl hovering just behind.

'I think I do remember your daughter, madam…' Megan began in her slow country burr. 'I believe she was with a gentleman.' She lowered her voice and her eyes, as though embarrassed by the information she was imparting.

'A gentleman?' Maude echoed hoarsely. It had

crossed her mind that Fiona might have a secret beau, but she'd dismissed it as too fantastic.

'His name is Major Wolfson as I recollect,' Megan added helpfully.

Maude had turned white and Rose sent her mistress a concerned look.

'And where might I find this fellow?' Maude croaked, glancing about as though anxious nobody should overhear the alarming news that her daughter might be a fallen woman.

'I've no idea, madam, but I do know he had business with the Duke of Thornley,' Megan said.

## Chapter Thirteen

'Might that be him, do you think, ma'am?'

'I don't think so, Rose; he is not in military uniform,' Maude answered, squinting at the broad back of a tall fellow who was striding away from them towards his horse.

The gig Maude had hired at the Fallow Buck had turned through wide crenellated pillars and rattled along a mile of meandering tree-lined avenue before pulling up in front of a sweeping set of steps. She'd watched the darkly handsome young man athletically descending the shallow flight of stone two treads at a time, his long leather coat flying out behind him. He was certainly a dashing individual, but in her mind's eye Maude had an image of her daughter's swain—if indeed one *could* term Major Wolfson such. Maude had a depressing idea her daughter was possibly viewed as a mistress rather than a wife by the scoundrel. But she strove for optimism and to believe him honourable if predictably mundane. He would assuredly not be so distinguished looking as the gentleman in the distance, who was probably the duke's son. Fiona, Maude inwardly sighed, would be true to form and attract a suitor with little to recommend him. Possibly this *major* had just the prospect of his army pension to offer a wife.

It had been a great sadness to Maude that Fiona had not found an eligible chap like her younger sister. Verity was a vivacious charmer and had her glossy chestnut hair and petite figure to turn a man's head, whereas Fiona, being rather too tall and too bland in looks and personality in her mother's eyes, had been overlooked by the bachelors who'd come into her daughters' orbit.

But Fiona had not helped herself, Maude thought crossly; as a dutiful mother she had often bitten her tongue about her eldest girl's frustrating lack of ambition to catch a man. *'Why can you not be more like your pretty sister?'* would have been too cruel a comment to fire at Fiona. But to Maude's chagrin it had nearly rolled off her tongue on more occasions than she could count. Then, after Anthony died, assailed by loneliness and grief, she'd been glad to have Fiona's company...until Cecil wormed his way into her life and she'd again resented her daughter being under her feet. But only at first.

Maude knew she'd been wrong about Fiona in many ways. She should have heeded her eldest child's warning about Ratcliff's swinish character. But the most startling thing for Maude was learning that the girl she'd known for twenty-five years had an inner steel and a sense of adventure that she'd overlooked. It had come as a shock when Fiona had bluntly told her that Cecil Ratcliff was a lecher and not only that, but she was also off to Devon to start a new life so she'd never have to see him again. Might her homely daughter surprise her one more time by netting an eligible gentleman who'd propose to her and give her everything her heart desired? If such a miracle were to come to pass, Maude knew that all their troubles would be at an end. She'd live with her newly married daughter and son-in-law in their lavish home and Cecil Ratcliff could go hang!

These mixed musings and fantasies had passed through Maude's consciousness as she gazed up at the magnificent house. With a deep sigh she collected her thoughts and got down to the job in hand. 'Well, here we are, then,' she declared briskly.

The stable lad driving the gig was peeking

nervously from under his brows at his grand surroundings. He'd never before been so close to
the ducal residence and felt like a trespasser. His
customer might be gentry from London, but he
didn't believe she was of a class that hobnobbed
with dukes any more than he was. 'Reckon I
should've taken you straight round the back,'
he muttered.

'Indeed, you should not!' Maude said in-
dignantly, despite also feeling awestruck. She
watched the handsome fellow galloping off
into the distance, then turned her attention to
the shrinking youth. 'Come help us down if you
please. I have urgent business with this Duke of
Thornley.'

The boy did as he was bid and watched, slack-
jawed, as the lady marched to the steps and
started up them. Arriving out of breath at the
top, Maude took an inspiriting lungful of air,
then hammered on the door.

His Grace had been on the point of returning
to his study, having spent some minutes conversing with his butler after Wolfson had left. 'Who
in damnation might that be?' He strode to the
door in front of the ancient servant, muttering
to himself, 'Has Wolfson remembered his manners and come to apologise?'

In fact, Thornley knew that the mercenary

had nothing to be sorry about. The man had told him plain truths, as he always did. Grudgingly, Thornley was coming to like the fellow, even though he had learned some worrying and rather humbling things from Wolfson today.

Flinging the door wide, Alfred stared at the two middle-aged women on his step. He could tell the mistress from the maid, not just from their attire, but from the air of entitlement exuded by the person closest to him. 'And, pray, who might you be?'

'I am Mrs…Ratcliff…' Maude announced in her crispest accent. In common with Rose she hated giving her name as Mrs Ratcliff, but knew she must, as unfortunately, that's who she was now. 'I have come to speak to the Duke of Thornley on an urgent matter. Would you fetch him, please?'

'I have no need to…you are speaking to him, madam.' Thornley looked her buxom figure up and down then cocked his head at the maid hovering behind.

A silence ensued during which Maude felt her temper rising. How dare he make her stand outside while he boldly gave her the once-over as though she were some auditioning servant! She'd not expected the fellow to be so…imperious in tone and presence. And why he attended his own door was beyond her. Anybody might be excused for thinking *him* one of the hired help. 'I do not discuss my business on the front step,' Maude burst out, her bravado wavering.

'Well, I suppose you'd better come in, then,' Thornley said, and stalked off. Over a shoulder he instructed his butler to show his visitor to the blue saloon and enquire whether she would like refreshment.

After ten minutes the tea arrived. Maude and Rose sat perched on high-backed velvet chairs in a sumptuously furnished room. The blue saloon lived up to its name: a hue of a summer sky, adorned with puffy clouds and fat-cheeked cherubs, decorated the ceiling while the soaring walls were lined with watered silk in a toning pastel shade.

The clock chimed four o'clock, making Rose jump. The duke's servant poured tea for Mrs Ratcliff, then put down the pot.

'Please give a cup of tea to my maid,' Maude said firmly.

Thornley's lackey did as she was told, but with a pronounced arch to one of her eyebrows. Then she left, leaving the visitors alone. Before entering the blue saloon the butler had found Rose a chair in the hallway where she might wait while her mistress had an audience with the duke. But Maude would not hear of that and had insisted her servant accompany her, more from feeling nervous than egalitarian. Nevertheless, Rose had given her employer a grateful look and the butler a smug sniff on passing.

'Perhaps the duke has forgotten about your arrival, ma'am,' Rose ventured in a whisper on hearing her restless mistress's teacup clatter on its porcelain saucer.

'Perhaps the bumptious fellow has not forgotten but has no intention of giving me five minutes of his precious time,' Maude returned bitterly.

'The *bumptious fellow* shall give you ten minutes of his time, madam, but not a moment longer,' Thornley said drily, having just entered the room and overheard his visitor's sniping.

Maude blushed, put up her chin and pushed away her cup. 'Then I will state my business without delay, sir. I am looking for my daughter and have a report that she might be in the company of a Major Wolfson. I have also heard that you may know of that fellow's whereabouts. If you do, I would be grateful to have his direction.'

Beneath his breath Thornley made a sound, part-chuckle, part-groan. So Wolfson's doxy was refined enough to have a mother worrying about her. Yet Alfred was sure the boy he'd sent to the

King and Tinker with a note for Wolfson had told him the courtesan's surname was Peake, not Ratcliff. Of course, he wouldn't be surprised to know the handsome major had more than one camp follower...

'I do know Wolfson but, alas, am not acquainted with your daughter. You have just missed the man, actually, but I expect you might find him at the King and Tinker, or perhaps the Pig and Whistle. I hope you are successful in your search.' Thornley turned for the door as though to leave. 'Do finish your tea...if you will.'

'That was *him?*' Maude exclaimed, jumping to her feet.

'Who was *him?*' Thornley asked a trifle impatiently.

'We saw a fellow leaving.'

'Yes...that was Major Wolfson, or Mr Wolfson as I believe he terms himself now.'

Maude almost stamped in frustration. 'Oh... but I might have asked him about Fiona and have missed the chance.'

'Fiona?' Thornley had again been on the point of quitting the room, but pivoted back to stare at Maude.

'My daughter... Miss Fiona Chapman,' Maude snapped, sure the fellow hadn't paid heed to a word she'd said. Obviously he thought himself too important to bother with her. Rather haughtily she said, 'Thank you for your time and hospitality, sir. We must go now.' She wanted none of his tea, or his condescension, and for two pins would tell him so.

'No…please…sit down…stay a while so we might talk.' Thornley sighed, feeling a weight sink to his stomach.

That morning he had sent his steward looking for Luke Wolfson so he might quiz the mercenary over his friend Rockleigh. In no uncertain terms, Wolfson had told him that Drew Rockleigh was an exemplary individual with excellent connections, but he was his own man and would be coerced into nothing against his will. But Wolfson had had more to deliver than his friend's character reference: the major had gone on to relate a deeply disturbing story that had left Alfred feeling shocked and ashamed and deserving of his hireling's rebuke.

He knew himself to be arrogant and impetuous and had never before thought to curb those traits. He was the Duke of Thornley and had been bred to do as he pleased and damn the naysayers. But Heaven only knew he regretted the day he'd concocted the kidnap plot because never had he imagined how awful might be the consequences.

So, this was the mother of the brave woman Wolfson had told him about. Less than an hour ago he had heard a tale about an abduction and a young woman's pluck and fortitude in coping with an ordeal that, Thornley was sure, might have deranged lesser females. He glanced at the lady who'd brought into the world such an intrepid soul. Yes…he could believe the connection true; Mrs Ratcliff was proudly challenging him with her stare—just like his late wife in that respect. Ethel would often tell him he might be a duke, but he was her husband first and he could get off his high horse.

Alfred felt duty-bound to inform the girl's mother about the dangers her daughter had faced and that the blame for Miss Chapman's ordeal could be laid at his door. But he didn't relish the doing of it. He hadn't wanted any lasting gossip surrounding his daughter's imaginary beau, so had known that at some time he'd have to expose all the details of his scheme to bring Collins to justice. He'd anticipated being hailed as a hero rather than an incompetent fool when his deception was made public.

The tale of Joan running off to elope had indeed pricked up the villain's ears and made him act, just as Alfred had intended it should. And Miss Fiona Chapman, an innocent in all of it, had suffered because of his half-baked plot. Luke Wolfson had impressed that fact upon him and Alfred knew that, had the two men been the same age, he'd not only have felt the full force of the mercenary's rage, but his fist, too.

Alfred would remain eternally grateful that the major had been in the vicinity to save the day; if Miss Chapman had been harmed Alfred's conscience would have tortured him till he died. A young lady's virtue, her dignity and self-respect—perhaps even her life—had all been at stake because of him. Alfred thought of his own daughter. He had put Joan at risk, too: she'd never have gone out late at night looking for Wolfson but for the plot's existence. Oh, Joan had been all for the intrigue and excitement of it all, but she was still a green girl and should be allowed to indulge those sensations within a parent's protection. Now Alfred accepted that Drew Rockleigh deserved praise not punishment for the service he'd done Joan. Neither of them wanted the marriage he'd been determined to force on them and having Joan blaming him for her unhappiness would be a constant torment. So, etiquette be damned! If anybody dared start a whisper that the Duke of Thornley's daughter had been compromised, either by her imaginary beau, or by Drew Rockleigh, he'd sue them to kingdom come!

'I think you have something bad to tell me,' Maude said hoarsely. She had watched the duke's harsh features altering shape beneath some inner conflict that had left him looking worryingly grave. Instead of feeling relief at his softening expression, Maude had been alarmed by the change in him. 'Fiona has come to harm?' Maude whispered.

When His Grace said nothing, but paced to and fro pulling on his lower lip, reflecting on a way to couch bad news, Maude let out a small wail. 'It is all my fault! I've been stupid and selfish and a very bad parent. Why have I failed her when all I want is the best for my daughter? She would have been safe at home, had it not been for me.'

Thornley gazed at the woman who'd just voiced virtually word for word the self-abuse spinning in his own head. He knew that he had many apologies to make and he might as well start straight away. Joan had chosen to be reckless, but Miss Chapman's reputation had been sullied through no fault of her own. Many folk were privy to Fiona's ill treatment, some of them very nasty characters. Alfred hated the thought of it, but feared the scandal would eventually get out and ruin this woman's daughter. 'Would you mind if your maid waited outside while we converse privately?' he croaked.

'I would not mind, sir,' Maude whispered, giving Rose a nod of dismissal. She would sooner be on her own if she were about to hear of a disaster befalling Fiona. Rose had served the Chapmans well over many years, and was as loyal as the day was long, but Maude knew that there were occasions when class differences must be observed.

When Rose had been settled outside on a hall chair Thornley closed the door and ambled towards Maude. Stiffly he went down by her side and clumsily took one of her hands, cradling it in his.

With increasing incredulity Maude had watched him approach her and lower himself on creaky knees. As soon as he touched her she instinctively withdrew her fingers with a hiss of alarm.

Thornley patted her digits in reassurance, but left them curled on her lap. Turning himself to a more comfortable position, he sagged on to his posterior, next to her armchair. 'First let me start by saying I have heard that your daughter has wit and courage and that it has sustained her through a very unpleasant episode. I can see from where your daughter might have got such qualities. Or perhaps you will tell me that Fiona favours your husband.'

'My daughter detests my husband…as do I… but we both loved her father very much,' Maude rattled off, still dazed to have made such an admission to a stranger.

'Indeed…that is a mixed blessing and I would hear more about it.' Thornley glanced at her, looking taken aback. 'But not now because I still have much to say. I must tell you something and beg your forgiveness when I have done for being the bearer of such bad tidings…' He frowned, wondering where to start to report to a mother that her unwed daughter had been vilely mistreated, and what's more, folk knew about it.

'My Fiona… She is not…' Maude licked her bloodless lips. Was he beating about the bush unable to say her daughter was gravely ill…and might *die*?

'Oh…no, no, she is in fine fettle!' Thornley burst out, having read Mrs Ratcliff's dreadful suspicions from her expression. He suddenly smiled, feeling rather better about everything. 'You are right, madam, there are much worse things might befall a parent than a scandal about a daughter. We are not at a wake, are we? Come, let us cheer ourselves up.' Thornley struggled to his feet while his visitor watched him with her eyes popping and her jaw sagging.

'I imagine—if you're anything like my dear departed wife—that you might prefer a drink of something stronger than tea.' He gave the bell pull a tug, then another. 'We must toast our children's good health, then worry about the rest later!'

## Chapter Fourteen

Had Fiona but known it, she would have been astonished to learn that her attitude mirrored that of the illustrious Duke of Thornley, a man she'd never met.

Things were not so bad, she impressed on herself in an attempt to combat pangs of melancholy. Gossip could not kill her, but when thrown over Fred Ruff's horse she might have slid off and cracked open her skull during that mad gallop. Worse still, once she was locked in that mildewed cell, bound and gagged, her captors would doubtless have gone off about their nefarious business. Had they met an abrupt end at the hands of the militia, she, too, would have expired, but not mercifully quickly, but in a drawn-out grisly way! It was the terrifying thought that she might slowly starve with nobody about to hear her muffled cries that had spurred her to immediately attempt to escape. She had much to be thankful for! She had her precious liberty, and her health, and good friends like the Jacksons…

And the memory of Luke Wolfson's hands on her body, trailing fire in their wake…

With a sigh Fiona cast him from her mind for the hundredth time that day. She had promised herself not to mope over him. She must accept that he was gone for good and probably hadn't given her, or their escapade, a moment's pause, since being reunited with his mistress.

Leaning her elbows on the wide gate at the side of the Pig and Whistle, she cupped her chin in her palms and gazed over meadow grass that swayed and gleamed beneath soft breezes and the setting sun. How would her mother take knowing about her eldest daughter's plight? Thank goodness Maude was in blissful ignorance of it all, she thought. But ever since Cecil Ratcliff set about defrauding the Chapman family Maude had toughened up, so she might cope better than expected when eventually Fiona recounted her tale. And she must; she'd hate it to come to her mother's notice on the grapevine.

Had her papa still been alive he would be distraught to know how badly things had turned out for his wife and spinster daughter. In his final months he'd mentioned leaving them financially secure, with no need to worry about paying the bills. But Anthony Chapman hadn't reckoned with his wife's silly vanity making her prey to a silver-tongued trickster. Her father's astute business deals, made to provide his widow with a comfortable pension, were now lining another man's pockets. Or they had been, Fiona reminded herself sourly, till her stepfather emptied his pockets at gaming tables and brothels.

It would have been easy for Fiona to rail at Maude, but she would not allow Cecil Ratcliff the added victory of turning mother and daughter against one another. He had often tried to drive a wedge between them, no doubt so he could mistreat both women under his roof without them seeking mutual support. He hadn't succeeded; though the parting between Fiona and Maude had been strained, there had been tears and affection on both sides.

Familiar laughter reached Fiona's ears, breaking into her introspection. Through one of the Pig and Whistle's mullioned windows she could see Peter and Betty Jackson. They were seated comfortably, partaking of an after-dinner tot, happy in each other's company. Her parents had liked to settle down together in such a way. But

Fiona had not seen her mother laugh in a long while now.

Earlier Fiona had eaten supper with Mr and Mrs Jackson, and a very good dinner of mutton hotpot it had been, too. Naturally the couple had been curious to know where she was heading, and why. After all they'd been through together, Fiona believed that they had proved their friendship and trustworthiness. She told them honestly that she'd travelled from London to take up employment in Dartmouth. Betty had said she'd heard of the Herberts and that nothing bad had reached her ears about the family. That had lifted Fiona's spirits a little. If Mr Herbert was good and kind he was sure to be sympathetic to her tale of the coach being delayed by highwaymen. And that was the extent of the story she would relate!

Fiona had wanted to stretch her legs before retiring to her chamber for the night. Tomorrow morning she must say farewell to the Jacksons, who were heading inland to Woodstone while she carried on journeying west.

Being considerate sorts, the Jacksons were trying to put a brave face on things for her. But Fiona feared human nature was much the same whether people were peasant or peer: salacious rumours would always be of great interest when a young lady's reputation was at stake. And heaven only knew there were stories about her now to give a gossip a field day.

The first twinges of self-pity assailed Fiona. Had fate been kinder to her, and that accursed vehicle of Toby Williams not broken down, none of it would have happened. The ruffians had been waiting for night to fall to rob innocent travellers braving the dark lanes. It had been very bad luck that Megan had misconstrued her identity from an overheard conversation at the Fallow Buck, then shared the misconception with her beau. Sam and Fred were not the sharpest tools in the box and had pounced too readily on the idea of her being the duke's daughter, hoping for high praise from their boss and a fat slice of profit from her ransom.

She owed her freedom, her comfort, perhaps even her life to Luke Wolfson. She should have thanked him properly rather than going off in a huff because his mistress had been waiting to welcome him at the King and Tinker. Now it was too late; he was no doubt halfway to London with his friends and had already forgotten her...

Her head dropped forward as she swayed on her feet, yearning to have his sweetly teasing fingers roving her skin once more. Fiona spun about to thump her back against the gate and stare up at the first stars studding a pale night sky. 'I'm glad he's gone…' she groaned in a whisper, desperate to convince herself of it.

'You're glad who's gone…dare I ask?'

Fiona snapped down her face, gazing unblinking at his beautiful gypsy features as though seeing a ghost. 'Jeremiah Collins…' She finally forced the fib through her quivering lips. 'What are you doing here, sir? I thought you'd travelled to London.' She made a small gesture, then turned away from him quickly lest she betrayed how happy and confused she was to see him.

'Who told you I'd gone to London?'

Fiona scoured her mind for an answer. In fact, Mr Robley at the King and Tinker had said Mr Wolfson had left with his friends but not where he'd headed to. She'd placed Luke in the metropolis because she brooded about him, and what he might be doing, far too much.

'I… Nobody told me…I just assumed you'd go there with your friends.' Fiona swiftly changed the subject. 'Mr Robley gave me your packet. I must thank you for your generosity. But it was uncalled for, Mr Wolfson. I am glad to have back my locket, but will replace its value with cash as soon as I'm able. As for the three sovereigns you gave me…' She dug in the pocket where she had stored his precious parcel of gold. 'I must return two to you straight away.'

Luke moved closer to her, enclosing her wrist as she would have thrust the parchment-wrapped money in his direction.

'You were glad I'd gone. Have you changed your mind now I'm back, Fiona?'

She looked away from those penetrative dark eyes. Of course, he'd known all along she was thinking…talking of him, whereas he probably had Becky Peake at the back of his mind. 'I'm certainly happy to have the opportunity to thank you properly for rescuing me,' she answered brittlely.

'My pleasure…' Luke raised her imprisoned fingers, chivalrously touching his lips to them.

Fiona avoided his gaze. She didn't need to look at him to know that his suggestive comment would have strengthened the amusement glimmering at the backs of his eyes. 'Why have you come here, sir?' she demanded, snatching back her hand. 'Is your purpose simply to mock me some more before you carry on with your life as normal? My life will never be normal again! I might be a disgraced woman but I'm certainly not a toy to be trifled with.' Again she thrust the coins at him and this time he took them with a sigh, slipping them into his pocket.

'I've never thought of you as such. Neither have I underestimated what you have endured. You're the bravest woman I know.'

His unexpected praise humbled Fiona; she even felt rather embarrassed by it. She'd heard simple sincerity in his voice and that was very pleasing. But she must not let his opinion matter too much; soon they would part ways for good.

'What *normal life* are you rueing the loss of, Fiona?' Luke asked, plunging his hands in his coat pockets. 'You've left home to get away from your stepfather and intend to take up paid employment in a profession that is likely to make you miserable. Do you still hanker for such an existence as that?'

'You don't know anything about me!' Fiona burst out. 'Who told you I dislike my stepfather?' she continued, ruining her determination not to speak about anything personal.

'You did… Have you forgotten already?' Luke replied. He approached her, moving a hand as though to draw her close, but Fiona whipped aside, greatly alarmed that he might have guessed Cecil Ratcliff had treated her in a very inappropriate manner. Nobody knew about that apart from Maude, and perhaps Rose. Not that Fiona or her mother had mentioned it to their maid, but Rose had a keen eye and a sharp mind.

Nothing much happened in the household that passed the woman by.

'So I have an idea of why you quit London to journey west. Do you know what brought me this way?' Luke asked quietly.

'How could I, sir, when you've made it your business to keep it all a secret,' Fiona retorted.

'I've not intentionally concealed anything from you. When we were outrunning the gang I said I'd no time to explain, but now things are different. So, in answer to your previous question—what am I doing here at the Pig and Whistle?—I've come specifically to see you, my dear. You wanted me to tell you about my involvement with Jeremiah Collins, didn't you? Are you still interested in hearing about it?'

Fiona raised her eyes to his and through the dusk could see his fixed gaze was no longer lit by mockery, but by another, truer emotion.

'Yes…if you will, sir.' Fiona dipped her head. 'An explanation is in order, I think, so must thank you for taking the trouble to come out of your way to give it to me.'

'Have you told anybody you suspect me to be in cahoots with the gang?' Luke turned his head to glance at the Jacksons, still ensconced by the tavern's fireside.

Disquiet needled Fiona as she slowly gave a

shake of her head. Perhaps his purpose in coming was to discover if she'd exposed him as a criminal, rather than to honourably explain himself.

Luke braced his hands against the gate, close to Fiona's side, and stared out over the darkling meadow. Somewhere out in the wilderness that held a tang of brine blown off the sea, a curlew called and was answered by its mate. After a moment in which they faced in opposite directions, enclosed in pastoral peacefulness, Fiona turned about and she, too, propped herself on the timber rail to gaze at the horizon.

'I quit the army last year, but still accept commissions suited to my profession,' Luke began in his rich baritone. 'I took on a contract for the Duke of Thornley. A day or so later I went back to see him to cancel it as the two of us didn't see eye to eye on vital aspects of the plan's structure and execution. My aim was then to return to London and forget all about the deal.'

Fiona digested that, then darted a bemused glance at his profile. Surely he was not about to tell her that the duke had somehow plotted to have his own daughter kidnapped by some villains! For what purpose? To prevent the young woman marrying the man she wanted? And why would Luke Wolfson's help be sought? Fiona found the answer to that last conundrum almost immediately: a duke would not deal directly with the scoundrels. He would need a go-between… somebody who might be able to infiltrate the gang and pretend to be in league with them. But the duke would not want his daughter harmed, just taught a lesson. And His Grace's mercenary would protect the girl while pretending to be her abductor.

Fiona had forgotten to seem aloof and rattled off the sum of her conjecture, moving closer to Luke in her eagerness to have his response to it.

'You've almost worked it out, sweet, so you'll understand my misgivings about strategic flaws.' Luke smiled sardonically. 'It was hardly going to fool a crook like Collins for very long.'

'Does the duke not *like* his daughter to risk her life in such a way?' Fiona gasped.

'He loves Joan very much and would have risked his own life before hers. The tale of Thornley's daughter running off to wed a lover was concocted. The duke's idea was for a woman to impersonate Joan, then when Collins was lured into the open in the hope of netting a huge ransom for the discreet return of the runaway bride, the villain and his accomplices would be captured and finally get their day in court.'

'Well, none of it came to pass!' Fiona snorted

derisively. 'And it would have been exceedingly good luck if it had succeeded.'

'Indeed…' he concurred.

Fiona stole a glance at Luke's rugged profile; he had sounded very scathing, as well he might! He'd cancelled the contract with the duke and had been on the point of returning to the metropolis when he found himself again embroiled in rescuing a damsel in distress, albeit the wrong one, and for no reward!

'So…if a false rumour had not been put about concerning Joan's secret elopement, those dullards Sam and Fred would have stolen my money, but left me be.'

'I'm sorry you suffered, but I'm not sorry that I met you.' Luke pivoted on the elbow he'd planted on the top of the gate, facing her. The hand idle at his side was raised so a leisurely finger could trace the delicate contours from her temple to jaw. 'I'm not sorry, either, that I had the chance to rescue you, or to get to know you better during that short time we shared. It wasn't enough. I still want more of you…' he said huskily.

Slowly he straightened, removing his lounging arm from the timber and very deliberately sliding it around her narrow waist to draw her closer. 'Just a day or so apart, yet I've missed you, and I don't believe you've not felt the same way about me. We've unfinished business, Fiona…that's the main reason I've come to find you.'

He lowered his face and intuitively Fiona angled her head sideways and back, sighing as they fitted together like pieces of a puzzle. He swept his warm lips across her throat to take her mouth in a leisurely, drugging kiss.

From behind a daze of sensation Fiona reminded herself that he'd still answers to give her. But the tantalising touch of his tongue tip against hers was enough to make her gasp and open up to his artful probing. When his hand caressed from her spine to the buttons on her bodice she instinctively put an arch in her back to entice the skilful fingers infiltrating her clothes to fondle her nude skin.

'You've no need to fret over gossip, sweet,' Luke murmured as he stroked the warm plump flesh he'd exposed beneath her chemise. 'And no need to fret over your employment, either. The fellow will understand you quitting your job, given the nature of what you've been through…'

'But he must not know!' Fiona's whispered cry was smothered beneath the sweet assault of his lips. She clasped his abrasive chin to force back his head an inch. 'Nobody must know what happened to me…' she breathed into his preying mouth. 'Or I will be unable to earn a decent living anywhere.'

'You've no need to earn your keep, Fiona,' Luke growled, tantalising a small ear with nips and kisses. 'I'll protect you…care for you…give you everything you'll ever want. Just tell me what it is you desire…'

A burst of intense joy swamped Fiona and she nestled her cheek against his shoulder. With a tiny sob of astonishment she realised that pure love was at the centre of the conflicting emotions this man aroused in her. In just a few days she'd finally fallen deeply, instinctively in love. And he must love her, too, or why would he want to marry her when he didn't have to…

Her lashes parted and the throb of joy faltered, then faded as her reason revived. He hadn't mentioned marriage…or love. And thank goodness that she hadn't, either!

What a fool she was! Fiona inwardly railed at herself. She'd simply read into his declaration what she wanted to hear. Yes, it was a proposal of sorts, but now, recalling it word for word, she saw it was similar to that delivered by her stepfather. He had also promised to give her gowns and trinkets, while attempting to thrust a hand beneath her skirts. And all the while he'd been raiding her inheritance—money put by for her dowry—so he could carry on carousing with his dubious friends.

She'd believed Luke Wolfson had a wedding on his mind because, unconsciously, that's what she wanted…what she'd always wanted. From the first moment their eyes had met through driving rain she'd felt attracted to him in a way that defied logic. Oh, he was wonderfully handsome, but it was more than mere good looks drawing her to him. She'd sensed between them existed an affinity that she'd never experienced with anyone other than her birth family.

When she'd been Jeremiah Collins's terrified prisoner she'd trusted Luke Wolfson would rescue her from the gang. And he had not let her down. But now he would; saving her from a life of servitude, or from her ruined reputation, was a chivalry too far. And why should he marry her? Did she think she now had a hold on this mercenary's affections because they'd shared intimacies a wife would allow a husband? How naive and unsophisticated he would think her, compared to Becky Peake!

If he guessed her awful mistake he might laugh…or feel embarrassed. He could be no more uncomfortable than she was! She must never disclose how close she'd come to throwing her arms up about his neck and blurting that she'd be delighted to be his wife.

Fiona had grown stiff in his arms, but didn't yet push away. Even relinquishing the bittersweet comfort of his warmth and strength was hard to do. She remained quiet, conscious of his silence, and of puzzles still unsolved.

Why would a man who already had a beautiful young mistress want an older, plainer woman in his bed? The solution she found made her burn with humiliation. She'd never save enough money to settle his fee, so he was offering to take payment in kind, allowing her to keep her precious locket, and to save her blushes was wrapping his lust in generosity. Then, when he'd had his money's worth, no doubt he'd turn her out. Perhaps he might even give her a reference to ease her path towards employment as a governess!

Disentangling herself from his embrace, Fiona raised her hands, intending to fumble beneath her collar for the clasp of the locket, but her fingers were arrested in mid-air and held steady at her shoulders.

'What are you doing?' Luke asked quietly.

Fiona shook him off, attempting to step back, but he gripped her elbows, jerking her against him.

'You mistake my character, sir. Thank you for your kind offer, but I still intend to keep a roof over my head by teaching children, rather than sleeping with gentlemen,' she said with a faux sweetness.

'Gentlemen? How many lovers did you anticipate having, Fiona?' he rasped.

'None...' She flung back her head, her tawny gaze clashing on eyes that gleamed between lengthy jet-black lashes.

'None? You intend to remain celibate? Do you not want children?'

'Only within wedlock,' Fiona answered coolly. She would not allow him to upset her fragile equilibrium with his taunts.

The throaty chuckle he gave lacked humour. 'You're after a husband, but not a lover, is that it?'

'I'm not looking for either, but if I were I'd want a gentleman I can respect and trust!' Fiona snapped.

'And desire?' Luke purred. 'I fit the bill on that score, even if you don't respect or trust me.'

Fiona had backed away against the gate, but he pursued with slow deliberate steps, bracing an arm either side of her, trapping her as he lowered his head towards hers...

'Mr Wolfson...is it you? Are you there, sir?

Is Miss Chapman with you? Oh, for a pair of young eyes! It is grown quite dark and I left my spectacles inside...'

# Chapter Fifteen

An expletive, forcefully ejected through Luke's teeth, preceded him straightening up. As he turned about he subtly brushed his mouth across Fiona's lips, still invitingly parted in a soundless wail of horror from recognising Mrs Jackson's cheery tones.

'Ah…it *is* you, sir!' Mrs Jackson was peering myopically into the twilight. 'And there *you* are, Miss Chapman. What a wonderful surprise to see your saviour again!' Betty beamed at the couple as she hurried closer. 'You two young people must have lots to talk about before we all leave this…' She cast a dramatic glance over a shoulder before whispering, '*This dreadful episode* behind us and finish our journeys.' She patted Luke's sleeve. 'But do both come in and join us. My husband will be pleased to see you, sir. You mustn't just go off as you tend to do without

saying a proper goodbye,' she playfully scolded
Luke. 'I've come to see if Miss Chapman would
like some warm milk or chocolate ordered before
bedtime. With so much to do tomorrow I expect
an early night is in order for us all.'

'I… Yes…that sounds nice,' Fiona burst out,
aware of a very ironic look singeing the top of
her head at the mention of bedtime. 'Chocolate…' She quickly gave her choice of bever-
age, relieved that Betty didn't appear to have
noticed anything untoward.

Perhaps the Jacksons were beyond being
shocked by her behaviour, Fiona wryly reflected.
When she'd first met the couple they'd seemed
alarmed that she was travelling without a companion. Heaven only knew what they'd think of
her now if they discovered what she'd been up
to moments ago with the gentleman at her side!

'You mustn't take a chill, Miss Chapman.'
Luke's mild tone was at odds with him briskly
pulling her cloak edges together.

'How considerate,' Mrs Jackson praised,
blinking adoringly at her hero.

It took Fiona a moment to recover from his
abrupt ministration and to realise the reason for
it: she glimpsed an edge of her lacy chemise
and, horrified, realised that her unhooked buttons had been exposed to view. Blood surged

into her complexion and she silently gave thanks for the dusk and for Betty's forgetfulness. Had the woman been wearing her spectacles…

Discreetly tugging at her clothes, Fiona accepted the arm that Luke extended to her. She knew she owed him at least a glance of gratitude for preserving her modesty, but she could not do it. Betty clutched Luke's other elbow and began chattering about the richness of the lamb hotpot they'd enjoyed for supper.

'Ah…capital to see you, sir!' Mr Jackson had made quite a sprightly leap to his feet on seeing Luke accompanying Betty and Miss Chapman into the tavern. Solicitously he began rearranging chairs so that everybody might sit close by the fire. 'I must shake you by the hand, Mr Wolfson, and do allow me to procure you some brandy. It is the least I can do after such a noble effort on Miss Chapman's behalf.' Peter Jackson glanced furtively about before hissing, 'Awful business!' He shook his head, continuing to pump Luke's fingers.

As Fiona sank back into her chair she wished the couple would quit referring, even obliquely, to her dratted abduction. She wished, too, that the hero of the hour would go away and leave her be! Yet seconds after the landlord had brought a bottle and glasses she learned that Luke was, indeed, staying for just a short while and her heart vaulted to her mouth in consternation.

'But surely, sir, it is best not to travel so late?' Peter had previously asked whether Luke intended taking a room at the tavern and had received a reply in the negative.

'I'm used to riding at night,' Luke said, taking a sip of the brandy Mr Jackson had insisted on pouring for him.

'You must make sure your guns are loaded and ready for use,' Mrs Jackson instructed in a motherly way.

'I always do, ma'am.'

A silence developed during which the married couple exchanged several significant glances. Suddenly Mr Jackson burst out, 'I have to say, Miss Chapman, that I'm sorry I was stubborn that night.' His veined cheeks flamed. 'It was my fault we got caught by those rogues. Had I listened to Toby Williams and turned back towards the Fallow Buck all might have ended differently—'

'And I must also say sorry.' Betty interrupted her husband's apology to insert her own. 'I wanted to journey onwards when we should have heeded the driver's advice.'

'There's no need for any mention of it.' Fiona sounded forgiving although the thought had

crossed her mind that they'd been foolish and
selfish to overrule Toby Williams. 'You've been
good friends to me and I'm pleased to see that
you are recovering well from that crack on the
head, sir.'

'It would take more than that tap to do me
down,' Mr Jackson boasted, conveniently for-
getting how he'd suffered and complained at the
time. 'Besides, it was my own fault.' His expression again turned sheepish.

'All is now forgotten.' Fiona glanced about at
her cosy surroundings to indicate she hoped the
matter closed.

'So graciously done…' Mrs Jackson leaned
towards Fiona, clasping her hand in gratitude.
'Are you sure you do not want to set the authorities on those rogues? They should not get away
with treating you so abominably.'

'No! I'm very well, as you can see…as I have
already said…' Fiona rattled off. Carefully she
disentangled her fingers, then rose to her feet.
'I think I shall ask the landlord for that chocolate. I'll order a cup for you, Mrs Jackson.' She
knew that the moment she was out of earshot
the Jacksons would again discuss her. But Fiona
needed to escape Betty's probing questions and
Luke's dark, preying gaze. Close to him she felt
stifled by the heat of his desire and the ambiva-

lent thoughts storming her mind were making her light-headed.

'I wish she would turn around and go home to her family,' Mrs Jackson whispered before Fiona had moved more than a yard.

A small, unseen grimace was Fiona's only reaction to the overheard remark as she carried on, with an admirably steady step, in search of the landlord.

'Hush…' Peter said. 'Now, we don't gossip, do we, my dear. Miss Chapman wants no more talk of it.'

'Hmmph… I'm sure that Miss Chapman considers Mr Wolfson as trustworthy as we, after all he has saved her virtue and her life.'

Peter shrugged in defeat.

'She is going to Dartmouth to be a governess, you see,' Betty hissed, gazing earnestly at Luke.

'Miss Chapman has told me all about it,' Luke said, finishing his brandy.

'Ah…she has, has she?' Peter mumbled, ignoring his wife's smug nod.

'Mr Herbert is known as good stock. We aren't personally acquainted with him, but we know people who are,' Betty carried on as though deaf to Mr Wolfson's heavy hint to change the subject.

'Yes…yes…' Peter cut across his wife. 'We

cannot vouch for people, though, can we, if we don't know them well?'

'That's why I'd sooner see the poor lamb go back home to her mother.' Betty pulled her shawl this way and that. 'She seems such a sweet, genteel young woman—things cannot be so bad that she must leave all she knows and loves in London to school a stranger's children.'

'Miss Chapman is independent and quick-witted—assuredly she knows what she is doing.' Luke knew that Fiona wouldn't appreciate being talked about behind her back…especially by him. He got to his feet, executing a farewell bow. 'Thank you for the brandy, sir.'

Peter lunged to his feet to again shake Luke by the hand and mutter good wishes and hopes for a renewal of their acquaintance. Betty extended her fingers, too, acting coy when Luke briefly raised them to his lips. Then with a smile and farewell that couldn't be mistaken for anything but final, he said, 'My best wishes go with you for a safe journey home. I'm off to the stables to see if my horse is sufficiently rested to set upon the road.'

Having found the landlord and asked for two cups of chocolate, Fiona dithered outside the kitchen door into which the fellow had disappeared. She was reluctant to return to the saloon and face more questions or well-meant advice. Part of her wanted to spend every available second that remained with Luke; she knew he was simply being polite in tarrying a while with the Jacksons. That other, logical, corner of her mind was urging her to avoid him completely because the pain of parting would worsen the more she saw him. She knew she must forget about him and his tacit offer of protection at a price.

But she couldn't; at present overriding all sense and reason was an unbearable thrill trembling her from head to toes, the like of which she'd never before experienced.

She was twenty-five years old yet had never before aroused such ardency in a gentleman. Now she had, and the man who wanted to make love to her was the man to whom she'd given her heart. Would it be so bad to lie naked with Luke Wolfson and bask in his passion if she couldn't have his love? The maelstrom of emotion battering her person caused her to sway on her feet and she sought support from the wall, her warm palms flat against cooling plaster.

She couldn't deny that his taunts had hit home: she *did* desire him…and she trusted Luke would treat her well as his paramour. If she could conquer her indignation and dreadful disappointment that another woman was sure, one day, to be his wife…what matter if she accepted the crumbs offered to her for as long as he tossed them her way?

'You seem to be lost in thought again,' Luke said huskily.

Startled, Fiona swung about, wishing she'd heard him approach. 'I've a lot to think about,' she blurted, managing a wavering smile.

'Me included?'

An immediate denial was teetering on the tip of her tongue. But the mockery in his eyes was directed more at himself, making him appear oddly vulnerable.

'Yes…' she murmured. 'You were on my mind, sir…amongst other things.'

'Were you thinking you might come to trust and respect me, Fiona, if I strive to improve my behaviour?'

'And how might you do that?' she asked, suppressing a smile. As well as being the most handsome man alive he had a self-deprecating humour she found appealing. Luke Wolfson, she realised, had qualities that any woman would find attractive in a husband. And no doubt he possessed other, sensual skills, temptingly tasted by her, but to which his mistress could fully testify.

Luke leaned his broad shoulders against the wall opposite and crossed his arms so they diagonally faced one another in the narrow corridor. 'I might quit seeking dangerous escapades as though a boy tasting excitement for the first time.'

'Is that why you're a mercenary? For the thrill of it?'

'Most probably...'

Fiona had to admit that did make him sound immature. Most soldiers would surely only risk their lives for their king or their pay. 'You really don't need the money from such work?'

His sensual mouth twisted aslant in a way that looked oddly bitter to Fiona. Most people would be happy to announce they were well off.

'My grandfather left me a bequest,' Luke stated distantly.

'My grandmother left me a bequest,' Fiona answered simply. She told him things she never mentioned to others. It was as though he held the key to her tongue as well as her heart.

'And what happened to it?' Luke asked gently.

Fiona's eyes slid sideways to merge with his dark stare. She could tell he knew...as he knew everything about her without her needing to utter a word. But he must never know she'd fallen in love with him; that was a secret she must bury deep.

'My stepfather spent it,' she informed him briskly. 'Which was typical of his selfishness. So now I am not a minor heiress, but a governess.'

'And what else has he taken?'

Fiona stiffened against the wall, her nails digging into flaking distemper. So...he had guessed that, too, had he? She lifted her eyes to his face but could read nothing there. His gaze was relentless, as always, demanding she bare her soul as well as her body to him. 'He...' Fiona moistened her lips. 'He took liberties and believed he had a right to my bed as well as my mother's, promising me nice things in return for my compliance.'

'He forced himself on you?'

'Not...to the full extent. He tried to kiss and touch me and he became unpleasant enough to make me want to leave.' Fiona lifted her chin, challenging him with a stare. If he felt disgusted to know she'd been mauled by a man charged with caring for her, he gave no sign. But there was a livid white line circling his mouth, stark against the depth of his tan.

'Did you tell your mother about it?'

Fiona nodded. 'She didn't believe me at first. Now she detests him as greatly as do I.' Fiona clasped her hands before her. 'I worry about her being left there alone with him.'

'And is she worried about you, do you think?'

'I believe she is…yes.'

'Will you go home, then?'

Fiona frowned at him. 'What is there for me to go back to? Nothing will have changed, and if it has, it will be for the worst. My stepfather has almost stripped the house of everything of value to fund his carousing.'

'You believe him a fortune hunter,' Luke stated.

'I believe he is a corrupt individual and I wouldn't be surprised to learn that what he told my mother about his background is a pack of lies.'

Luke's thick eyebrows were drawn up in enquiry.

'He said he hailed from Surrey and had been decorated during his army career, even serving under Wellington. He was a very smooth talker, at first…until he had my mother pinned beneath his thumb.'

Luke frowned. 'His name?'

'Cecil Ratcliff.'

'I also came under the Iron Duke's command, yet I don't believe I'm acquainted with Ratcliff.'

'Then you may think yourself fortunate!' Fiona said pithily.

Their eyes merged through the murky flickering shadows thrown by the corridor's wall candles. For a moment Fiona felt tempted to cross the tiny space that separated them and launch herself into his arms. She knew he would comfort her and how she longed for such. But then he spoke quickly and harshly, breaking the spell.

'There's a better life waiting for you than teaching other people's brats for a living.'

'There's a better life waiting for you than pursuing criminals for pay you don't need,' Fiona shot back. 'You, sir, are in the privileged position of being able to play at having a career and may stop at any time you choose. I am not so lucky.'

'I take what I do seriously,' Luke said quietly. 'And if you think that money brings with it happiness and contentment, I can assure you it does not.'

Fiona sensed he was about to add something, but he turned from her, shielding his expression while pacing along the corridor. Puzzled by the change in him she thought he might leave without another word, but he retraced his steps. Cocking his head to one side, he stared pitilessly at her until, flustered, she blurted out, 'I have applied for a teaching position and I intend to take it up. I would be a poor wretch indeed if I backed away from a new challenge before giving it a try.'

'You deserve better,' Luke returned.

'It is what I want to do.' It was far from the truth, but she'd bristled at his domineering tone. 'It is what I *shall* do,' she added determinedly, hoping to convince herself as well as him.

Luke extended dark fingers towards her, trailing a fingertip down the side of her forearm. 'I want you…you know that,' he said throatily. 'Why do you persist in making things hard for yourself?'

Fiona threw up her face to the ceiling and gave a sob of laughter. So he thought it would be hard for her to bow and scrape for her pittance of a salary, did he? No…being relegated to the outer circle of his existence while he lived his charmed life with his wife and their children… now *that* would be hard for her.

Then she thought of Becky Peake and wondered if the brunette might get Luke down the aisle. Their attachment obviously ran deep and Luke must trust his mistress, too, or he wouldn't have brought her with him on such a dangerous mission.

That led Fiona to reflect on another puzzle to which she'd not yet had an answer. Who had

off as Fiona flushed to the roots of her silky fawn hair. She had dearly hoped to keep from him that she viewed Becky Peake as a rival.

'Oh…I thought you'd be sitting with your friends, Miss Chapman.' The landlord had barged backwards out of the kitchen door and swung about to face her. He was holding a tray laden with two cups of chocolate. Seeing Fiona's companion, he gave a low bow, dropping the tray obsequiously close to his knees.

'Major Wolfson…what would you like, sir?'

Luke glanced at Fiona, a wicked glint just visible beneath lazy lids.

'Nothing from the kitchens, thank you… I'm just off to the stables.'

'Ah, settling your shot, then, and on your way, are you, Major?' the landlord said, disappointed to know such a flush fellow was leaving so soon. Every local innkeeper knew how free Major Wolfson was with his tips. Having batted a look between the couple he mumbled about taking the drinks through to the saloon.

'Are you returning to London now?' The question burst out of Fiona.

'Eventually… I've a score to settle first.'

'With the Duke of Thornley?' Fiona asked with a frown.

'No… I've said all I needed to, to His Grace.'

'You're not going after Jeremiah Collins?' Fiona gasped in shock. 'Why?' Their differences now seemed unimportant; she was anxious that Luke might again risk his life rather than give up being a hireling. 'I wish you would not go after him, sir. You are badly outnumbered by his gang and might be ambushed and captured.' Seeing that her comment had not made him stop and reflect, she blurted, 'Besides, if you provoke Collins he might spread dirt about me from malice.'

'I've said I'll take care of you in every way necessary,' Luke returned quietly.

'There are some things that cannot be put right with a pair of duck-foot pistols...or a gift of sovereigns.' Fiona sounded exasperated. 'I'll not allow my future to become a game of chance, dependent upon men's whims and favours.'

'I'll not abandon you, Fiona.' Luke took a step towards her, a crooked smile softening his hitherto stern expression.

'And what of Becky Peake? Did you abandon her? Will you renew your acquaintance with her when back in town and spread your time and generosity between us?' Before he could answer she carried on, her tone now level and composed. 'Thanks to you I'm on my way to take up my position in Dartmouth tomorrow.' She evaded him by pacing slowly to and fro until he again propped himself against the wall, hands plunged into his pockets. She knew he was watching her from beneath heavy lids and kept beyond his reach. 'You have helped me in putting my life back on track, and in return I'd like you to also have a future in front of you. If you pursue that fiend Collins…' Her voice tailed away and she kept her back to him to protect the glitter of tears in her eyes at the dreadful idea of him being killed or maimed.

'I came to Devon to rid the area of the gang and I'll leave when the job's done.'

Fiona pivoted on a heel. 'But…you've cancelled the contract with the Duke of Thornley!' she argued, coming closer to him in her agitation. 'Why make it your business?'

'Because it is my business and I don't need a contract. Now it's personal between him and me. And Collins knows it.'

'Miss Chapman…come along, my dear, your chocolate will get cold.' Betty Jackson had hove into view and seen the couple, face to face, in the corridor. 'Do have another brandy with us before leaving, Mr Wolfson,' she cajoled. 'It will save my husband sinking the lot and falling asleep.'

'Thank you, ma'am, but I'm setting off now.'

Luke turned a relentless gaze on Fiona. 'Come with me!' His demand was honeyed with persuasiveness.

Fiona drew a ragged breath, hovering for a second on the cusp between agreement and refusal before giving an almost imperceptible shake of the head.

Luke continued to drill his eyes into a crown of fawn hair as though waiting for her to change her mind. 'Miss Chapman…' he finally murmured, before stepping away from her and giving a nod that encompassed both ladies. 'I wish you all safe onward journeys.'

'And we return you the same sentiment, Mr Wolfson. Oh, indeed we do!' Betty exclaimed.

'Don't worry, my dear, I'm sure you'll see him again.' Betty gave Fiona's quivering arm a squeeze as the door closed on Luke's departing figure.

Fiona mumbled something indistinct in response to the woman's comfort. She was just overwrought with all that had gone on! she told herself impatiently as a tear trickled from the corner of an eye.

'I know he likes you.' Betty winked and tapped the side of her nose. 'Just between us… I remember my courting days.'

Fiona bit her lip, realising that the woman was hinting she'd seen more than she'd let on when they'd all been outside earlier.

# Chapter Sixteen

Cecil Ratcliff shoved away his half-empty coffee cup. With a look of utter distaste he picked up the piece of soggy toast on his plate, then in a fit of temper flung it to the floor. At breakfast time he desired eating broiled kidneys and poached eggs, juicy ham and freshly baked bread, not a slice of thinly buttered toast without so much as a dollop of jam to tempt the palate.

The woman he'd employed as a servant, since his wife absconded taking her maid with her, barely raised her head at the sound of his snarling. Dolly carried on sweeping out the fire, although there was no fuel in the outside bunker to bring in and burn in the grate. The scuttles were empty, too, and only a few small logs remained piled by the fireside. In an attempt to hide the gaping hole beneath the mantelpiece the maid continued scrunching up old copies of *The Times* and lobbing the paper balls over the fender.

'Get me something palatable for breakfast,' Cecil snapped, irritated that his servant had ignored his tantrum.

Dolly pushed herself to her feet. 'Nothing in the larders, Mr Ratcliff. I had to cut the mould off that bread before I could toast it.'

That blunt remark brought a furious glow to Cecil's unshaven cheeks. 'Go to the grocer's, then, you insolent chit. Tell them to send the boy round with every supply we lack.'

Dolly had only been with him for three days. Already she'd had enough. He was a mean swine who expected all the luxuries of home provided by a single servant for a pittance of pay.

'Did you hear what I said?' Cecil roared as the maid continued swiping together her sooty palms. 'You insubordinate hussy, get to the shop and put in my order,' he bellowed.

'You want goods from a grocer, you find yourself one who'll take your order,' Dolly returned shortly. 'Every shopkeeper around says the same—they'll not be coming back here till you've paid what you owe.' Dolly pulled off her apron and flung it on the floor. 'You can have back your job. I'm not surprised the other one went. You're a slave driver, that's what you are.'

Dolly was glad she'd not unpacked her things. She'd had an inkling she might not be staying long. Having stormed up to the attic room that had been her chamber for the two nights since she'd arrived, she jammed her few belongings into her carpetbag's open mouth and was lugging it downstairs in a trice.

Cecil was waiting for her by the banisters, a faint smile turning down the corners of his mouth. 'Don't you want to have your pay, Dolly?'

Dolly hesitated. Even if it were only pennies, it would come in handy. 'If you want to give it to me, sir, I'd be much obliged to have it.'

Cecil nodded slowly. 'I think you deserve something…'

As she reached the bottom tread he held out his closed fist, but instead of opening his fingers to reveal a few coins he backhanded Dolly, knocking her to the ground.

The maid was allowed to crouch, whimpering, at his feet for no more than a few seconds. Ratcliff hoisted Dolly up by her collar and dragged her to the door. Flinging it open, he tossed her on to the top step, then with a boot against her backside sent her crashing to the pavement.

On hearing Dolly's howl Cecil slammed the door, then set off towards the drawing room with a satisfied smirk. Within moments he'd forgotten about the servant and was putting his mind to more important matters. There was not much left in the house to sell, but the small portrait on the wall would fetch something at the pawnbroker's and Solomon had expressed an interest in seeing it.

Cecil gawped, open-mouthed, at the space where the picture had hung. He was sure that Dolly hadn't taken it. For the short while she'd been in his employment the lazy slut had rarely moved from her warm spot in the kitchen. He glanced about at dusty surfaces on a few unattractive items of furniture that remained. Cecil tried to bring to mind when last he'd clapped eyes on the canvas, but since Maude had bolted, he'd been out more than usual and came home every night deep in his cups. He always went straight to bed and hadn't set foot in the drawing room in days.

Maude… His thoughts pounced on his wife and his eyes narrowed. The woman he'd married hadn't been the biddable mouse he'd taken her for. She'd certainly surprised him by running off. Perhaps she'd not fled empty-handed, but had stolen a valuable painting to speed her path away from him.

Spitting an oath, Cecil pulled out drawers in

the sideboard and emptied the few remaining bits of silver cutlery on to the top.

'Ah…Mr Ratcliff…back so soon,' the pawnbroker purred, beetling from the back of his shop to welcome his prolific client. 'Now, what have we this time?' The elderly fellow slid his spectacles up the bridge of his nose and passed a jaundiced eye over the mismatched collection of knives, forks and spoons that Cecil had emptied on to the counter.

'I thought you said you might bring a painting in for me next time, sir,' Solomon mentioned.

'Yes, I might…if I can find it,' Cecil snapped. He didn't like the fellow's familiar tone. But Solomon paid good prices so Cecil bit his tongue. 'It's probably of little value in any case: very small and dull, and the frame is damaged.'

'Ah…I know it, sir,' Solomon said, lowering his eyes. 'Your wife's late husband bought that one from me some years ago.' Indeed Solomon did know it and would have been very pleased to see it again. After he'd sold it to Anthony Chapman for a few pounds he'd realised it had been a Dutch master and worth a lot more than he'd got for it.

Cecil had picked up on the pawnbroker's sly interest and he ruminated on the reason for it while fingering the silverware on the counter. 'Mr Chapman knew about art, did he?'

'No…no…' the pawnbroker lied. 'As you say, the painting is small and dull…unattractive.' He shrugged. 'But business is business and I take a look at everything. Bring it in when you find it.'

'I will,' Cecil said through his gritted teeth, pocketing the cash Solomon handed over for the cutlery.

For some minutes Cecil stood outside the shop with his head sunk towards his chest while he cogitated. Although it was easy for a person who didn't want to be found to lay low in the heaving metropolis, he had a hunch that his wife was no longer close by. He imagined mother would have followed daughter; he'd not been able to break the bond between them despite his best efforts to divide and conquer. Previously Cecil had had little interest in Fiona's whereabouts… but he did now.

Maude had only recently run off so Cecil was confident that somebody in the coaching company would know in which direction she'd travelled. With a brisk step he set off to find the proprietor. On rising that morning Cecil had not been bothered about bringing Maude home, but suddenly he was determined to catch up with his errant spouse.

\* \* \*

'There is a gentleman below asking to see you, Miss Chapman.'

Fiona's heart vaulted to her mouth. She'd been sorting through the few things in her travelling trunk, but now dropped the lid on it and gazed, wide-eyed, at the landlord's wife. 'Is it Mr Wolfson?' she eventually forced out as her heart continued to batter at her breastbone.

Mrs Brewer shook her head. 'He looks to be a well-to-do fellow and needs to speak to you urgently and privately, so he said. He wouldn't give his name.'

Her disappointment at knowing Luke had not come back was subdued by a prickle of uneasiness. Fiona quashed her fears with logic; it was highly unlikely her stepfather would have discovered where she was, let alone put himself to the bother of pursuing her.

'I'll be down directly. Perhaps you would have one of the lads bring down my trunk. Is the Dartmouth coach soon due in?'

'Should arrive before noon—the weather is as fine as can be, so I'm sure we'll be hearing a blast of the horn soon.' The landlady followed up the information with a reassuring beam.

Fiona followed the woman down some narrow creaking stairs to the saloon bar where a stout gentleman was standing with his back to her, his hat caught beneath an arm. He twisted about on hearing Fiona pass over the threshold.

'You are Miss Chapman?' he clipped out, giving her a sharp top-to-toe summary.

'I am, sir, and perhaps you would acquaint me with your name?' Fiona had bristled and taken an instant dislike to the fleshy-faced fellow staring at her through a pair of round spectacles balanced on his bulbous nose.

'I, Miss Chapman, am your employer. Or I was.' Mr Herbert strode to the door and closed it. 'For your own good,' he explained his move to closet them privately. 'I doubt your reputation could be more damaged, but in the spirit of attempting to do what I can to help, I'll keep what I have to say very quiet and concise.'

Fiona felt her stomach lurch; the horrible man need not add anything at all for her to know that gossip had started about her and the highwaymen. But she put up her chin and politely waited for Mr Herbert to do his worst.

'I expect you now realise that I am Mr Stanley Herbert. Word has reached my ears that a misfortune overcame you and your fellow travellers en route to Dartmouth.'

'It did, sir,' Fiona confirmed levelly, realising

he had pursed his lips in readiness to have her admit to her disgrace.

'And is it true that you, Miss Chapman, suffered abduction at the hands of these miscreants?'

'I… Yes, that's correct…but I am in good health, as you can see, sir.' Fiona suddenly felt heartsick. She had no wish to be constantly reminded of the vile incident, but her greatest fear was that her livelihood was about to be whipped away.

'Physically well, you may be, Miss Chapman, but I think you know that your life, and your prospects, have been irreparably damaged.' Mr Herbert's voice was low and slow, as one might enunciate an opinion on an immeasurable tragedy. He blinked rapidly behind his glasses. 'I was annoyed to find you did not arrive at the appointed time. Now I know the circumstances behind the delay, I can sympathise with your dreadful plight, but of course my duty to my daughters' moral welfare is paramount.' He shook his head, approaching her. 'Here…take this…' Mr Herbert handed over five shillings. 'It is an amount of compensation and I hope it will help you. I also hope you find work in another area where people remain in ignorance of your stigma.'

Fiona marched to the table and tipped from her palm on to its surface the coins he'd given her. 'I have no need of your sympathy or your charity, sir.' Her pride had revived and her tiger-ish eyes clashed on his affronted stare. 'I can see now that we would not have suited one another in any case, so am glad to have met you sooner rather than later.'

Mr Herbert's chest expanded and he grew florid. 'Indeed, Miss Chapman, we would not have suited!' he wheezed out. 'My daughters have had a lucky escape. I will bid you fare-well.' With small fast steps he strutted to the exit, then returned to retrieve his five shillings. With his puffed-out chest straining his waistcoat buttons, he again approached the door and shut it noisily behind him.

It was the sound of the fanfare from the approaching mail coach that startled Fiona from her daze. She had been standing stock still, her head thumping from the effort of trying to decide what to do next. After she settled her bill at the Pig and Whistle she would have some change from the sovereign Luke had given her, but there was nowhere near enough in her purse to get her back to London. Even should she decide to return to the metropolis she would never again set foot in her stepfather's house.

Her friends, the Jacksons, could not help her, either. They had all parted company earlier that morning, with hugs and tears in abundance. The couple had given her their direction and insisted on having Fiona's promise to write to them as soon as she had settled in at the Herberts. Then they had climbed aboard the trap that was taking them home. Even Mr Jackson had looked suspiciously dewy-eyed as he took the reins and called out to Fiona every good wish for her future health and happiness.

So she was quite alone and regretted having pressed Luke to take back his coins. How she needed them now! But she did not rue for one minute having refused to take Mr Herbert's conscience money. She was glad she had found out what a horrible man he was.

But beggars couldn't be choosers, she impressed on herself when her indignation had been tempered by realism. Unpleasant as her work and her life might have been at Dartmouth she would have had shelter till she could find the means to move elsewhere.

Fiona's troubled thoughts were dragged to the present by the clamour in the bar next door. New arrivals had disembarked from the coach and trooped into the inn for refreshment before journeying on.

Fiona propped her warm forehead against the cool glass of the mullioned windowpane and watched the hubbub outside. The team of horses was being unharnessed from the dusty contraption and the busy ostlers brought to Fiona's mind memories of Toby and Bert Williams.

'There's a lady turned up on the coach asking for Mr Wolfson.'

Fiona spun about to see the landlady closing the door behind her. Mrs Brewer looked slightly awkward. 'I know the major has gone on his way, but my husband said that the two of you were friendly…so do you know where he has headed? The lady seems anxious to catch up with him.'

'Did she give her name?' Fiona asked, although sure she already knew the answer to that. So Becky Peake had not given up her chase! Fiona was assailed with a mixture of anger and admiration that her rival would continue to humble herself for Luke Wolfson's sake.

Suddenly the door was flung open and Maude hurtled in. 'I thought I recognised your voice. Oh, Fiona, my dear child! How glad I am to have found you!'

The landlady diplomatically withdrew on realising that a family reunion was about to take place. Of course she'd heard the rumours about what had happened to Miss Chapman, so could imagine that the poor mother—if that was who the woman was—had much to say to the ruined daughter.

Shocked to the core at the sight of her mother surging towards her with Rose trotting at her side, Fiona gripped the nearest chair for support. 'Mama! What…what on earth—?' The rest of Fiona's stuttered question was cut off as Maude enclosed her daughter in a breathtaking hug.

'Oh, my dear, I'm so, so sorry that you have suffered abominably…'

Fiona gently disentangled herself as her sense returned. She held her mother's hands and gazed into Maude's wet eyes, feeling very close to blubbing herself. 'How did you know where to find me?'

'The duke said that Mr Wolfson would be at either the King and Tinker or the Pig and Whistle, and would know your whereabouts.' Maude gulped. 'He wasn't at the first inn so I came here in the hope of questioning him. But now I don't need to, for I have found you!'

'You've spoken to the Duke of Thornley about me?' Fiona pounced on one of many astonishing facts circling crazily in her mind.

'Yes…yes…or I wouldn't have known to come here,' Maude garbled.

'And His Grace told you that Luke Wolfson knew me?'

'Well, he did, but he wasn't the first to mention that fellow and you in the same breath. A young hussy at the Fallow Buck said that you were with the major and she pointed me in His Grace's direction to find out more. So off we set to Thornley Heights and I met the duke and what a tale I heard!' Maude wailed.

'Young hussy?' Again overwhelmed by her mother's report, Fiona found one thing to immediately ask about. Overriding all else was the thought of Becky Peake being still in the vicinity to hound Luke.

'Her name was Megan,' Rose interjected helpfully, having hitherto listened to and watched the fraught exchange from a distance.

Fiona drew her mother, tottering, towards a chair and made her sit down. Then she sank down beside her on the rug. For a moment she remained quiet and still, assembling her thoughts. Then she raised her head and gave her mother a wobbly smile. 'It is good to see you, Mama, and I wish that we had better news for one another. But we must not despair. We will get by… we always do.' She enclosed her mother's shoulders in a hug as Maude stifled a sob. 'First you must tell everything that has happened to you and then I'll tell you my news…good and bad.'

'Oh…I know, you are ruined,' Maude wailed beneath her breath. 'The duke told me so and very sorry he is, too, because it is all his silly fault that you got dragged into this. But what good is sorry?' Maude wrung her hands. 'He seems a decent man and has said he will make amends…but how is that to be achieved?' Maude flung up her hands in exasperation. 'When I demanded he tell me, he had no answer to give. What will he do? Will he buy you a husband?' She snorted her dubious opinion on the likelihood of that.

'I don't want a husband bought for me, Mama,' Fiona returned forcefully. She threw back her head, moist eyes blinking at the ceiling. Oh, she knew that in the circumstances paying a nice chap to marry her and salvage her reputation would be a sensible, if humiliating, option. Indeed, Fiona had heard of instances when a genteel woman had been discreetly married to a fortune hunter following an unfortunate slip on the lady's part. But Fiona knew she had not made a slip and she knew there was only one man she wanted.

Luke Wolfson had desired taking her with

him, as his mistress, and suddenly she was regretting turning her back on that offer more than she was sorry for having given him back his shiny gold coins.

'Tell me what else the duke said, Mama.' Fiona sat back on her heels and waited for her mother to resume her account. Her hopes of keeping bad news from reaching her mother's ears—or at least breaking it to Maude herself— had been dashed. Fiona realised that Mr Herbert would not be alone in having heard the gossip. The countryside was probably buzzing with tales of the lady and the highwaymen, each version more lurid than the previous one, thrilling everybody with its awfulness.

Some twenty minutes later mother and daughter had finished talking and were gazing quietly at one another.

'So...this Wolfson is just your saviour rather than your beau?' Maude said, a touch disappointedly. 'When I spoke to His Grace, he was cautious in what he said about you and the major. Perhaps he thought I might have a fit of the vapours knowing you had an admirer.' Maude glanced at Rose who had taken a chair by the window and appeared to be absorbed in some crochet work, pulled from her reticule. 'I wondered if you might have succumbed to Wolfson's charms, you know, Fiona.' Maude managed a weak chuckle. 'I saw him leaving the duke's house, you see, but had no opportunity to talk to him. He is very handsome.' Maude angled her face to watch for Fiona's reaction.

'Yes, he is…' Fiona agreed in a murmur, a tiny smile tilting her full lips.

'You like him, but fear that he is put off by those rogues having manhandled you.' Maude slapped her lap in exasperation. 'And how I wish I might have given that Mr Herbert a piece of my mind. How dare he speak to you so! But none of this would have come about but for my stupidity…' Maude ended on a sorrowful sigh. 'If only I had not married Cecil.' She clutched her daughter's hands, bringing them to her bosom. 'If I could turn back the clock I would. Please forgive me for being a silly vain woman.'

Fiona nodded vigorously, unable to speak. She hated seeing her mother upset, but her burgeoning sorrow at having let Luke go off and leave her was closing her throat with anguish. Piously she'd told him she'd sooner be a governess than a mistress, but even before Mr Herbert had dismissed her, she'd known she'd told a lie and would fly to him in an instant if she could.

The night through she'd tossed and turned upstairs in her comfortable bed. At one point she'd got up and padded to the window to stare at the heavy moon, knowing he was somewhere close, beneath the same silver orb. And with a fervour she'd not employed since her dear papa was on his deathbed she'd prayed for the well-being of a man she loved. Then she had felt annoyed with him for troubling her so. He had rejected what most people wanted despite having the where-withal to provide himself with a permanent home in polite society. It was a great puzzle to Fiona why Luke chose not to enjoy the safety and comfort his wealth and status could provide.

'What will you do?'

Maude broke into Fiona's introspection with a quavering demand for information. She'd been watching her daughter's delicately sharp features being shaped by fierce concentration.

'The first thing I will do is get us some re-freshment.' Fiona stood up, determined to buck up on seeing such concern in her mother's eyes. 'It will all seem a little better after a nice cup of tea and some of Mrs Brewer's ginger cake.' At the door Fiona hesitated and turned to look back at her mother. 'Have you left Mr Ratcliff for good?' She refused to give her stepfather any-thing other than a formal title.

'I shall never go back to him! I'd sooner enter

the workhouse!' Maude declared dramatically. 'And I'd not be surprised to see him there, too… or the Fleet! He has sold everything we once had.'

'Apart from your late husband's small painting, ma'am,' Rose reminded without looking up from her needlework.

'Oh…we have something to sell!' Maude gleefully clapped her hands. 'I had quite forgotten about that picture packed in the trunk.'

Fiona was pleased to see her mother's smile and went off to find Mrs Brewer and order their tea. But she knew there were still many problems ahead of them all. If the Duke of Thornley were prepared to make amends to them in some way then she'd as soon he compensated her mother so Maude might have a modest home and shelter.

She needed nothing for herself; she knew with a kind of serene acceptance that fate had already decreed her future. Luke Wolfson was a dangerously enigmatic man but wherever he was… that was where she would go…in the hope he still wanted her.

## *Chapter Seventeen*

Megan moved closer by sidling from table to table, furiously polishing the wooden tops, hoping to eavesdrop on the conversation between the two men. The landlord of the Fallow Buck was a gregarious fellow, willing to pass the time of day with any patron and he seemed to have a lot to say to the haughty-faced individual.

It was a name overheard that had drawn Megan closer…and there it was again… *Mrs Ratcliff.* Megan knew *that* woman…and her daughter, Fiona Chapman, and she reckoned that this traveller must be a relative, come looking for the two of them.

She resumed swiping her cloth over ale-spotted oak as she noticed the gentleman was watching her from beneath his brows. Perhaps he thought she had crept closer because she fancied him.

The landlord wandered off and Megan was about to follow him to probe for information about the stranger when he spoke to her.

'And what might your name be, my dear?'

Innocently, Megan glanced up at him. 'I'm Megan. Would you like me to get you some refreshment, sir?' she asked politely.

Cecil Ratcliff slumped down into a chair at the table Megan had been cleaning. 'Indeed you may…a bottle of port and a plate of beef with bread and cheese and pickles,' he listed out. 'And if a decent cigar is to be had in this place, bring that, too.'

Megan dipped her head. One of those, was he? Plenty of wants but most likely a tight-fist… like his wife, if indeed he was Mrs Ratcliff's husband. Megan went off to the kitchens and while preparing the food alongside the landlord, got answers to the questions she casually asked. She learned that the fellow was indeed Mr Ratcliff and he *was* enquiring after his wife and stepdaughter.

'He seemed a churlish sort,' the landlord summed up Cecil Ratcliff, while slicing juicy beef from the bone. 'I don't reckon his wife will get to keep that picture. I wish I'd not mentioned seeing it now.'

'Picture?' Megan echoed with a frown.

'Mrs Ratcliff couldn't get the lid of her packing case shut. I gave her a hand and noticed she'd got a small painting wedged inside. I only mentioned it in passing, but Ratcliff seemed glad to know about it.' The landlord raised his bushy eyebrows at Megan. 'Perhaps it's an heirloom… and, no, he is not having one of my cigars so say we've no stock.'

Megan turned away with the loaded plate of food, heading for the door. She reckoned that Sam might want to hear about Mr Ratcliff arriving in Devon and about an heirloom.

Jeremiah Collins had been snapping and snarling at his men since the fiasco with Miss Chapman. In turn Sam had been snapping and snarling at Megan. Collins didn't like deals to turn sour on him and the kidnapping escapade had netted him just a few pounds from Wolfson when he'd been expecting ten times as much in ransom. Megan wanted her and Sam to be married because she loved him despite his faults and bad connections. Once they were wed she was sure she could lure Sam away from Collins's gang. But in the meantime she was certain if she gave Sam some useful information to pass to Jeremiah then all might be well again between them and they'd start walking out together once more. Perhaps, before Ratcliff was reunited with his family, he might be tricked into believing that his stepdaughter was still in danger and stump up a ransom. That would be sure to put a smile on Collins's face. As far as Megan could see there was no risk in such a plot...but much to gain...

The Duke of Thornley was also beset by thoughts of Cecil Ratcliff and had been since the day Maude had come to visit him, looking for her daughter.

Following his talk with Maude that day he'd brooded on what she had disclosed about her wretched marriage. Alfred had liked Maude and wanted to do everything he could to make her life comfortable and that of her blameless daughter. He felt he owed them both that much. He'd guessed what Maude wanted above all else was for her and Fiona to be rid of the man making their lives a misery. So he'd acted on that hunch. Alfred wasn't sure that the document in his hand would do the trick, but it was certainly intriguing enough for him to harbour a glimmer of hope.

The duke's man of business had returned from London just that afternoon, bringing with him a report of his investigations into Maude Ratcliff's reprobate of a husband. With a sigh Alfred tossed the parchment on to the shiny yew

table and sat down, chin cupped in his hands.
It all seemed outlandish, but then, of late, much
of his life was like that, so he imagined other
people's lives were, too. He made a snap decision to send servants to scour the coaching inns
and find Maude…perhaps now reunited with
Fiona…and invite her to Thornley Heights so
he might share with her some astonishing news.
Of course, were it authentic, it would present the
woman with a fresh set of problems. But Thornley felt it only right to give Maude the chance to
have her say on it.

'I hoped I'd be seeing you again quite soon.'

'Always happy to oblige,' Luke drawled as he
circled Jeremiah Collins, levelling a pistol at the
man's chest. 'But I think you're lying.'

'How astute you are, Wolfson,' Jeremiah
scoffed through his gritted teeth. In fact, he was
cursing his unexpected visitor to damnation and
also the fellows who were supposed to be guarding the churchyard. He imagined that Wolfson
had overpowered the dolts. 'And what have you
done with Ruff and Dickens?' he smoothly enquired.

'Nothing that a good physician won't be able
to cure.'

'I'll knock them out again when they come

round.' Jeremiah chortled. 'I must get myself some better help.'

'You won't need it. You're packing up business. We're off to see the magistrate.'

'I don't think I'll come…but thank you anyway for the offer,' Collins spat caustically. 'I guessed from the start you were up to no good.' In fact, he'd known nothing of the sort. When the major turned up in Devon, offering his good connections and expertise in exchange for a slice of the profits in kidnapping the Duke of Thornley's daughter, Jeremiah had been keen on the idea. He hated those above him in the pecking order, and though Wolfson fell into the category, the major had sounded like a man carrying a chip on his shoulder. He'd seemed a kindred spirit to Jeremiah…but of course it had been a clever ruse on Wolfson's part.

Influential as he was in his own way, Jeremiah would never have had the audacity or the opportunity to attempt the kidnap of a powerful aristocrat's child. When the major had outlined his scheme and told him he had Thornley's ear, and that of their mutual friend, the Duke of Wellington, Jeremiah had listened intently.

Naturally, Jeremiah had had the major's credentials checked by a militiaman who was not averse to taking a bribe. Everything had checked out as it should. Still, Collins had been wary. Why would a fellow who moved in such exalted circles want to bite the hand that fed him? He'd demanded an answer direct from Wolfson and had been told that there were private reasons— not for discussion—for him wanting to even scores and make some money in the process. Jeremiah had accepted that as it fitted in with the major's brooding moodiness. But he bitterly regretted now letting avarice blind him to the fellow's true character. He'd fallen for it hook, line and sinker rather than making Wolfson prove himself further.

By the time Jeremiah's suspicions started outweighing his greed it was too late. Those numbskulls that worked for him had taken it upon themselves to abduct the wrong woman.

'And how is Miss Chapman?' Collins jibed although inwardly seething, and investigating every angle to outwit and kill his daunting adversary.

'She is very well,' Luke said, pocketing the pistol. At present he had no need of it. Ruff and Dickens were out cold and tied up out of harm's way. Luke knew he could take Collins easily in a straight fight and the man didn't appear to have a weapon on his coatless person. Nevertheless, Luke was on his guard. The smuggler could have a knife concealed, probably in a boot, just as Luke did himself.

Luke glanced to right and left in the church. All was quiet and still and the candles burning at the end of the pew where Jeremiah had been seated, drinking brandy, shed a blurry light on his foe's sinister features.

Then he heard it: a scratching noise and a faint shout.

Luke's dark eyes whipped back to Jeremiah. 'You've somebody imprisoned down there?'

'Nobody important.' Jeremiah flicked some indolent fingers. 'Not to me at least; perhaps you'll think differently as you're smitten with the man's stepdaughter…or has that fire already extinguished?' Jeremiah smirked. 'I told you I'd buy back the buttoned-up spinster when you'd done with her.'

Luke had withdrawn the pistol again and was walking backwards towards the stairs that led below, keeping Jeremiah in his sights. He could scarce credit what the man had said, yet didn't think that Collins was lying, either.

'You've got Ratcliff?'

At Jeremiah's bored nod Luke snorted a harsh laugh. 'Why? You fool! The man's being dunned, he's hardly going to find a ransom for himself or a stepdaughter who loathes him.'

'Being dunned, is he?' Jeremiah tutted sarcastically. 'I doubt those creditors know he has a valuable painting. Or rather his wife has it in her possession.'

'Bring him up!' Luke snarled. Of all the things that could have gone wrong during his mission to bring Collins to justice he hadn't thought it would be something as unpredictable as Cecil Ratcliff's untimely appearance!

He'd had from Fiona's own lips that she and her mother detested Ratcliff, but Luke couldn't allow Jeremiah to murder the fellow, which he would once he discovered no cash was to be had for Ratcliff's release.

Fiona was a sweet fair-minded person; she had every reason to loathe the man her mother had married, but she wouldn't want his death on her conscience. She'd blame herself for running away and drawing her stepfather into danger. And the thought of Fiona's future happiness being threatened stabbed at Luke's guts like a hot knife. He'd known for a long while that he was falling in love with her, but had suppressed the emotion by trying to convince himself that he was confusing lust with finer feelings. He regretted propositioning her when he could just as easily have asked her to marry him. It seemed incredible that in such a short time he should be so enslaved and ready to settle down. But with calm acceptance he knew it to be true. There'd been nobody in his past, and he sensed that neither would any woman in the future match up to Fiona as his future wife and the mother of his children.

'Get him up here!' Luke's bellow brought Jeremiah to his feet.

'I'll bring the fellow up when Mrs Ratcliff arrives and hands over the painting.' Jeremiah threw back his head and hooted a guffaw. 'You really don't know, do you, that the whole family is now congregated in the neighbourhood?'

Luke lunged at Jeremiah, curling a large, savage hand about his throat, prepared to throttle the devil to get every scrap of information out of him.

'Mrs Ratcliff was first to come searching for her daughter, then the stepfather turned up. I have spies out—these things soon reach my ears…sooner than they do yours, by the look of things,' Jeremiah wheezed out merrily. 'I imagine you might have some explaining to do when the chit's belly starts to swell.'

Shoving Collins away before he succumbed to the temptation to strangle him, Luke gritted with specious softness, 'Bring the fellow up here.' He raised the pistol. 'Or I will kill you and

God knows you'll not be meeting your maker before time.'

A few moments later Cecil Ratcliff was pushed, stumbling, up the same stone stairs from which, not long ago, Fiona had emerged into dim candle flame. Luke, staring, thought his eyes were deceiving him. Then, on striding closer for a better inspection, he noticed the cunning light in the fellow's pale eyes and knew he wasn't mistaken.

Luke glanced at Jem Collins. 'This is Cecil Ratcliff?'

'The very same,' the smuggler croaked through his crushed windpipe, his mean eyes darting between the two men.

'Tell him who you are.' The pistol moved slightly to encompass the prisoner.

'Cecil Ratcliff. And who pray are you?'

'Your erstwhile commanding officer, Rowland…not forgotten me already, surely?' Luke said softly. Lieutenant Charlie Rowland might have cut his sparse hair short and shaved off his beard, but he was still recognisable as the army deserter and all-round blackguard Luke knew of old.

Cecil licked his lips. 'I've no idea what you're talking about.'

'Of course you have—you're still up to your old tricks, then. But your time's up now, just as it is for him.' Luke jerked his head in Collins's direction.

'What in damnation?' Jeremiah snarled, glowering at his prize. 'If your wife's not on her way with that canvas, you've not long to live.' In a deft swooping movement that attested to much practice, Jeremiah had whipped a blade from his boot, then leapt to hold it to Cecil's throat.

'His wife's not on her way.' Luke advanced on the two men. 'His wife's in Bedlam, and since committing her he's had at least another two bigamous marriages that I know about, not including the one to Miss Chapman's mother. He's also had more sojourns in the Fleet than you've had kegs of brandy off Dawlish Beach.'

'Don't listen to him…he's lying. I don't know him,' Cecil spluttered before realising that both men were enemies and his greatest peril was from the fellow pressing the knife to his jugular.

'You've got yourself a pig in a poke, Jeremiah,' Luke stated coolly. 'The authorities will be almost as keen to apprehend this felon as they will you. You might as well let him go. He's bankrupt…he always is…' Luke cocked the loaded pistol in a very deliberate way. 'Who's carrying the message to Mrs Ratcliff?'

Jeremiah licked his dry lips. His informant in the dragoons had told him to take care if cross-

ing Wolfson as the man had a fearsome reputation with a range of weapons, both on and off
the battlefield.

Jeremiah knew he risked a bullet in the brain
before he'd finished slicing his captive from ear
to ear. But he managed a careless shrug, his free
hand gesturing obscenely his refusal to answer
any questions.

Luke suddenly barked a laugh. 'Ah…I see…
Dickens was on his way, was he, when I caught
him saddling up outside.' Luke got great satisfaction from knowing that Fiona's mother wasn't
about to burst in and swoon at the sight before
her.

Jeremiah knew he must upset Wolfson's equilibrium to have a chance of escaping. At present
his lethally composed opponent would be difficult to conquer. If Wolfson overpowered him,
his next stop, after gaol, would be Gallows Hill.

'Whoever you are, I doubt you knew that this
fine major has been tumbling your wife's daughter. What do you think about that, eh?' Collins
muttered close to Cecil's ear, but loud enough
for Luke to hear.

Cecil darted a resentful glance at Luke. So
he'd had more luck bedding the wench, had he?
But Cecil wasn't about to let on that Fiona had
rejected him. He gave as listless a shrug as was

possible with Jeremiah's heavy arm about his neck. 'She's a harlot ready to lift her skirts for any fellow. She's soothed many an itch for me.' He growled a ribald laugh.

Luke knew it for a provocative ploy, yet even so he was consumed by an irresistible urge to leap at the sneering pair and batter them.

Collins glimpsed a flicker of raw emotion stretching Wolfson's lips flat on his teeth and seized his moment. He gave his captive an almighty shove, reinforced by a boot against Cecil's backside that sent him crashing into Luke. Luke stumbled under Ratcliff's unexpected weight, giving Jeremiah the second he needed to lunge forward. Momentum had taken Cecil to his knees and, caitiff that he was, he cowered there, arms up over his head, as Collins charged forward with the knife, steel glinting in the candlelight.

A vicious knife-swipe sliced Luke's shoulder, but he managed to protect himself from further injury by swaying backwards on his heels. Swinging his head round in a brutal movement, he caught Collins's profile. When the smaller man staggered from the blow Luke followed up by delivering a single hefty jab to the smuggler's chin, snapping together his sagging jaw. Once Collins was sprawled senseless on the flags Luke

removed the blade from his opponent's limp
fingers.

He swung a look over a shoulder as he heard a
scurrying sound and was just in time to see Cecil
Ratcliff frantically crawling on hands and knees,
then jumping to his feet to flee from the church.
Following a frustrated curse, Luke turned back
to Collins and hoisted his comatose form on to
his shoulder, then went outside in pursuit of the
other man.

'Be still or I'll use this pistol,' Luke shouted at
the fugitive dodging between headstones. 'You
know I can hit you from this distance.' In a sliver
of moonlight Luke saw his quarry duck down
behind a rock angel. Quickly, keeping Cecil in
his sights, he flung Jeremiah over his stallion,
lashing together the unconscious man's hands
and feet with the reins as a precaution.

Free of that burden, Luke began to stalk Ratcliff through the graveyard, shoving the pistol
back into his coat pocket. He knew he had no
need of it. The bigamist looked to have grown
fat on his three years of parasitic living since de-
serting from the army. Had he not absconded he
would have been court martialled, possibly executed for thieving supplies from the army store
he'd been charged with overseeing.

Cecil stood up slowly as though about to turn

himself in, but instead he threw the fistfuls of stones he'd gathered from the ground. Luke crouched down as a pebble scored his scalp, but Ratcliff's desperate tactic had gained him little other than a few more yards of turf covered. Luke sprinted forward, tackling his wheezing torso to the freshly dug soil beside an open grave.

'I can make it worth your while to let me go,' Ratcliff gasped, struggling to get free of the forearm on his throat, pinning him down. 'I've that painting to recover, Wolfson. You can have it, I swear,' he cravenly wheedled. 'Once I catch up with my wife she'll hand it over in a trice. It's yours…and on good authority it's valuable…'

'You've got two choices in the matter,' Luke said with deceptive softness. 'You can beg forgiveness for ever having laid your filthy hands on Fiona Chapman, or you can spend the night in there.' Luke jerked a nod at the open grave. 'I'll blanket you with earth to make sure you keep warm.'

'You're no better than me where that chit is concerned. Will you apologise to her for bedding her?' Cecil spat. 'What does it matter? She's ruined now. Collins told me what's gone on. No gentleman would touch her with a bargepole once he knows smugglers have taken their sport with her. She'll end as a penny whore in Whitechapel if I don't put a roof over her head. You might as well keep your mouth shut on it all, Wolfson, for the sake of those two women. They've no choice but me.'

'You're wrong about that,' Luke said as he hit Ratcliff in the mouth with all the force he could muster from close range. He dragged the snivelling wretch up by the collar, in much the same way that his prisoner had hauled Dolly to her feet days before.

'I'm tempted to kill you, but I won't.' Luke thrust Cecil from him as though he felt contaminated by his proximity. 'You're not worth a murder charge. The law can decide your fate.' He grinned suddenly, and drew the pistol from his pocket. 'Two for the price of one…not a bad night's work.' Shoving Cecil in front of him, he headed back to Star.

# Chapter Eighteen

'Please calm yourself, Mama,' Fiona whispered.

She sent a glance over a shoulder to where the Duke of Thornley had diplomatically withdrawn to allow mother and daughter to digest his solemnly imparted news that Cecil Ratcliff was a bigamist, amongst other things.

Maude scrunched her wet handkerchief in her fist. 'The cheating swine! To do something so vile and immoral to an innocent woman is beyond bearing!' She scrubbed again at her blood-shot eyes.

'Yes, I know, Mama,' Fiona soothed. 'But you are not his legal wife after all—you said you regretted marrying him so perhaps it is not all bad.'

'I have allowed a man—an odious individual at that—to take intimate privileges only given under vows to a husband,' Maude spluttered in a voice of suffocated outrage.

Fiona drew her mother towards a chair and made her sit down, then shot a look at the fellow hovering by the window with his hands clasped behind his back.

Earlier that afternoon, mother and daughter had been drinking their tea and discussing where to head on departing the Pig and Whistle, when the duke's servant had turned up with a message for Maude. Thankfully it contained just an urgent summons to Thornley Heights. Had it been any more explicit Fiona knew her mother might have swooned dead away in the tavern's saloon bar, then even more people would know that, unbelievably, the scandal surrounding the Chapman women had just deepened.

The letter had intrigued both mother and daughter and they'd agreed that they should accept the invitation and go straight away to see His Grace. So they'd packed up their things with Rose's help, then all ridden in the coach provided by the duke to solve the mystery.

Obliquely, Fiona had been glad to have a distraction to prevent her constantly thinking about Luke. Had he been injured in the confrontation with Collins? Had he sensibly decided to avoid danger and return to London after all? But the most pressing uncertainty was where to go to find him.

At the Pig and Whistle she'd been mulling over ways to tell her mother that she'd fallen in love and was prepared to follow Luke Wolfson to the ends of the earth if need be. She'd now need to bite her tongue on that secret a while longer; it would be too cruel to add to her mother's anguish when Maude was already on the point of hysterics.

Fiona glanced up as the drawing-room door opened and a young woman entered. Having approached the duke for a brief conversation, the petite brunette then hurried over to Fiona and Maude.

'Papa has allowed me to come and speak to you, Miss Chapman. I'm so very sad to hear of your troubles.' Joan cast a sympathetic look on Maude's bowed head.

'You must be Joan Thornley.' Fiona straightened from her crouching position close to her mother's chair.

'I am… Oh, sorry to be rude—I should have introduced myself straight away.' Joan held out her hands and warmly clasped Fiona's fingers. Following a quick glance at Fiona's mother, still propping her contorted features in her hands, Joan drew Fiona aside. 'I know you have also suffered through no fault of your own,' she whispered, looking chagrined. 'I very much regret that as well.'

'Hush…I am fine…' Fiona said kindly, as the young lady began blinking back guilty tears. 'But I'm not sure my mama will quickly recover from this dreadful blow.' Fiona knew Maude must feel the greatest fool alive. Although her mother now hated Cecil, at one time the woman had thought herself in love with her second husband. She had put her faith and trust in a man who'd given nothing but lies and deceit in return for sincere affection and loyalty.

'I expect Major Wolfson acquainted you with our half-baked scheme to catch the smuggling gang.' Joan had kept her voice low while looking very sheepish.

'Yes…he did…'

'You were very brave, Miss Chapman; I couldn't have asked for a better impostor—' Joan broke off, blushing and biting her lip. 'Sorry, that was a daft thing to say.' Soon she'd bounced back to resume excitedly, 'It must have felt as though you'd been swept up in a Gothic novel. Luke Wolfson is such a handsome and brave hero and the whole thing is exceedingly romantic.' Again Joan frowned at what she'd said. 'I know why Papa got cross with me. I do sound like a very silly and flighty girl sometimes. Yet I'm almost twenty.'

'It *was* quite thrilling—in hindsight, of course,' Fiona ruefully admitted. 'I was terrified at the time, but tried not to let on to those villains. Besides, I trusted in Mr Wolfson to rescue me,' Fiona concluded softly.

'If I tell you something, will you promise not to breathe a word to a soul?' Joan asked.

Fiona had been on the point of returning to her mother's side, but noticed the duke had pulled up a chair close to Maude and was talking to her in an undertone.

'I am disgraced, too!' Joan hissed, rather tactlessly. 'But thankfully only my papa and the major's friend know about it. Oh, and Pip, too. He drove the gig that took me to see Mr Rockleigh, you see, but Papa has threatened the boy to keep quiet on pain of losing his livelihood. My father is still very angry at me for taking such a risk, but eventually he'll calm down—'

'You went to see Mr Rockleigh?' Fiona interrupted Joan's rattling report. She recalled Luke had told her that his friend Drew Rockleigh had set off back to London.

Joan nodded. 'I was trying to help with the plot to capture Jeremiah Collins, you see. I knew only the major could outwit the devil. So believing Wolfson at his friend's hunting lodge I went off to find him, late at night, behind Papa's back.'

'I'm guessing your plan went awry.' Fiona sounded calm despite her shock at hearing what the young woman had done.

'Mr Rockleigh was on his own at his hunting lodge.' Joan grimaced. 'Thankfully Papa has now seen sense over trying to make the poor man marry me. *I* compromised *him* if anything…' Joan sighed. 'I refused to have him, but I expect Mr Rockleigh must hate me for causing him such trouble, especially as he brought me home safely.'

A small muffled noise from Maude drew Fiona hurriedly back to her mother's side, fearing yet more bad news was to be had.

'You are very good to us, sir,' Maude gulped. She put away her handkerchief and turned to Fiona, making an effort to compose herself. 'His Grace has kindly invited us to stay the night at Thornley Heights as his guests, Fiona. Then in the morning he will escort us to London to sort out this terrible mess.'

'Oh, capital!' Joan burst out. 'I love to have company and I adore London.' She gave her papa a twinkling smile, just in case he had intended leaving her behind. 'I shall pack a few things after dinner. I'm so looking forward to it.'

She linked arms with Fiona as though they were old friends. 'We have so much to talk about.'

'I must let Rose know what has been decided.' Maude made to rise, but the duke stopped her with a hand on her arm.

'My daughter will send a message down to the servants. I expect your maid is taking refreshment.'

Fiona smiled although privately feeling rather melancholy. She yearned to see Luke again, but accepted any meeting would be delayed by this latest calamity. There was no urgency to be with the man she loved, other than to revel in his closeness. She knew to abandon her mother would be selfish; besides, she trusted that Luke would still want her, whether it was in a day, or a month's time, that they were finally reunited.

He might be a gentleman who in his time had dallied with a variety of women, but she believed him fair and honest. She was sure that he'd fulfil the promise he'd made to care for her and protect her.

Given time, and a successful result against the smugglers, she guessed that Luke would journey to Dartmouth, believing her to have taken up employment with the Herberts. He wasn't fickle; he'd not give up his pursuit of her too easily. And if he did…then he was not the man she believed him to be.

'I have spent far too much time lately riding in carriages…' Fiona mused, partly to herself, gazing out of the window at drifting fluffy clouds.

'I'll warrant none of those contraptions were anywhere near as luxurious as this one,' Maude returned, nestling further into supple hide squabs. Although they had been journeying for almost two hours the woman was still in awe of the splendid crested coach that was taking them to the metropolis. She ran her appreciative fingers over the upholstery for the hundredth time.

'Papa does own some very nice vehicles,' Joan piped up. She had insisted on riding with the ladies rather than with her father. So Maude and Rose shared one spacious seat and the two younger women sat opposite. The Duke of Thornley was travelling ahead with his valet in another impressive conveyance, flanked by liveried outriders. 'When I turned seventeen he bought me a landau so I might parade around Hyde Park with my friends.'

'Do you visit London often?' Fiona had wondered why the younger woman wasn't enjoying the London Season. Most spinsters of Lady Joan's age and elevated status wanted to be part of the vivacious social whirl in town in springtime.

Joan pulled a face. 'Since Mama passed away my father has withdrawn into his shell. And taken me with him,' she added rather wistfully. 'But I don't begrudge comforting him as best I can. My parents liked to spend time in Devon and were so very happily married...' Joan frowned and shot a look under her brows at Maude.

'Lucky people indeed...' the woman muttered sourly.

'So you will relish this unexpected outing,' Fiona burst out, keen to keep a light atmosphere. She'd been surprised that Joan was not even engaged. She was a very pretty young woman and with such wealth and connections would attract a horde of eligible suitors. But Joan obviously knew her own mind and had rejected her father's choice when hapless Drew Rockleigh compromised her. He was a very handsome fellow, Fiona recalled, but other than that he might have nothing to recommend him.

'Indeed, I am delighted to be going to town!' Joan had been peering out of the window at passing scenery, but now settled back and clapped her gloved hands in excitement. 'When we arrive in Mayfair the first thing we must do is arrange a big party…' She hesitated and glanced at the unhappy woman in the corner. 'If you would like to, of course.'

'That sounds a splendid idea.' Maude bucked herself up. She might be dejected on her own account, but she knew she must not look a gift horse in the mouth. There was never likely to be a better opportunity to re-launch her daughter into society and find her a husband. Maude knew it was Fiona's last chance. A twenty-five-year-old spinster was more of an age to be a debutante's chaperon at the marriage mart, than her friend or rival. Maude discreetly assessed Fiona's profile; her daughter had turned up her face to allow the sun streaming in the carriage window to gild it. She seemed prettier, Maude decided, her hair blonder and her complexion peachier. Her daughter's usual air of serenity seemed subdued by a vibrant, if rather secretive, happiness. Maude had guessed that Fiona had a hankering for her handsome rescuer and was harbouring fantasies of a happy ending with him. What girl would not fall in love with such a dashing hero? Before Maude had even learned of the service Wolfson had done her daughter she had thought he appeared to be a charismatic man.

Of course the major knew all the details of Fiona's disgrace so could not be counted on for anything other than his discretion—which the duke, during their private talk yesterday, had assured her Wolfson had gladly given. If Fiona's dreadful ordeal leaked out she would be shunned, but Maude's flagging spirits where her daughter was concerned were boosted as she reminded herself that they now had the patronage of the Duke of Thornley. Few would dare question the calibre of the friends of such a rich and influential man.

Maude settled back with an air of resignation. As far as her own situation was concerned she knew she must make the best of a bad hand. She *had* wished her marriage to Cecil had never taken place…and it seemed she'd got her wish, albeit courtesy of a very shocking and humiliating set of circumstances. She lifted her chin an inch, knowing she must find some of the grit her daughter had in abundance and stare down any malicious gossips.

Fiona heard her mother's tiny satisfied sigh and, feeling pleased by it, she relaxed. She could scarce credit that so much had happened in so short a space of time.

Having spent a comfortable night in a sumptuous chamber, mother and daughter had risen early, as had the rest of the household. The duke had said at dinner the previous evening that he wanted to set off for London immediately after breakfast and indeed that had happened. At the crack of dawn the house had been a hive of industry as the servants finished the preparations for their master's trip to town and served up a huge repast that seemed to Fiona barely necessary as she was still feeling full from the twenty courses or so of dinner from the previous evening.

Despite the thick mattresses and silky smooth sheets Fiona had slept little with her mind crammed with worries. At one point she had given up trying to count sheep and had got up and stared out of the window into blackness where Luke's face seemed to haunt every cloud and shadow. Now, the rocking of the coach and her exhaustion combined to lull her and her lashes dropped over her weary eyes.

She wasn't sure for how long she slept but she awoke with a start and quickly looked at her companions to note they, too, had nodded off. She realised then what had brought her awake: the coach was slowing down and bumping over ruts formed by a multitude of other carriage wheels that had turned into this tavern courtyard. Inwardly Fiona groaned; she had been inside many such establishments lately and would have preferred to journey on.

'Why are we stopping?' Maude came awake with a start and craned her head out of the window.

'It is the Halfway House,' Joan said, rubbing her sleepy eyes. 'We always break our journey here. Papa will bespeak us a private room so we might have some refreshment.'

'Oh, no!'

Fiona had been gazing at some drizzle trailing down the leaded windows when she heard Joan's muted gasp of dismay. Moments ago they had been shown to the back parlour of the Halfway House. Joan had been about to take a fireside chair while Fiona continued to stretch her stiff legs, promenading to and fro in the cosy room. Now she returned to Joan's side, but the young woman, with a wary glance at her father who was ensconced with Maude on a sofa, skipped to the door. It had been left slightly ajar by the landlord who'd gone to fetch their food. Quickly Joan pushed it shut.

'What is it?' Fiona asked in concern.

'*Who* is it? That's what you should have asked.' Joan swivelled her eyes in a show of exasperation. 'I just spied Mr Rockleigh in the corridor! I hope Papa does not see him. I think they are under a very fragile truce following my visit to the man's lodge.' She sighed. 'Oh, what a bother and such bad luck to run into him here!'

'Are you sure it was him? Was he alone?' Fiona frowned.

The two young ladies stepped to the window so they might talk more privately under the guise of observing the worsening weather.

Joan shook her head. 'Oh, he was not accompanied by his friend, the major,' she explained quietly. 'He had a dark-haired young woman with him.'

'I see…' Fiona tried to curb her dreadful disappointment. Just for a moment she had imagined that Luke might be under the same roof as her, but she realised it was more likely his mistress was instead. It was a puzzle why Luke's friends had not already reached London and the only solution Fiona could come up with caused her heart to thump in anxiety. Had Becky Peake and Drew Rockleigh been waiting for Luke to join them before journeying on? Fiona felt the pain around her heart increase as her mind pounced on a dreadful reason for his delay in turning up. Luke might even now be lying murdered in that desolate graveyard that the Collins gang used as a hideaway.

'I hope he is planning on leaving soon,' Joan fretted in a whisper. 'Papa is unpredictable. He might blow his top, or sink into one of his moods if they unexpectedly come face to face.' She shot a look at the door. 'Perhaps I should go and see if I can find the dratted fellow and warn him to conceal himself.' She nibbled at her lower lip. 'I must find an excuse to slip away...'

'I'll go,' Fiona said hoarsely. 'We've not been introduced, but I know what Mr Rockleigh looks like. I'll explain the situation to him.'

'Oh, would you? That is very kind.'

Joan's grateful smile helped Fiona swallow her misgivings over her impetuous offer. She felt desperate to have any news of Luke that she could, although she was naturally reluctant to accost people she didn't know. A meeting with Becky Peake was especially daunting to her. Yet she also had a morbid wish to come face to face with her rival and perhaps with womanly intuition gauge just how entwined in Luke's life the woman was.

Fiona hurried out into the corridor with her mother's bewildered expression imprinted on her mind. Of course the woman would be sceptical about her excuse that she was in need of a little fresh air. They had all only recently come indoors after all...and it had turned to rain.

## *Chapter Nineteen*

The Halfway House was a far larger inn than any that Fiona had previously frequented.

The maze of intersecting corridors that ran into back and side annexes was busy and she was relieved that most of the travellers appeared too harassed to bother about her slender presence weaving through the throng.

A very rotund fellow barged impatiently past, causing Fiona to ram a flat palm on the top of her bonnet to prevent it being knocked askew. She then resumed scouring the crowd for a pretty brunette or a strikingly fair-haired gentleman. Instead of clapping eyes on either of those individuals she rounded a corner and spied a handsome tanned face.

She might only have got a glimpse of his profile before other people surged forward to block her view, but it was enough for Fiona to recognise Luke. She'd know him anywhere, she realised, even in a darkened room. Her senses were attuned to him, like an animal scenting its mate. And then her fanciful yearning was quashed and she was jolted to harsh reality.

Becky Peake was with him. The crowd surrounding the couple dispersed and, snatching her chance, the brunette pressed her mouth to her lover's. Luke removed his mistress's arms from about his neck and turned…

Astonishment transformed his features, then he took a pace forward, shaking off Becky's fingers as she again reached for him.

'I thought you and your mother were staying at Thornley Heights.' Luke had reached Fiona in a few long strides, taking her hands in his.

Fiona moistened her lips, wondering how he knew she'd been the Duke of Thornley's guest, or that Maude had joined her in Devon. But seeing him being kissed by the mistress he'd said he'd finished with had ignited a fiery reaction within that overpowered her reason. She snatched back her hands. 'We were at His Grace's house, but left this morning to travel to London,' she answered frostily.

'I need to speak to you on a very important matter, Fiona,' Luke said huskily. He thrust his fingers through his glossy raven hair. 'Actually, there are numerous things I must say to you privately.'

'I see…and these matters are so vital that you travelled in the opposite direction to that in which you expected me to be.' She glanced past at the woman watching them through narrowed eyes. 'Your mistress is waiting for you, sir. I doubt we have anything left to say to one another.' Fiona knew she was acting like a jealous shrew, but she couldn't control herself. She was desperately keen to know what had occurred between Luke and Jeremiah Collins, but then realised he might have forgone a confrontation with the smuggler in favour of chasing after his paramour.

Luke's mouth slanted in sardonic contemplation of Fiona's indignant, blushing face. 'If you allow me to explain, my dear, seeing me with Becky will seem quite insignificant to you, as indeed the meeting is.'

Fiona raised furious eyes to his. 'Your arrogance and conceit is breathtaking, Mr Wolfson. Why would that woman matter to me?'

'I wasn't convinced last time you said you were indifferent to what I get up to,' he drawled, taking her arm and steering her towards the door that led outside into the courtyard. 'I'm no more persuaded now. But you will listen to everything I have to say whether you like it or not.'

'Unhand me!' Fiona hissed, trying to wrench her elbow from his grip.

But he forced her with him into the cool damp afternoon and before she knew it they were protected from the drizzle and from view by a large privet bush. When Luke removed his hand from her arm Fiona flung herself around to glare at him with sparking tawny eyes. 'To my previous complaints about your character I now add that you are the most ill-mannered man alive. Don't you dare rough handle me! And you have abandoned your mistress without giving her the courtesy of a word of explanation.'

'She needs none. Becky knows about us and that she is no longer my mistress. And I didn't want her farewell kiss just now.'

That steely announcement stunned Fiona into silence for a few moments. 'What does she know about us?' she eventually asked hoarsely.

Luke rubbed a hand about his bristly jaw; Fiona recognised then the weariness about him and his dusty dishevelment. He looked like a man who had ridden hard and had little rest. Suddenly she felt ashamed of her behaviour.

'We'll talk about that later. I've some news about your stepfather that I think you should know immediately although I'm loath to upset you.'

Fiona put an unsteady hand to her forehead.

So, gossip about Cecil Ratcliff's bigamy had already spread. 'I know what you are going to say,' she murmured. 'So it will not come as a shock… although it is a surprise that the scandal is already out.' She sighed in defeat. 'The Duke of Thornley reported to my mother yesterday that Ratcliff is a bigamist who uses aliases.'

'Is that why you didn't travel on to Dartmouth? Did you forgo your employment to comfort and support her?'

Fiona guessed that he'd been to the Pig and Whistle looking for her. He would have learned from the landlord that a crested carriage had taken mother and daughter to His Grace's home. Luke obviously didn't know, though, that her employer had also turned up at the inn with no good deed in mind.

'Mr Herbert learned of my kidnapping and came to the Pig and Whistle to say he thought me unfit to be near his daughters following the incident.' Fiona's voice betrayed just a hint of the hurt she'd felt at being so rudely rejected.

'He insulted you? The bumptious dolt! I've a mind to go to Dartmouth and—'

'You will not!' Fiona interrupted quickly, gripping Luke's arm in emphasis. 'Please do not… It will just make matters worse.' She allowed him to draw her closer in comfort, leaning into his warmth and strength as though it were the most natural thing to do. 'I would have had no option but to quit the position in any case when Mama showed up.'

'Bad luck and heartache seem to dog you, don't they?' Luke said softly, gently soothing her with caressing fingers that moved from her cheek to cradle her scalp. 'Did you mother travel west looking for Ratcliff, or for you?'

'Ratcliff?' Fiona raised her eyes to Luke's face. Then her puzzlement transformed to horror. 'Oh, no! Never say the swine is close by.' She gazed back at the inn, inside which her mother was comfortably ensconced with the Duke of Thornley.

'He is…but there's no need to fret, Fiona. He is under guard and can't bother you.' In as few words as possible Luke explained how he had come across Ratcliff as Jeremiah Collins's prisoner and recognised him as a thief and deserter who'd served, under a different name, in his regiment.

Their eyes remained locked together for several moments after Luke stopped talking. Finally Fiona dragged her wide amber gaze up to the heavens. 'It is too much!' She took a pace away, then quickly returned. 'So not only is he *not* my mother's husband, but he is *not* Cecil Ratcliff, either? *That* name is one of his aliases, I take it.'

Luke gave a grave nod. 'He has changed his name several times to escape justice. His crimes are many after all and he knows a long prison sentence is the best he can expect once apprehended.'

'Why did Collins kidnap him?' she asked in despair. 'The spendthrift has nothing but IOUs to hand over.'

'I gather he pursued your mother towards Devon because she stole a painting from him. He believes it valuable…and Collins somehow came to hear about it. He wanted to attempt to trade Ratcliff for the canvas.'

'*Stole it?*' Fiona burst out in an outraged hiss. 'That small painting belonged to my father, and whatever that odious man might think about his rights to it, *we* believe it to be ours.'

'If Ratcliff were your mother's legitimate husband, the law would see it differently, but never mind that now,' Luke added gently on noticing moisture beading Fiona's lashes.

Fiona smeared away the angry tears and composed herself with a little sniff. 'The fiend should rot in gaol for what he has done.'

'And will your mother feel the same way about his fate?'

'I think Mama would like the chance to throw

the key to his cell into the depths of the sea!' Fiona replied flatly.

Luke released her and prowled to and fro, looking reflective. 'Do you want me to turn him over to the authorities?'

'Why…where is he?' Fiona marched after Luke, cocking her head to read his expression. 'What have you done with him?'

'Nothing…yet. He's locked away in a barn and can't escape. Drew's gone off to guard him. But I wanted to speak to you first before delivering him to the magistrate.' He gazed solemnly at her. 'I couldn't add to your woes and I couldn't be sure your mother wouldn't choose to stay loyal to Ratcliff, no matter what. If you want him set free…just say.'

'You would do that for me even though he has a catalogue of crimes to answer to?'

'I'd do anything for you, Fiona…you should know that by now…' Luke said huskily. Suddenly he was again before her and his mouth swooped, covering hers in a hard swift kiss. 'If I let him go he'll simply disappear from your lives. It's how he operates. Once his fraud is uncovered he runs for cover, then emerges elsewhere to prey on another unsuspecting female.'

Fiona bit her lip, thinking. She glanced up at Luke and gave him a faint smile; he had been very kind, considering their feelings before making any decision on Ratcliff's fate. 'He should be punished...' she uttered slowly.

'I agree...'

'But it is up to Mama, she must decide.'

'Shall we approach her now and bring an end to the matter?'

Fiona nodded. 'Mama is sitting with the Duke of Thornley...'

'*Thornley's* inside?' Luke snapped his gaze to the inn.

Fiona smiled ruefully. 'He's been very good to us. We overnighted at Thornley Heights and he is accompanying us to London in order to help sort out the mess we're in.' Fiona shook her head ruefully. 'We none of us had any idea that *the mess* has met us halfway.' Fiona sighed. 'Perhaps His Grace might turn back when he finds out and that will disappoint Joan. She is very much looking forward to her sojourn in town.'

'Joan is inside, too?' Luke's dark eyebrows shot up.

Fiona suddenly clapped her hand to her mouth in consternation. She had forgotten her promise to Joan to run an errand.

'I was out in the corridor looking for your friend, as a favour to Joan. She caught sight of

Mr Rockleigh and wanted to warn him to keep his distance from her father.'

'You know about that fiasco, do you?' Luke's tone held a mixture of amusement and exasperation.

'The kidnapping plot had some bad consequences,' Fiona said with some understatement.

'And His Grace is obviously feeling very guilty over the way it affected you,' Luke observed. He dipped his head, teased a delicate earlobe with his lips and warm breath. 'I rode this way looking for my friend simply to enlist his help. I'd rather have followed you to Thornley Heights, but I needed Drew to guard Ratcliff while I attended to other things. Drew and I served under Wellington together so he knows of Charlie Rowland, as we knew Cecil Ratcliff to be.'

'You have put yourself to some trouble over the vile wretch.'

'I had to—I knew you would never be content until the matter was settled. So you may tell Joan that my friend Drew is out of harm's way and no need to fret on that score.'

'And Becky Peake?' Fiona breathed.

'No need to fret on that score, either.' Luke dropped his hands away from her, but his loving expression intensified. 'Becky might claim that she wants only me…and she does…but we both know it's not true. She appreciates the things I give her and I've appreciated her company. But for me it's over. And for her…another generous man will do.' He smiled ruefully. 'I caught up with her and Drew quite quickly because they'd been enjoying staying at a variety of inns on their leisurely return to town.'

Fiona's lips softly parted in astonishment. 'You mean, your friend has stolen Becky from you?' she burst out.

'Not exactly—he's providing a service,' Luke answered diplomatically. 'And I've no objection to that whatsoever. Neither has Becky, although she was delighted to see me, as you witnessed. She likes to keep her options open—it's what women in her position do.'

'I see…' Fiona could feel the heat travelling from her throat to her cheeks. Was he obliquely giving her a first lesson in the ways and expected behaviour of his paramours? Had he just hinted that his mistress was expected to go quietly when her time was up? 'I should return to the others,' Fiona said. 'They will all be wondering where on earth I have got to.'

On cue, Joan appeared in the doorway that led back inside the tavern. 'Oh, there you are, Fiona,' she called. 'I thought I spied your bonnet behind that bush.' Joan rushed outside, then came to an abrupt halt on seeing somebody else, better concealed behind the privet.

'Major Wolfson!' Joan beamed and gave Fiona a rather arch glance. 'Well, this is a nice surprise. You are travelling with your friend, I expect.' She turned to Fiona. 'Have you warned Rockleigh off?' She grimaced. 'Papa is sinking some brandy and one never knows how that might affect him. He'll either be very mellow, or a bear with a sore head.'

'Mr Wolfson has just told me that his friend has already left,' Fiona quickly informed her. 'There was no need or opportunity for me to speak to him.'

'Oh...' Joan sounded a trifle disappointed and slipped her hand through the crook of Fiona's arm. 'Perhaps he will turn up in London.'

'We might not need to travel on...' Fiona shot a glance at Luke, hoping he might take over explanations. Her head had started to pound with the amount of information crammed within it. And then there was the question of her future with Luke, if indeed she had a future with him. She believed that his relationship with Becky was finished and that he still wanted her to replace the brunette. But for how long? Would he allow her to be taken on by one of his friends when he grew bored with his *buttoned-up spinster*?

'Let's go inside and find the others, then everybody will hear what I have to say,' Luke said, leading the way back to the tavern.

'So…the blackguard is safely apprehended?'

The moment Luke had finished his concise account of capturing Jeremiah Collins the Duke of Thornley demanded absolute confirmation of his arch-enemy's fate.

'Delivered to the magistrate and under lock and key,' Luke replied before taking a sip of brandy.

'Capital! I owe you a sum of money, sir,' Thornley boomed out. Then he glanced at the ladies. 'We'll speak of it later.'

'There's no need. I went after Collins on my own account rather than yours.'

His Grace looked rather taken aback at that blunt comment, but appeared not to take offence. He employed the decanter instead, then offered Luke a refill.

'What of Dickens and Ruff?' Fiona asked. She knew that the young smuggler deserved his comeuppance, yet still felt sad that, with his life before him, Sam might have forfeited his future with Megan for the noose…or if he were lucky, years of hard labour.

Luke shrugged. 'I told the dragoons where to find them tied up. I imagine Collins's two cohorts have now joined him in gaol.'

'Quite rightly!' His Grace announced. 'Those types deserve no quarter. With Collins gone I expect another gang will form in time. It is the unfortunate way of things along this coast.'

Fiona knew it to be true; she recalled how savage young Sam had been when she made her escape from her dank prison. If pushed to choose between obeying his master, or sparing her life, he would have followed Jeremiah Collins's orders.

After a moment Fiona realised that her mother had remained very quiet, seated alone on the sofa. She sat down beside Maude and took her chilly hands between her palms. The woman had listened quietly to Luke's account of finding Cecil incarcerated by Collins. She had looked too shocked and despondent to speak a word on hearing that he had followed her simply to lay his hands on the painting she had in her possession. Fiona guessed that her mother harboured a grain of duty, if not affection, for the man she'd believed to be her husband.

'What should Mr Wolfson do with Ratcliff,

Mama?' Fiona asked quietly enough for their conversation to be private. 'He will free him on your say so—'

'No!' Maude hissed in an undertone. 'I would not have some other poor wretch go through what I have had to endure at that man's hands. I have some concern for Cecil. I'm not sure why after the way he has treated me. But both men *must* be punished. It is the only civilised way.'

Fiona's fingers tightened on the thin digits in her clasp. 'You are right…and I'm proud of you for being so strong.' She gave her mother an encouraging smile.

'I'm so proud of you!' Maude croaked, raising her glistening eyes to her daughter's face. 'I cannot describe how sorry I am that any of this came about, my dear.'

'Hush…' Fiona rubbed vigorously at her mother's quivering fists, clasped together in her lap. 'All will get better now.'

'Are we still to go to London, Papa?' There was a great deal of persuasiveness in Joan's voice, indicating the answer she hoped to receive.

'I suppose so, my dear, if it is what you all want.' He glanced at Maude.

Maude turned her enquiring eyes on her daughter.

'Miss Chapman?' The duke turned to Fiona for her decision.

'Yes…let's carry on to town, if we may.' Fiona gave Luke the most fleeting of glances and thought she saw him respond with an almost imperceptible nod. From that she drew comfort that he wanted her to know that once his business in Devon was finished he would come after her.

# Chapter Twenty

'Wake up, Fiona… Wake up!'

Fiona blinked her heavy eyes. Then, as the sound of a voice calling her name penetrated the fog in her mind, she pushed herself on to an elbow amidst plush coverings on her comfy feather bed. Her mother's wide-eyed visage wavered into view behind the burning candle the woman was holding aloft.

Fearing yet another disaster was about to be revealed, Fiona swung her legs over the edge of the bed, ready to get up.

'What has happened, Mama?' There was a tinge of weary resignation in Fiona's tone as she searched for her slippers in the wavering light brightened by a glow of logs smouldering in the grate.

'The duke has asked me to marry him.' Maude sank down on the edge of the mattress.

So vacant-eyed did her mother seem that Fiona sensibly removed the flame from her weak fingers lest she dropped it and set fire to the blankets. Having deposited the sconce on a side table, she sat beside her mother, studying her expression.

'Do you think he is a madman?' Maude slurred in a whisper.

Fiona blinked, moistening her dry lips. 'Perhaps you misheard him, Mama.' She was aware that her mother smelled of sherry.

'*Will you marry me, Madam*, were his exact words.' Maude livened herself up. 'He has taken quite a lot of port. Perhaps he is drunk, not mad.'

'And what response did you give?' Fiona breathed.

'Well, I said I would marry him, of course, before quickly retiring for the night. I thought it best to humour him in case he acted yet more bizarre.' Maude giggled. 'Me…a duchess…just think, Fiona—'

'You *would* marry him?' Fiona interrupted. 'But you don't love him and are barely acquainted…' She bit her lip, aware of being a hypocrite. She barely knew Luke Wolfson but she believed she loved him and wanted to be his wife.

'I didn't know that vile creature I walked

down the aisle with a year ago; yet I thought I did.' Maude gave a fierce wag of the head. 'Love! Pah! I need no more of that. I loved your papa and now I know that was enough! At least the Duke of Thornley has his credentials all about him.' The grand furniture and velvet bed hangings in the chamber drew Maude's appreciative eyes. 'No person would dare gossip about you if you are the Duke of Thornley's ward.' Maude sighed. 'I doubt the fellow will recall it in the morning when he is nursing a sore head.' She stood up unsteadily and started to disrobe. 'That will be a shame, for he is a nice gentleman… He reminds me of your papa.' Maude unlocked her packing case and haphazardly pulled out some things in search of her nightgown.

'Had Joan retired for the night at that point?' Fiona found it hard to believe that His Grace would have proposed while his daughter was listening.

'She went up to bed just after you, so we were alone. There were no witnesses.' Maude sighed, pulling ineffectually at her gown in an attempt to get her arms out of the sleeves.

Fiona helped her mother with her buttons, then to don her nightgown. She watched the woman climb unsteadily into the other huge four-poster and draw up the covers to her chin.

Although shocked by what she'd heard Fiona could find no questions to ask.

Her mother might fear His Grace was under the influence, but Fiona doubted the Duke of Thornley, drunk or not, would blurt out something so consequential without realising the enormity of what he'd done. The man had said he wished to make amends to them, but to offer her mother marriage? Fiona couldn't deny it was a solution that would rectify everything in one fell stroke. Her mother's shame and embarrassment over Cecil Ratcliff's bigamy would disintegrate and her own situation would be vastly improved. There would certainly be no need for the stepdaughter of a duke to become a gentleman's mistress…unless she really wanted to…

On hearing the first soft snore coming from her mother Fiona massaged her tired face with her fingers. She wished she, too, could climb back into bed and fall fast asleep, but she knew such comfort would be denied to her. She had slumbered for more than an hour already and now felt depressingly alert following her rude awakening.

They had arrived in Mayfair late that afternoon and had been shown to a magnificent chamber on the first floor of the west wing of their host's mansion. Joan had wanted the guests to have maids, but Maude had politely refused. Fiona knew that her mother was concerned that the duke's servants would see the state of their oft-darned nightgowns and petticoats.

Earlier, on rising from the dinner table following a lengthy and delicious meal, Fiona and Joan had played a few hands of rummy while their parents continued depleting the decanters. Fiona had then retired for the night, wanting some private time to mull things over in her mind and think of Luke. Surprisingly, he'd barely entered her mind when she fell asleep shortly after her head snuggled into the downy pillows.

But she concentrated on Luke now while perching on the edge of the bed. She knew he would not yet have returned to London. They had all parted company at the Halfway House; the duke's party had set on the road towards London and Luke had set off in the opposite direction to relieve Drew Rockleigh of his duty guarding Ratcliff. The man she'd believed to be her stepfather would by now be in prison.

Fiona wondered if Becky Peake and Drew Rockleigh might also have arrived in town. But those two were swiftly pushed to the back of her mind. It was Luke who dominated her thoughts. Would he soon come to visit? If he did, and again propositioned her to be his mistress, what then?

With a sigh, Fiona sank down on to the bed and curled up, resting her cheek on her clasped hands. She had promised to go shopping with Joan tomorrow, and she was determined to enjoy the outing, so she must empty her mind again and fall asleep or she would make a very dreary companion.

'Are you getting up, Mama? Fiona pulled back the curtains, allowing sunlight to stream into the bedchamber.

Maude burrowed further into the covers, avoiding the golden beams. 'My head is aching,' she whimpered.

Fiona redrew the heavy curtains till just a chink of light remained. 'It is almost two o'clock. I am going out with Joan soon. Will you come?'

'I want to…but I cannot…' Maude mumbled. 'I shall not take another glass of sherry in my life, I swear.'

Fiona went to sit by her mother, shaking her shoulder to gain her attention. 'Do you recall what you told me last night?'

Maude peeped over the edge of the blankets. 'Yes, I do.' She struggled to a seated position. 'Was His Grace at breakfast earlier?'

'He was. He looked bright as a lark and as though he can hold his drink far better than you.'

Maude sank into the pillows. 'Well…I expect that he is a more regular tippler and I suppose a serious talk with him must be in the offing.'

'Indeed…' Fiona said on standing up. She knew it was best to leave her mother to ponder alone on something as personal as another marriage proposal. She didn't want to influence Maude on her future because she realised her time at home had come to an end. Her life had changed the moment she set off for Devon and would never be as it once had, whatever transpired between her and Luke. Fiona had tasted freedom and found it suited her despite the pitfalls that were the price to pay for independence.

'I know you very much like that fellow Wolfson and so I suppose the other news I told you came as a blow.'

Fiona turned back to frown at her mother. 'What news are you talking about, Mama?'

Maude again struggled up, looking concerned. 'I should not have said anything… I would not have, had I been thinking straight when I came up to bed.'

'I fear you were thinking straight, Mama, because you told me nothing about Mr Wolfson. You only repeated the duke's proposal.'

'Oh…' Maude bit her lip. 'I didn't tell you

what His Grace overheard while at his club yesterday afternoon?'

Fiona shook her head and perched again on the edge of the mattress, feeling curious. The Duke of Thornley had taken himself off to St James's within an hour of the travelling coaches rolling to a stop in front of his magnificent Mayfair town house. Joan and a host of servants had been left to attend to his guests while he sought the company of his gentlemen friends. But His Grace had returned in good time, and good spirits, to dine with them all.

'You said it concerned Mr Wolfson,' Fiona prompted. Her mother's reticence in finishing what she'd started was making her uneasy. Had Maude been told something very detrimental to Luke's character?

'Are you in love with him?' Maude asked bluntly. On seeing her daughter's immediate blush she gave a sigh. 'I'm sorry, my love, but His Grace heard some gentlemen talking about Luke Wolfson's betrothal.'

'Betrothal?' Fiona breathed.

Maude nodded. 'It might just be baseless gossip, but I'd sooner you heard it from me, my dear, than from others.' Maude patted at Fiona's fingers, tilting her head to read her daughter's expression.

'Well…if it is true that he is taking a wife, I suppose it is his own affair,' Fiona said with a levity she was far from feeling. She stood up with a ready smile and bid her mother farewell, aware of Maude watching her quick retreat from the room.

A few minutes later Fiona was descending the stairs, with her temples thudding, lost in troubled thought. Luke had informed her that he had never asked anybody to marry him and she'd believed him speaking the truth. Since that conversation had taken place he had been in Devon. If he were to be married, he must have recently proposed to somebody in the West Country… so had Becky persuaded him to make an honest woman of her?

The pounding in Fiona's head increased. She also believed Luke had told the truth about finishing with Becky. But the scorned mistress might be back in town by now and playing games. Perhaps Becky had been starting rumours in the hope they might become true for her. Fiona sighed, pulling on her gloves, in readiness to depart for the shops. She would not cast Luke into the role of liar and cheat. She would put her trust in him and not torment herself with overheard gossip. Impatient as she was to know more about it she must wait till he came to see her then ask him calmly about the rumours.

Fiona spied Joan waiting by the great door and speeded up towards her. She had said nothing to the duke's daughter at breakfast about their parents' blossoming friendship. Fiona guessed that if His Grace had meant his proposal to be taken seriously he'd want a sober talk with his intended bride before he mentioned a word about it to his daughter.

A gentle nudge in the ribs from Joan made Fiona drop the mother-of-pearl buttons she was examining.

'Look! Mr Rockleigh is just over there and he has seen us. I'm sure his companion is the brunette he was with at the Halfway House. Now I've had a better look at her I can tell what sorts *he* consorts with!'

The rattling information certainly gained Fiona's attention. Startled, she followed the direction Joan was indicating with a pair of lively eyes.

'I believe you're right…it is Mr Wolfson's friend,' Fiona murmured with surprising calm considering that Becky Peake was glowering at her from beneath a feather-embellished bonnet.

'He's coming over!' Joan squeaked while apparently absorbed in selecting a reel of French lace.

Indeed, Drew Rockleigh was approaching

them and Fiona's heart began hammering beneath her ribs. She took a calming breath and drew herself up in her shoes. Her immediate instinct had been to march over to Becky and demand to know if Luke had asked her to marry him. But she knew she must not. With perfect attention to etiquette Drew Rockleigh had abandoned his *demi-rep* companion to examine fripperies at the counter while he joined them.

'How nice to see you, Lady Joan,' Drew said suavely.

'Is it?' Joan returned tartly. 'I am surprised, sir, that you feel that way, all things considered.'

Drew gave a gruff chuckle and turned his attention to Fiona, growing serious. 'And you must be Miss Chapman. Luke has spoken about you. I'm pleased to be able to introduce myself to you at last.'

'I'm glad to meet you, too, sir.' Fiona returned a pleasant greeting although anxious to know *what* had been said about her. She didn't wait long to find out.

'Luke has often praised your courage,' Drew informed her. 'And from what he has told me, I must add my admiration to his. But enough has been said on the unfortunate matter and I'm sure you'd sooner leave it be.'

'And I, too, would sooner no more was said on

*the unfortunate matter,*' Joan chipped in sourly, drawing another wry glance from Drew.

As Rockleigh turned his attention to Joan and they continued to have a prickly exchange Fiona felt her eyes drifting in Becky Peake's direction. The woman appeared to have been waiting to gain her attention. Fiona was beckoned, then, when she hesitated in obeying the audacious summons Becky again crooked her finger.

As though to reassure Fiona that their meeting would be discreet Becky screened herself behind rolls of fabrics standing on end. Women like Becky knew their station in life; a genteel female would be sullied by talking to a notorious courtesan.

The temptation to find out more about Luke's betrothal was irresistible; Fiona's womanly intuition was telling her that Becky wanted to speak to her about that very subject. Stepping away from her companions, still engaged in a bout of lively bickering, Fiona joined Luke's mistress in a colourful forest of silks and satins.

'You're Miss Chapman,' Becky stated bluntly.

'I am, and I believe you're Miss Peake,' Fiona returned, meeting the woman's challenge in similar vein.

'Luke has told you about me, then.' Becky sounded triumphant.

Fiona wasn't prepared to reveal anything about her private conversations with Luke, so merely replied coolly, 'Did you want to discuss something in particular?'

'Of course…' Becky smirked. 'And you know very well what it is, don't you? Now don't go all coy or pretend that it's a surprise to you that Luke and I are lovers.'

'I never act coy, nor do I employ pretence,' Fiona retorted clearly.

'I'm glad to hear it.' Becky felt grudging admiration for her rival's forthright manner. She might be genteel and past her prime, but it was plain Fiona Chapman was no shrinking violet. 'I shan't pretend, either, then,' Becky said. 'I know Luke wants a dalliance with you. But we've no need to be jealous of one another. You're not his first fancy and you won't be the last, but he always comes back to me.' Becky was a robust liar; most of what she'd said she knew to be false. Luke had made it clear their relationship was over. Then when she'd quizzed him over Miss Chapman, the strange look in his eyes had told her everything she needed to know but he wouldn't say. He was in love—not with the simpering miss who'd come to town to try and hook him for the second time, but with the quiet mouse he'd rescued from Jeremiah Collins. At close quarters Becky could grudgingly see that the refined lady who'd stolen Luke's heart had qualities a man might find attractive. Her eyes were a fascinating shade of hazel and her fawn hair was thick and glossy. She was not as buxom as Becky, but her figure was nicely curvaceous.

Becky might profess not to be jealous, but Fiona guessed the opposite were true. She wasn't going to get dragged into a catfight over Luke Wolfson in the middle of a drapery. She'd been wrong in thinking that Becky was about to crow about being Luke's future wife. And it would be the height of bad taste for her to bring up the subject of his rumoured betrothal, much as she craved finding out more about it.

'Don't sulk.' Becky gripped Fiona's arm, tugging her back as she would have moved away. 'Luke will give you a pension when he grows bored with you. He's very generous, if you please him.' Becky deliberately fingered the pretty gem pinned to her collar. 'You're not his usual type, but he'll take fair-haired women, for a change.' She twirled a long brunette ringlet about a finger. 'Even if he does wed Miss Ponting, he'll keep me close by.'

Becky smiled on seeing a flicker of raw emotion clouding Miss Chapman's cat-like eyes. 'Ah…he has not let on about her, has he? He

chased after a debutante a few years ago.' Becky
sighed theatrically. 'But back then, you see, he
was a lowly lieutenant with nothing but his looks
to recommend him.' Becky gained a mean comfort from the hurt intensifying in Fiona's eyes.
'The foolish chit took her mother's advice and
rebuffed him. But now he is one of the most eligible bachelors around she is trailing after him
like a puppy dog.'

An insolent look raked Fiona from head to
toe. 'She is rather like you in a way—older now
than she wants to be and hoping she'll not get
left on the shelf.' Becky crossed her arms over
her middle in a contented way.

'If you have nothing of importance to say,
then please do not waste any more of my time.'
Fiona managed to dismiss the woman's spite although she was feeling light-headed with tension
and close to tears.

'His marriage does not bother you?'

'Not in the slightest,' Fiona returned with
barely a betraying tremor in her voice.

'I think you *do* employ pretence…' Becky
chortled. 'You're a poor liar, Miss Chapman.
Quality such as you want husbands, not lovers.
You thought he'd do the decent thing because of
your connections.' Becky glanced past Fiona at
the Duke of Thornley's daughter. 'Luke's still a

bachelor because he favours keeping company with me rather than getting leg-shackled to any snooty madam.'

'And you're welcome to him,' Fiona uttered in a suffocated tone. With that parting shot, she slipped out from behind the rainbow screen of fabrics, passing Drew Rockleigh, with a strained smile, as he made his way to rejoin his companion.

Fiona's heart was beating a slow tattoo beneath her bodice as she pored over her hostile exchange with Becky. The woman had seen through her defensive pride to the core of her being. Of course she wanted to be married to the man she loved, but Becky's few coarsely spoken remarks had finally helped her bury her hopes and dreams beneath reality.

Luke *had* finished with his mistress and he *did* want her as Becky's replacement—Fiona trusted that to be true. Becky had lied on that score, but there was a ring of truth to the younger woman's talk of Luke's past. Some years ago he'd chased after a debutante and been turned down. Since then his prospects had improved and the lady who'd spurned him was in town to let him know she'd changed her mind. Now Fiona knew exactly what the Duke of Thornley had overheard and recounted to her mother when they were both tipsy.

Fiona had wondered whether she'd cope with being Luke's mistress, shut away in a corner of his life when he married and raised a family. She'd wondered if she might endure that twilight existence that would grow darker as they aged until his time and affection for her finally extinguished. A brusque exchange with a woman who knew Luke better than she did had lifted the blinkers from her eyes. It would be intolerable and she ridiculed herself for having thought she might equal Becky's role and attitude where Luke Wolfson was concerned. Over the past frantic weeks many people had praised her courage. But once intimately bound to him, would she ever be brave enough to quietly withdraw from his life when he wanted her to rather than have him despise her?

Fiona focused on Joan, noticing the young woman was waiting impatiently for her.

'What did *she* want?' Joan nodded at the door through which Becky Peake and Drew Rockleigh had departed. 'I saw you having a quiet word with her. I won't tell, I promise.'

'It was nothing important,' Fiona answered, bringing her quavering tone under control with a cough. 'Did you win?' She swiftly changed the subject to avoid any further mention of Becky.

'Win?'

'You sounded as though you were sparring with Mr Rockleigh.'

'Oh, that… I always win. I imagine he lets me,' Joan admitted ruefully. She looked thoughtfully at Fiona. 'Were you sparring with *her* a moment ago?'

Fiona's answer was a neutral smile. 'I was on the point of buying some nice buttons a moment ago.' She opened her reticule to find some coins. 'My blue pelisse could do with brightening up.'

'As you won't admit to fighting over Mr Wolfson I imagine you lost the battle—'

'I did not!' Fiona blurted before realising she'd been tricked into saying too much.

With an arch look Joan led the way back to the button display.

## Chapter Twenty-One

Two more days had passed before the moment arrived that Fiona was both longing for and dreading. As she placed down her novel on the dressing table and peered wide-eyed at her reflection in the mirror, she again pondered on what might have delayed him.

Over the past long days and nights she had tormented herself with the idea that he had by now proposed to Miss Ponting. Becky's boast that Luke would sooner keep his freedom and her company than get leg-shackled seemed less likely the more Fiona had thought about it. Besides, her mother had now confirmed what Becky had told her about Luke's connection to the Pontings. He *had* courted Harriet a few years ago and been rebuffed.

The duke had taken Maude to the theatre one evening and the Pontings had been there, too, her mother had reported. High-instep people, Maude had described them, although nowhere close to being in His Grace's league, the woman had added with a smirk. The daughter was rather an obvious beauty, she had carried on with a sniff, being too blonde and too pale of complexion. Maude's attempt to encourage Fiona had had the reverse effect, especially when she'd let slip that gossip was now rife about Luke Wolfson renewing his pursuit of Harriet.

Fiona knew she should not feel so hurt or surprised by the news. A well-bred, eligible bachelor would naturally want to pass his name and wealth on to future generations of Wolfsons. In the past he'd seemed quite bitter when mentioning family life, but surely if he intended to quit working as a mercenary, a wife and children would figure in his plans…

As Miss Chapman was still seated and appeared to be entranced by her own reflection, the maid added, 'Mr Wolfson is waiting for you in the morning room. Shall I arrange for tea?'

'Umm…no…I believe his visit will be brief. Is my mother back?' Fiona asked normally despite blood streaking so rapidly through her veins that she felt faint. Slowly she gained her feet, gripping the edge of the mahogany table and swaying into it for support until her knuckles turned white.

'Not to my knowledge, Miss Chapman.'

Fiona was glad that Maude and the duke were still out on a shopping excursion. She knew that Joan was with her friends, visiting an exhibition of Greek artefacts at a museum. In fact, Luke's timing for a very private conversation between them could not have been better. Perhaps his mercenary's propensity for meticulous preparation had made him plan it that way. But she was glad that there would be no witnesses and that she might have an hour or so in which to recover from this final parting.

When Fiona entered the morning room Luke stayed quite still for a moment, simply regarding her with hungry dark eyes. Then he relinquished his lounging position by the mantelpiece and strode to meet her, immediately taking her cool hands in his warm grip.

'I've missed you,' he said huskily, his fingers tightening on hers.

'I've missed you, too,' Fiona replied, believing him sincere. He seemed about to embrace her and, much as she yearned to have him do so, she slowly withdrew her hands and put distance between them. He looked wonderfully distinguished and handsome, as usual, but she knew the closer they were, the more he touched her, the harder it would be for her to say what she must. Several times she'd rehearsed this little farewell speech and her good wishes for his future, yet phrases slipped away to hide in the corners of her mind.

'What's the matter?' Luke asked bluntly, moving to a position where he could read her expression. 'Are you cross that I've not turned up sooner?' He gave her a boyish smile. 'I've a good excuse for the delay.'

'I'm sure you have…' Fiona wouldn't let rancour into her voice. He owed her nothing, not even an explanation for his tardiness. They both knew that his business was his own. The only offer he'd made was to care for her as his mistress.

'Are you interested in hearing where I've been?' Luke asked, plunging his hands into his pockets.

'I have some news for you, actually,' Fiona blurted, achieving a level, conversational tone. She could tell he was alert to her reserve despite her best efforts to conceal it. In turn, he'd become guarded. 'It is a rather exciting and very unexpected turn of events.' Fiona injected some lightness into her voice.

Luke raised his thick eyebrows in polite enquiry, but Fiona sensed that he was brooding on the reason for the change in her. He had, unseen by family and friends, snatched a farewell kiss from her in a fleeting private moment before she'd boarded the coach at the Halfway House. Then he had mounted Star and, from a vantage point on the brow of a hill, had watched the cavalcade of Thornley vehicles till it disappeared from view. The blossoming intimacy and affection between them Fiona had hugged to herself like a warm shawl as the conveyance dipped and swayed over ruts on the final leg of the journey to town. But that serenity was gone now, crushed by reality. If she succumbed to the longing to be with him at any cost, she risked an intolerable future veering between joy and despair.

'My mother has received a marriage proposal from the Duke of Thornley. She has accepted. The betrothal is not yet common knowledge so you are one of the first to be told. His Grace is to put an announcement in *The Times* at the end of the week.'

'That is a surprise.' Luke's response held mild interest.

Fiona was somewhat taken aback by his attitude. She knew him for a cool, undemonstrative man, nevertheless she'd expected more of a reaction than that. 'So…it will affect me,' she added briskly.

'In what way?' Luke asked, strolling to again prop a hand against the mantelshelf.

'In…in the matter of…our attachment,' Fiona stammered out, cringing inwardly at her jumbled explanation. She so wanted to match his composure. She elevated her chin, squarely met his attentive eyes. 'You asked me to be your mistress on two occasions. I expect you have taken from my…affectionate responses…that I have tacitly agreed to your proposition and my words to the contrary were sham modesty.' She plunged on quickly, as warmth fizzled in her cheeks. 'I admit I was tempted to accept when everything in my life seemed turbulent, but now my circumstances have changed.'

'And have your feelings for me changed?' Luke's tone was flinty. 'Or are you simply trying to tell me that the stepdaughter of a duke deserves better than a retired army major?'

'I am trying to tell you that being shunned by my family, and in time by you, sir, is what I find unacceptable,' Fiona flared at him. Every good intention to remain logical and unruffled fled from her mind to be replaced by indignation.

'You are able to easily turn your emotions on and off, are you?' he asked quietly.

'No…I am not!' Fiona enunciated. 'Brave you might think me, but I am human and have weaknesses. I cannot bear the hurt awaiting me if I turn my back on every code I've known. If I go with you I risk heartbreak and ostracism.' Her tawny eyes raked his impassive features. 'Do not cast *me* in the role of mercenary,' she added in a suffocated whisper. 'Or imply that I have misled you. That would be too rich, coming from you.'

Luke glanced at his dark hand stark against the pale marble supporting it. 'What has Becky Peake told you?' His tone was pitilessly demanding.

Fiona's lips parted in surprise, then were pressed together in a mutinous line. Of course, he might have visited Becky and his friend Drew before coming to see her. Becky had been shamefully spiteful to her in the drapery so Fiona imagined that, of the two, Rockleigh might have mentioned witnessing the clandestine conversation between the two women.

'What did the infernal woman say?'

Luke strode towards her so fast that Fiona skittered backwards. Again he stopped himself touching her although she saw that he wanted to. His outstretched fingers were jerked back and rammed into his pockets.

'I've had a report of your meeting from Drew so you might as well tell me.'

'It matters little what we spoke about as I'd already heard the news she wanted to flaunt in my face. My mother told me about some gossip that is flying around town about your betrothal. Becky Peake merely confirmed she'd heard it, too, although apparently it doesn't bother her one bit as she is confident of remaining your mistress when you take a wife.'

But for a muscle tightening close to his mouth Luke would have appeared unmoved by what he'd heard. 'I told you I had finished with Becky. Do you think me a liar?'

'No…' Fiona admitted faintly. 'I think you were telling the truth and poor Becky isn't happy about being put off.'

Luke barked a laugh. '*Poor Becky* is already ensconced in an apartment owned by a young viscount. So her talk of undying devotion to me is far-fetched.'

Fiona blushed. 'I see…I'm sorry,' she said automatically.

'There's no need to be. I'm happy she is settled so quickly. I believe Drew made the introduction—the viscount is a friend of his.'

'Would that I had some of her spirit,' Fiona muttered ironically.

'Explain that…'

She averted her face, but gave him his answer. 'Becky saw a future with you as nothing to be afraid of, no matter what you chose to do, or who else you chose to spend it with.'

'I imagine you are again hinting at me having once courted Miss Ponting. I recall telling you that I had never proposed. Do you think I have lied about that?'

Fiona bit her lip, unable to remember Becky's exact phrasing about Luke's pursuit of a debutante. 'Whether you fell to bended knee or not is unimportant—you wanted Harriet Ponting as your wife!' she argued with renewed vigour. 'Had she been receptive to your suit you would now be her husband.'

'But she wasn't and I'm not,' Luke pointed out mildly. 'There is nothing for you to take exception to…not even the fact that I briefly paid attention to a woman in my youth.'

*'Your youth?'* Fiona echoed sharply. 'You are now thirty and chased after Miss Ponting not that long ago. I hardly think you were a green boy at the time.'

'Very recently you accused me of being woefully immature… How much worse do you think I was when aged twenty-five?' he asked with mordant self-mockery.

The moral high ground seemed to be slipping away beneath her and Fiona keenly felt her lack of sophistication. 'You think it all amusing, don't you?' she stormed, a teary sheen burnishing the gold in her eyes. 'Well, I do not.' She marched away from him, then swung about, quivering fingers clasped in front of her. 'You're right— you are still woefully immature. I am not a toy to be trifled with. I am a human being and deserve some consideration and respect. You might pick your mistresses on a whim and perhaps you also chose Miss Ponting with the same lack of care.' Fiona edged up her chin, despite feeling utterly forlorn. 'Thankfully her parents were vigilant on her behalf and I can look after myself. I will never accept such cavalier treatment from you or any other man.'

'So...of what are you accusing me, Fiona?' Luke asked. 'You seem to think me fickle, incapable of true feelings...yet at the same time the idea of a serious past attachment to Harriet Ponting upsets you. Which is it you want me to be? A rogue or a gallant?'

*I want you to be only mine...* Fiona bit her lower lip to prevent the plea exploding from her. She gasped in a calming breath. 'I did not know that you might soon be wed.' While gazing soulfully into his earthy brown eyes she blurted,

'Did Miss Ponting break your heart when she rejected you? I have sensed on occasions that you feel hurt…bitter even…about something in your past.'

In exasperation Luke turned his face up to the ceiling with a gesture of disbelief.

'I'm sorry if you think it's an impertinence to ask…but can you not see that it makes a difference? You should have told me if you are still brooding on another woman.'

'I'm not bitter or brooding because of another woman…not in the way you mean, in any case,' Luke said quietly, dark fingers pinching the bridge of his nose as though to ease his strain.

'In what way then are you feeling bitter?' Fiona persisted. For a moment she thought he would either ignore her question or take himself off. But again he raised his eyes, this time to moderate his expression rather than his temper. Suddenly he seemed steelier, master of his emotions.

'You asked me once why I worked as a mercenary when I'd no need of the money.' He glanced at her. 'The truth is I did need the money from those endeavours…not to pay bills but for my own self-respect.' He paced to and fro as though undecided whether to say more. 'My grandfather bequeathed to me everything he owned and it was a considerable amount of cash and property. I was nine years old when he disinherited his son in favour of his grandchild. When I was twenty-seven I took what should have been my father's birthright. By then it no longer mattered that my father had hated me from the moment I'd usurped him. All the family I'd known were dead…my benefactor the last to go.'

Fiona became very still, shocked at what she'd heard. She was tempted to move to comfort him. But she feared if she did he'd bottle up the rest and she wished to ease the burden of his unhappy memories.

'My father and grandfather had fallen out over a joint business venture that failed—cargo from the Indies that was lost in a storm. My father never recovered financially, but my grandfather made back his money and more besides. The rift between the men never healed and worsened when I was dragged into their fight.' He studied the floor this time, stubbing the toe of a boot against the oak boards. 'My mother blamed me and also my father and his kin for destroying our happy family and her comforts. She separated from my father although a divorce was out of the question. She took me to live in the Berkshire countryside with an elderly aunt of hers while my father stayed in the city.' He paused. 'I attended

Harrow school, but was never invited to my father's home. By the time I went up to Oxford he had been dead two years. He'd drunk himself close to death many times, but he couldn't recover from tumbling down the stairs in a bawdy house.' Luke gave a sour, reflective laugh. 'I spent most school holidays with Drew and his family in Kent. The Rockleighs are fine people.'

Fiona could not bear listening to the strengthening huskiness in his voice. She rushed to him, tentatively touched his arm, her heart squeezing when she felt the tension in him.

'You feel guilty, but you should not,' she whispered. 'It is not your fault that your elders…people who should have cared for your well-being… made you a pawn in a spiteful game. You were just a boy.'

'I know…' Luke nodded. 'But still I do, even after all this time. Had my grandfather gone first I would have gladly given everything to them the moment the bequest was executed.' Luke curled his fingers over the small white digits soothing him. 'My father expired over a decade ago and my mother followed him to the grave a few years later. She'd requested to be buried in the Wolfson plot, by my father's side. My grandfather was eighty years old and still holding grudges. But I fought him and eventually he relented and allowed his daughter-in-law to be laid to rest on his land.' He paused. 'My mother always wished to stay with her husband, but she did her duty and removed me from living beneath his roof and his wrath. But she never let me forget she'd suffered for it.'

'Oh, I'm so sorry…' Fiona hung her head, feeling ashamed. 'I shouldn't have pressed you to say anything about it. I know you have aired some very private thoughts. I swear I'll never betray your trust.'

Luke turned to fully face her, gazing down at her with immense gravity. 'My inheritance was a curse, not a boon, and that's why I wished to carry on earning my living. If I brood on anything in my past it's that, not a failed love affair. When a moody young man I vowed I'd give away the lot the day the will was read. My mother despaired on hearing that plan. In her eyes such an action was a greater insult than that perpetrated by her father-in-law.' He frowned. 'If she'd outlived the old boy I would have given her whatever she desired.'

'I do understand why you would want to do that.' Fiona's voice trembled with sincerity. 'But…I'm glad you didn't have a chance to test the scope of your generosity, or her avarice.' She sighed. 'Money and corruption are often bedfellows. And if it helps you at all…what you have told me has made me reconsider my own situation.' Quickly she explained, 'Ratcliff let slip that he knew about my small bequest. Perhaps he wormed his way into our lives to lay hands to it.' In her sweet attempt to boost Luke's mood Fiona enthused, 'In any case, I no longer care about Ratcliff. We…my mama and I…have you to thank for our salvation where he is concerned. The Duke of Thornley and Joan also owe you a debt of gratitude for apprehending vile Jeremiah Collins.' She smiled shyly into his velvet-brown eyes. 'So, you see, being in possession of your hateful inheritance has done good, in its way. Without his grandfather's wealth spurring him to soldier on, Major Luke Wolfson might have retired to the life of a town fop.'

'*Town fop*…is that how you see me?' But he chuckled gruffly, hugging her to him. 'I think you, Miss Chapman, are all I need to stay hale and hearty and happy.'

Fiona's smile faded. Now he seemed to have returned to his normal self, anxieties were again pricking at her mind. She felt more closely bound to Luke following their intimate talk. But she was still haunted by uncertainty over his feelings for Miss Ponting. Carefully she withdrew from his possessive embrace and gazed up into his preying eyes.

'I'm sorry to ask, but I must know—are you still in love… Is Miss Ponting right to hope… to expect…?'

The unfinished question throbbed between them, timed in seconds by the pendulum of the large wall clock.

'I know I should have told you I'd fallen in love,' Luke eventually said very softly.

'Will you marry her?' Fiona's voice was a hoarse whisper.

'If she'll have me…' Luke's smile was barely there. 'First I have to impress on her my sincere apologies if she believes I have ever treated her with a lack of consideration or respect. Of all the people I have ever known she is the most deserving of such homage.' He paused for a moment following that vehement declaration. 'I must also convince her of my intention to improve my behaviour. And I will change, for her…just for her…because no other woman will do…so if she turns me down…'

Luke left the rest unsaid. He approached Fiona and stood very close. Very slowly he smoothed the satiny line of her jaw with gentle knuckles before tilting up her chin so she couldn't avoid his eyes. 'Please look at me, Fiona,' he begged.

After a fractional hesitation Fiona raised her lashes, her heart wedged dizzyingly in her throat. She yearned to hear him say that he loved her, but he simply rewarded her shy smile with another tender caress.

'I love you, Fiona... Oh, I want you, too... You're a fire in my blood and have been since the first night that I met you. Even drenched through you looked ravishing to me. I recall almost telling you so at the time and earning your mistrust because of it.'

Fiona remembered very well the incident on that first night they'd met. He'd given her his coat to wear and she'd felt spellbound while they'd talked by the firelight.

He skimmed his lips over a satiny crown of fawn hair. 'I've tried to fool myself that seducing you will suffice and ease my desire to be with you. But it won't do. I want to be by your side in and out of bed. Most of all I want to protect you and our children from every disappointment and harm. I know I can't do that, however hard I try.' He tilted up her chin with five curled fingers. 'There'll be times when bad luck and worries will afflict us as a family...but we'll fight it all together...if you'll be very kind and have me as your husband.'

As the little muffled sob of joy broke in her

throat he enfolded her to his chest, rocking her within his embrace.

'I can't lie and say my intentions towards you were honourable from the start. After such a short acquaintance you can't blame me for thinking that the need for you was simply a base one.' His tone was growing increasingly wolfish, but he slid a reverential kiss on her brow. 'I soon realised that what I felt for you ran far... far deeper than lust.' He chuckled on seeing the blush spreading on her cheeks, then took her mouth in a profoundly drugging kiss.

Just a touch of his tongue teasing her lips made Fiona melt into him. She opened up immediately to the skilful caress, her hands climbing his muscled chest to rest on his shoulders before her slender fingers linked behind his head, urging him closer.

*He loved her...wanted to be her husband...* The wonderful words circled soft as butterfly wings in her consciousness. And her own declaration was filling her mind ready to burst forth. But she couldn't relinquish the exquisite sensation of their fused mouths to utter anything at all. His hands were undoing buttons on her bodice, then unlacing her chemise. Fiona shivered in glorious anticipation as finally...finally warm firm fingers slid, then moulded over her silky, sensitive skin. Arching her back, she gave herself up to the stroking hands drawing her closer to a blissful frenzy.

Luke growled deep in his throat, lifting her and settling her calves about his hips before striding to the sofa. He went down with her, his mouth pressing hot and hard against her lips, the delicate dips at her collarbone, before moving lower to tantalise thrusting rose-tipped breasts peeking at him from between the loose edges of her gown.

Fiona cried out in delight as he suckled the sensitive little nubs, drawing first one then the other into his mouth to be tasted and tantalised with tongue and teeth.

'I love you, Luke,' Fiona gasped, bucking and writhing beneath his erotic fondling.

'I should ask you properly to be my wife.' Luke cupped her enraptured face between his palms. 'You deserve better than this,' he groaned. 'Yet if you don't quit wriggling, sweetheart, I might not be able to stop.'

'No…don't stop…' Fiona burst out, drawing a rough laugh from him as she tugged his face again down to hers.

Gently he kissed her. 'You are a very wanton young lady…much to my surprise and delight,' he murmured. In a swift abrupt movement he sat

Fiona up, tugging together her clothes. Then he gazed into her smoky amber eyes just visible beneath a dusky fringe of bashfully lowered lashes.

'Let me put your mind at ease over that youthful courtship.' Luke brushed a thumb over Fiona's lips, pulsing from his passionate assault. 'I did kiss Harriet Ponting a couple of times during our courtship. When her father told me not to call on her again my pride was badly dented, but I wasn't heartbroken. Two years later I inherited my grandfather's wealth and the Pontings made it clear they'd welcome my visits.' He paused. 'I felt no inclination to get to know Harriet again. In fact, when our paths have crossed I've simply been polite to the family.' He frowned as though aware he seemed callous. 'I realise now it was infatuation…not love. I had decided to get married before my grandfather died and my army pay was all I had to offer. I wanted a wife to accept me for who I was rather than for what another man's money made me.'

Fiona leaned forward and pressed her soft lips to his cheek. 'You have my love and my respect and if you wish to give away your inheritance, I will not object.'

'I know, Fiona…and that's why I'm determined to keep it so that every luxury and comfort will be yours.' He sank from the sofa to humbly plant a knee on the floor, taking both her hands in his. 'Will you marry me, Miss Chapman? I swear I'll improve and be worthy of you and our children.'

'I wouldn't have you change a single thing, sir, for I very much like you the way you are.' Fiona shaved his jaw with her palms, savouring the abrasion against her stroking fingers. 'I would still adore and want you even if you carry on with your dangerous missions.'

'Would you indeed?' Luke gently teased.

'Well…as long as you were at home with me for a good deal of the time,' Fiona amended stoutly.

'Or perhaps you could be my accomplice and join me on my travels. We make a good team, you and I,' Luke said. 'We could set up in business ridding the country of outlaws…'

'Now you're mocking me…'

'No…I'm not…I'm trying to tell you…in my woefully immature way…that I've no further need of such thrills. Those ghosts that refused to let me enjoy my inheritance have gone now.' Luke rose to sit beside her, drawing her back against the sofa with an arm about her waist. 'You, Miss Chapman, have brought about a rather wondrous change in me. For many years I've craved finding that contentment I knew as a youngster, before my grandfather blighted my life with his riches.' The crooked smile he gave her was appealingly bashful. 'I suppose what I'm trying to say is that you have soothed my troubled soul…and helped me find peace…and I can't do without you.'

'I'm so glad about that,' Fiona whispered, nuzzling his cheek.

'As a lad I loved the fields and open spaces about my grandfather's estate in Essex, even during a cruel winter. I'd like to settle down in the country and raise our family. But if you prefer a lively social life we can live at our Eaton Square town house during the Season. Wherever we are…London or Essex…I'll be happy so long as you're with me.'

'I feel the same way about you.' Fiona laid her head against his muscled shoulder, feeling quite serene. 'And I think I might like country living. I'd barely set foot in rural parts before seeking employment in Devon. Yet as soon as I returned to London I knew I missed that vivid scenery. In town all seems grey by comparison.' Fiona gazed up into Luke's face, harking back to the first time their eyes had merged through the dusk. His complexion had been glistening with rain, his snowy linen shirt a stark contrast against his bronzed skin and she'd thought him as dangerous and foreign as the alien landscape.

'I thought we were very different people. Yet it seems we are quite alike.' After a harmonious silence she tilted up her face to his. 'Is there no villainy in Essex to occupy you while I fill a nursery with our sons and daughters?' Just an hour ago Fiona would have been astonished, and not a little embarrassed, at the thought of talking so openly about having babies. But it seemed the most natural thing in the world to chat with Luke about bearing his children.

'Surely it's a bit early to talk about that, when you've not yet accepted my marriage proposal, Miss Chapman,' Luke reminded her, not wholly in jest.

'Oh, of course I'll marry you,' Fiona answered on a yearning sigh. 'I would marry you tomorrow, Luke Wolfson, if I could.'

'Tomorrow?' Luke asked, an amused glitter in his eyes.

Fiona nodded vigorously. 'Today…' Her tone held utter conviction. 'I would marry you this minute, Luke.'

'Good… Do you want to know why it's taken me a while to join you in town?'

'Was it to do with my stepfather?' Fiona asked doubtfully.

'No… Ratcliff was quickly taken into custody in Devon. He will be dealt with in due course.' Luke drew a jewellery box from his in-

side pocket. 'I went shopping to get you this.'
He turned the casket, lifting the lid to display a
domed emerald encircled by glittering diamonds.
'I have lots of inherited gemstones, but I wanted
you to have something of your own that was free
of the taint of the Wolfson family's sadness.'

'Oh, Luke…it's beautiful…' Fiona cried,
touching a single digit to the rich green stone.

Easing the ring from its velvet nest, he slid it
on to her betrothal finger.

'I would have become your mistress knowing you loved me, you know.' Fiona moved her
fingers allowing the light to spark on the gems.

'But you might have left me at some time,'
Luke replied wryly. 'I couldn't risk that.' He
drew her into his embrace. 'I wanted to tell you
sooner that I loved you. I almost did on occasions. But there never seemed to be a right time.
The smugglers…Becky…your mother and stepfather…they all got in the way.' His mouth covered hers in a kiss of wooing sweetness that
nevertheless was powerful enough to leave her
lolling against the velvet cushions, craving more.

A sudden crash of a doorway and voices outside made Fiona grip tight to Luke's shoulders
and stifle a giggle. 'Mama is back with the duke.'

'I can't wait long for us to be man and wife.'
Luke stroked her cheek. 'I expect your mother

and stepfather will have a glittering affair despite both having been widowed.'

'Mama does class it as her second marriage. She says what occurred with Ratcliff was a pantomime. They do talk about having a large party, too.' Fiona's eyes darted to the door as though she expected the newly betrothed couple might burst in on them at any moment. She struggled up to a decorous sitting position beside Luke.

'Do you want such a celebration for yourself?' Luke asked, his sultry gaze roving her beautifully flushed face.

'No...not at all.' Fiona twisted the weighty stone on her finger, polishing it with a thumb. 'I've never been one for lavish entertainment.' She gave him a twinkling smile. 'I might make a disappointing hostess, you know.'

'Nothing about you disappoints me...' Luke paused. 'And I'm hoping you won't disappoint me now and look shocked when I ask if you will...'

'Whatever it is, I will...' Fiona suggestively coiled her arms about his neck, resting her head on his shoulder. 'I trust you, you see, Luke, and love you so very much.'

Luke rewarded her devotion with a sweetly seductive kiss. 'When I went shopping for your betrothal and wedding rings I stopped off to get a special licence,' He breathed against her bruised lips. 'I want you as my wife before the sun sets on today.'

Fiona held his face back from hers, searching his eyes for humour. But there was none, other than that wry self-mockery that seemed to be his constant companion.

'Are you brave enough to risk coming with me and throwing in your luck with mine? Shall we share one last adventure before we settle down to sensible domesticity and a barrage of questions in the morning?'

Fiona nodded, eyes brimming with joy and excitement. 'Of course, but I insist on having some terms, sir.'

'Name them,' Luke said gruffly.

'I must leave my mama a note or she will fret dreadfully.'

'Agreed.'

'And…' Fiona hesitated, afraid that he might think her next request unattractively outlandish and very forward.

'Tell me…for I've a mind to carry you off and have my wicked way with you without delay,' Luke groaned.

'I should like to spend our wedding night in the open beneath the stars, with a fire to warm us and the scent of roasting game in the air,'

Fiona breathed, her eyes vivid with excitement. Familiar, delightful sensations were tormenting the depths of her abdomen, and her breasts tingled and grew weighty as erotic thoughts flooded her mind.

Luke dropped his head to hers and just touched together their smiling lips. 'We certainly are made for one another, Fiona... That memory haunts my mind, too. I feared it might remain an unfulfilled fantasy to make love to you on the ground beneath the stars.' His tongue tip circled her lips, plunging to taste hers. 'Are you sure you wouldn't rather a feather mattress and silk sheets for your first time?'

Fiona blushed, nipped a corner of her lower lip with small pearly teeth in an unconsciously alluring way that drove Luke wild with desire.

'An earthy bed it is, then,' he growled, thrusting ten fingers into her dishevelled locks and tilting her face to his so he might feast again on her lips.

'I hope the night is mild.' Fiona's murmured comment was gruff with laughter.

Luke's kiss deepened, shooting spears of heat through her.

'I won't let you get cold, sweetheart. You'll be burning till dawn, I promise...'

\* \* \* \* \*

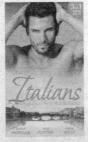

# MILLS & BOON®

## Want to get more from Mills & Boon?

Here's what's available to you if you join the exclusive **Mills & Boon eBook Club** today:

✦ *Convenience – choose your books each month*
✦ *Exclusive – receive your books a month before anywhere else*
✦ *Flexibility – change your subscription at any time*
✦ *Variety – gain access to eBook-only series*
✦ *Value – subscriptions from just £3.99 a month*

So visit **www.millsandboon.co.uk/esubs** today to be a part of this exclusive eBook Club!

# MILLS & BOON®

## HISTORICAL

**AWAKEN THE ROMANCE OF THE PAST**

## A sneak peek at next month's titles...

**In stores from 2nd October 2015:**

- **Christian Seaton: Duke of Danger** – Carole Mortimer
- **The Soldier's Rebel Lover** – Marguerite Kaye
- **Return of Scandal's Son** – Janice Preston
- **The Forgotten Daughter** – Lauri Robinson
- **No Conventional Miss** – Eleanor Webster
- **Dreaming of a Western Christmas** – Lynna Banning, Kelly Boyce & Carol Arens

0915/04